SUNRISE OVER STRAWBERRY HILL FARM

ALISON SHERLOCK

Boldwood

First published in Great Britain in 2023 by Boldwood Books Ltd.

Copyright © Alison Sherlock, 2023

Cover Design by Alice Moore Design

Cover photography: Shutterstock and iStock

A CIP catalogue record for this book is available from the British Library.

Paperback ISBN 978-1-80426-448-5

Large Print ISBN 978-1-80426-447-8

Hardback ISBN 978-1-80426-449-2

Ebook ISBN 978-1-80426-446-1

Kindle ISBN 978-1-80426-455-3

Audio CD ISBN 978-1-80426-454-6

MP3 CD ISBN 978-1-80426-453-9

Digital audio download ISBN 978-1-80426-452-2

Boldwood Books Ltd
23 Bowerdean Street
London SW6 3TN
www.boldwoodbooks.com

For Sian Maidens, with whom I've enjoyed many wonderful camping holidays and who never picks on me during Uno. With much love x

1

Flora Barton gave her grandmother a wide smile as she tried to pretend that her heart wasn't completely breaking into two.

'Well, these numbers look great, don't you think?' she lied in an overly bright tone, gesturing at the iPad screen on the kitchen table.

Flora and her grandmother, Helen, known to most people as Grams, locked eyes briefly before they both looked away. She couldn't get anything past Grams, so Flora let her fake smile slip as she then turned to their friend Joe with a sigh.

Joe Randall was their neighbour in the tiny rural village of Cranfield in the middle of the English countryside. In addition, he was a great businessman who had achieved success helping quite a few local farms diversify and turn a profit in an increasingly uncertain time in the trade.

But some farms were seemingly beyond help and, unfortunately, Strawberry Hill Farm was one of them.

'Thanks for all your hard work sorting this out these past few weeks,' Flora told him. 'We really appreciate it, especially all the extra hours you had to put in when you're already so busy.'

She glanced at the clock and saw that it wasn't even seven o'clock in the morning yet. Joe had managed to squeeze in a very early meeting with them in his packed diary.

Joe gave her a sympathetic smile. 'I wish I had been able to do more,' he replied. 'But at least the decent price we've been offered for the plough means that now all your farming equipment has been sold, you should have enough money to pay off your debts.'

'Just the tractor left,' said Flora, gulping away the emotion which was threatening to overwhelm her.

They had sold nearly everything to keep Strawberry Hill Farm afloat, but without any crops to tend, what on earth was she going to do now that she wasn't a farmer any more? It had been her only job since she had left college so her CV was non-existent.

A ray of April sunshine shone through the nearby window as the sun rose above the horizon, lighting up the farmhouse kitchen. After so many months of endless rain, Flora felt as if the weather was mocking her. It was the rain that had done the damage year after year. It had flooded all their fields but two and ruined every crop that they had tried to sow. Without any income from the fields, Strawberry Hill Farm had been running at a loss for a couple of years.

They had let their farmhand go to reduce costs, but even that hadn't been enough. The only thing left to keep the farm afloat was to sell the farm machinery. That left them just the empty fields slowly being reclaimed by nature and the farmhouse – their home.

Flora glanced over at Grams. Her tiny elderly grandmother was pulling a baking tray packed with various pastries out of the Aga.

When she was little, Flora had been unable to say the word Grandma and so it had become Grams and the nickname had stuck, even amongst her friends.

Grams was eighty years old but had yet to lose the fierceness which had helped her survive a busy life working the land over many years. However, Flora knew that deep down Grams' heart was breaking too over the fate of Strawberry Hill Farm.

But whatever happened in the future, she and Grams would always remain together. They had a very close and loving relationship, and despite everything that had been thrown at them, they had hardly ever exchanged a bad word.

'Right, who wants a breakfast muffin?' asked Grams, whose baking always filled the farmhouse with its sweet tempting aroma. She placed a plate piled high with banana and apple muffins in the middle of the large oak table.

'Actually, I've got another early meeting to go to,' said Joe, standing up and glancing at the muffins with regret. 'Shame really as you know how much I love your baking.'

Flora nodded in agreement. Everyone loved Grams' baking.

'It's fine,' said Grams, reaching up to give him a hug. Her diminutive stature meant that she barely came up to his chest. 'I'll pop a few in a bag that you can take with you. You won't keep that business brain of yours whirring on an empty stomach. The right breakfast sets you up for the day.'

'Try not to worry about the farm,' Joe told her, before turning to give Flora a hug. 'We'll keep trying to find a way out of all this for you both.'

'Thanks,' murmured Flora, grateful for his kindness. She knew that he had done his best. But some things were just not salvageable.

After he had left, Flora looked once more at the plate which was piled high with double the amount of muffins that Grams normally baked.

'Have you invited the girls for breakfast and not told me?'

asked Flora, raising her eyebrows in surprise. 'Because I'm not sure I'll be able to eat all this by myself.'

The girls were her best friends, Harriet, Libby and Katy, who also lived in the tiny hamlet of Cranfield. She had known Harriet and Libby since childhood and Katy had arrived in the village the previous autumn, at which time their cosy threesome had become an awesome foursome of close friendship and support. And Flora needed their support now more than ever.

Despite everything, at least she and Grams still had their home, she reminded herself. Although without any income from the land, even that was now under threat. She glanced around. It was a large but comfortable farmhouse kitchen, full of oak beams, a huge oak table and the homely aroma of coffee and freshly baked bread. The only thing missing was her grandad.

Grams and her husband Bill had lived at Strawberry Hill Farm for all of their sixty years of happy marriage. Flora's grandad had inherited the farm from his own parents and it had been in the family for almost a century. Having lost her mother to illness when she was only eight years old, Flora had been delighted when she and her father had come to live at the farm soon afterwards. Her grandparents were so steady and loving, in stark contrast to her father, who had sunk into a deep depression after the loss of his wife.

He had first remarried a year later and everything had changed once more. Flora's new, glamorous stepmother had no desire to live on a farm, nor to be the wife of a lowly farmer either. Her dad's own reluctance towards inheriting the family farm had turned into a full-blown crisis when he and Flora's stepmother moved out soon afterwards. That marriage had lasted six months and two more had followed since.

Her father was always seeking out someone to fill the hole left by the loss of Flora's mother. His search had led him everywhere but back to Strawberry Hill Farm to visit either his parents or his daughter.

Flora knew that the memories of her mother kept him away but had always secretly hoped that the lure of his only child would have brought him back home. But it had never happened.

Left behind, Flora had blossomed under her grandparents' care and attention and they had encouraged her to pursue her love of art. She had always adored painting and they had all been delighted that she had received a place at art college. During her first summer break, she had returned from a holiday in Africa armed with new ideas to freshen up the farmhouse. Consequently, the thick walls of the kitchen were painted bright orange and the cupboard doors a vivid blue. It wasn't the traditional colours for a country kitchen, but her grandparents adored it and suited their sunny natures.

But all too soon afterwards, Flora's grandfather had grown ill, leaving Grams overwhelmed with trying to cope with working the land by herself. So Flora had abandoned her art course to return to the farm to help out. When her grandfather passed away a short time later, Grams had tried to encourage her to return to college but Flora had refused. She would never have wanted to be anywhere else other than by Grams' side when she needed her.

She had been young, only nineteen years old, and her carefree college days were suddenly over. As Grams grieved for her beloved husband, Flora became aware of the responsibility of ensuring the farm that had been in the family name for over one hundred years survived. It was a huge burden and weighed heavily on her young shoulders.

So she had even abandoned her beloved painting to work every hour, do anything and everything that she could to help the farm carry on. In fact, she loved working the land, never minding the early starts and late finishes as it meant that she could enjoy the beauty of the sunrises and sunsets – her favourite times of the day. But any work/life balance was impossible with so much to do. She enjoyed a weekly cocktail session with the girls, but everything else had been sacrificed. And it still didn't feel as if it had been enough, especially now with the future of the farm so uncertain.

Grams brought over a mug of coffee and sat down at the table.

'I'm getting things ready for our visitor. Have you forgotten?' she asked. 'Lorenzo's grandson is arriving over the next couple of days.'

Flora made a face as she selected a muffin from the pile and picked at a piece of apple on the top. 'I still don't understand why he's coming here,' she said.

The timing couldn't be worse and the farmhouse wasn't exactly up to welcoming any visitors.

'Nico is coming here because he's the grandson of one of my oldest friends,' Grams told her. 'The letter I received last week said that he has something he wants to discuss with me. I have no idea what that is, but of course we will make him welcome. He couldn't be sure on the exact date when he was going to arrive, but I'm sure he'll be here soon.'

'So, remind me again. You and Lorenzo were...?' prompted Flora.

'Just good friends,' said Grams with a smile to herself. 'He came to the farm to work during the summer of 1961. We had such fun all those years ago, your grandfather, Lorenzo and I. We were all young and carefree, only in our late teens, and we have remained friends ever since, despite Lorenzo returning to Italy that same year. Did I tell you that his son is a very famous footballer over there? And an even more famous playboy!' added Grams, laughing. 'Can't wait to hear all about that! Paolo Rossi is apparently always in the news over there with his scandalous love life. I'm sure his son has inherited the same good looks and charm that all the Rossi men seem to have.'

Flora grimaced. The last thing she wanted was some over-bearing charmer turning up at the farm. Having been abandoned by her father all those years ago, she had deliberately built a hard shell around her heart to any kind of romance. Because if her own father could walk out on her, then surely every other man would do the same? Men were an alien species to be approached with caution, hard to understand and always likely to let her down. Apart from her grandad, of course. She missed him terribly and so did Grams.

She looked across at her grandmother. Helen Barton had a weatherworn face, but her eyes sparkled bright against her grey hair and rosy cheeks.

'I think a playboy might be just what you need,' Grams told her with a wicked glint in her green eyes. 'Have a bit of fun. You're thirty-one and I can't remember the last time you went on a date.'

Flora took a bite out of the muffin, the delicious flavour reminding her just how good a cook her grandmother was.

'I went out with Tyler Smith last autumn,' she replied, before wolfing down the rest of the muffin.

Grams rolled her eyes. 'Tyler is a nice lad and a good farmer, but he's as dull as ditch water,' she said with a sad shake of her head. 'You need someone you can laugh with. That's the one whom you should fall in love with.'

'Love?' Flora raised an eyebrow at her grandmother. 'I haven't got time for love. I need to check on the fields.'

'Why?' asked Grams, looking surprised. 'There's nothing growing in them any more.'

'I know, but how else can I avoid this awkward conversation?' said Flora, with a wink. She quickly got up and went to walk outside when she stopped to return to the table to drop a kiss on her grandmother's forehead. 'You don't need to worry about me,' she said in a soft voice.

'I will always worry about you,' replied Grams, reaching out to take Flora's hand in hers to give it a tight squeeze. 'You're our lovely girl and always will be. I just need to know that you're happy.'

'Of course I'm happy,' said Flora quickly. 'I'm here with you, aren't I?'

Flora squeezed her grandmother's hand before dropping it to walk out of the kitchen door.

Once she had pulled on her wellington boots and shrugged on her wax jacket, she went around the side of the L-shaped farmhouse to walk down the hill on which the farm was set. At this highest part of the farm, the land fell away towards the river in the valley below and the view was spectacular across the rolling hills and green landscape of the English countryside.

The glorious surroundings always kept her calm, especially at that moment when it was bathed in early-morning sunshine. Flora would be heartbroken if they ever had to leave the farm. But if she couldn't find a way of bringing in any income, what choice might they have in the future?

She glanced at the strawberry field on her right as she headed down the wide stony track. The strawberry plants were just peeping up from the ground where she had sown them the previous autumn but would benefit from being bathed in warm sunshine and the gentle incline which helped drain any rain away. Facing south, this field never flooded, so, over the summer, the bright red fruits which had given the farm its name all those years ago were the only crop which had made any profit.

Further across, the next field was much larger. It too was bathed in spring sunshine and never flooded, but it lay empty. That particular field hadn't produced any decent crops in a couple of years and with costs spiralling, Flora had left nature to reclaim it. Slowly, the field had become a wildflower meadow, fresh green growth showing everywhere. In its wild way, Flora rather preferred it than the other regimented fields that had been farmed until recently on the other side of the hill.

But those larger fields wouldn't be farmed any more either. The hill on the other side dropped sharply away and the farm's remaining fields were all on a floodplain at the bottom, boggy and sodden for most of the year. It had been an ongoing battle for ages, but the last two winters had been the worst, with the wettest weather on record causing the winter harvests to fail for the second year in a row. And now, with the sale of the farm equipment, they couldn't be farmed any more anyway.

At the bottom of the hill, Flora continued along the wide stony track into the woods. After being bathed in the early-morning sun, the woods briefly felt darker and cooler until she stepped out into a leafy glade where the trees had been cleared a long time ago.

In the distance, she could see the glistening water of the River Ley through the trees as it wound its way from nearby Cranbridge village onwards through the countryside.

Around two decades ago, when the flooding had caused problems further down the river one winter, Flora's grandad had dug out a large amount of earth to widen the bank of the river on their land and created a huge natural pond. It had helped slow down any floodwater, using nature to protect the villages and farms upstream from any damage.

Over the years since, nature had slowly reclaimed the space and it had become a magical place to Flora. Fed from the river and safely away from the muddy fields, the water was crystal clear. The sun was dappled as it lit up the water through the surrounding circle of trees. Birdsong filled the air, and on the far side of the pond, a couple of moorhens were preparing their nest for the arrival of their chicks.

It looked almost fairy-like that morning and, for a moment, her hands twitched to paint the view before the light changed. It had been years since Flora had painted anything, since leaving art college in fact. All of her paints and drawing pads were under her bed, gathering dust.

Much like her, thought Flora, allowing herself a smile of grim humour.

She was becoming fed up of being the sensible one, as her friends always told her she was. She wanted wild passion and excitement in her life before it was too late. Harriet and Katy had both found unexpected love in recent months and Libby was always travelling off to somewhere exotic with her job as a flight attendant, dating pilots and visiting amazing places.

Flora secretly envied her friends' happiness and rich lives. But she didn't have the luxury of excitement when she had to keep the farm afloat for both her and Grams.

Her twenties had passed by in the blink of an eye and it was likely that her thirties would go the same way. She hadn't even dipped her feet in the water in front of her in recent years, as the busy summers on the farm had taken up so much of her time.

Well, it was sunny now, she thought, looking at a wide ray of light across the water.

The sensible part of Flora reminded her that it was only April and the water would likely be freezing cold. But the other part of her, the part that she had thought hidden so deep inside that it rarely surfaced anymore, suddenly sprang to life. It told her that she had nothing to lose but the feelings in her toes if the water was that cold.

She suddenly decided that, for once, she was going to do something ridiculous and impetuous. She was going to follow her heart and just enjoy herself without the ever-present worry of money, work and duty.

Flora swiftly moved forward to stand next to one of the large boulders on the side of the lake and flung off her wellies. Next came the socks and then her jeans. She quickly shrugged off her jacket before taking off her jumper and T-shirt in one swoop of her arms.

Then, in just her underwear, she stepped around the boulder and waded into the clear water. She gasped at the extreme cold, but she went further in until she was standing up to her shoulders in the water. It was sharp, almost painfully cold on her skin, but it reminded her that she was still young and free. That she was still alive.

Why had it been so long since she had done this? she wondered. Perhaps she should begin taking a few risks now and then, she decided.

She sank down into the freezing water and lay on her back, floating and staring up at the blue sky above. She spread her arms out wide and, for the first time in such a long time, she felt at peace.

But just as she had reached a calm state of mind, she suddenly heard a deep male voice call out from somewhere nearby.

'Is this a private party or can anyone join in?'

Flora quickly rose up in the water, spinning around to find out who had spoken.

She stared in horror as she saw a handsome man, leaning on the bonnet of a red Ferrari and smiling at her whilst Flora stood there in just her underwear in the middle of the lake!

2

Nico Rossi had woken up in the driver's seat of the Ferrari with a crick in his neck and an aching back. The classic sports car might be glorious to look at, but it was certainly not a great choice for sleeping accommodation.

He had arrived in Cranfield in the middle of the night after a long drive from the port of Dover. In the darkness of the countryside, the car had bounced along the potholed lane leading to Strawberry Hill Farm. However, it was so late that he hadn't wanted to wake up his grandfather's elderly friend. After a search on the internet came up with no hotels in the vicinity, he had crept the car past the farmhouse and followed the lane where it became a track and parked up where it ended.

He had endured a restless, uncomfortable night in the narrow seat, but dawn had brought glorious spring sunshine. Feeling exhausted, he had clambered out of the car and made it as far as leaning on the bonnet, willing himself to wake up in the fresh air and wishing he had a strong cup of espresso to drink.

He hadn't even realised he had parked next to a small lake in the darkness the previous evening. It was certainly a beautiful setting, somewhat magical with the rays of sun shining across the water. He felt a moment of peace after so many days of upset and misery.

However, his solitude was broken as an attractive brunette arrived nearby. He had been about to call out a greeting when he found himself watching in total bemusement as she suddenly stripped off down to her underwear and waded into the water right in front of him! At first, he thought he must have been dreaming, but to his surprise – and immense pleasure – he realised that she was most definitely real.

She was currently standing up to her waist in the water glaring at him. 'Who are you?' she snapped, trying to cover her bra with her hands. 'You're trespassing on my land!'

'Then I suggest you come out of the water and arrest me,' replied Nico smoothly, his English perfect despite his words carrying a soft Italian accent.

He couldn't help but smile at her. She looked so delightfully indignant, standing there with her long dark hair plastered against her creamy skin. She looked like a beautiful but extremely angry water nymph.

'I shall call the police!' she carried on, with a toss of her long hair, which caused the water to ripple out from where she stood.

'From over there? That's a trick I'd like to see,' he replied. 'Especially because I can see your mobile sticking out of your coat pocket.'

They both glanced over at her pile of clothes, still lying on the boulder at the side of the lake, before looking back up at each other.

He guessed that the water must be absolutely freezing cold, considering it was April, and finally stopped teasing her. After all, he did try to be a true Italian gentleman, despite his infamous surname.

'It's okay. Come on out,' he called. 'I'll turn my back to give you what's left of your dignity.'

He did as he had promised, turning away to head around the car and open the door. He reached in to find a towel from the bags that filled the space behind the driving seat. In fact, every nook and cranny of the Ferrari was crammed with as many of his possessions as he'd been able to pack. He then checked his mobile, and by the time he had done all that, he was aware that the woman had come to stand on the other side of the car now fully dressed.

He straightened up and looked across the bonnet at her. Even from that distance, he could see the flash of her green eyes and the water droplets on her thick dark eyelashes. Her face glowed from a life seemingly spent outdoors, he thought. Her skin still gleamed wet from the water as she stood there in a jumper and jeans, holding a wax jacket.

'Here,' he said, holding out the towel for her to take. 'I thought you might need this.'

She hesitated before taking it from him, shooting him a look of distrust as she did so. 'Thank you,' she said, before using the towel to dry her face and hands.

'I apologise for disrupting your wild swim,' he said, digging a hand into his jeans pocket. It really was quite cold in the morning air. 'I didn't mean to frighten you.' He looked around. 'I must confess that I didn't think fairy-tale glades like this even existed. I can see why Nonno raved about the place so much over the years.'

'Nonno?' she said, with a confused frown.

'My grandfather. Lorenzo Rossi.' He moved around the car to stand in front of her. 'Nico Rossi,' he said, holding out his hand. '*Buongiorno*.'

'I'm Flora Barton,' she told him, taking his hand to give it a firm shake. 'Helen Barton's granddaughter.'

Up close, she was even more beautiful than he had initially thought, although those incredible green eyes were still flicking him sceptical glances.

'Well, Flora,' he said. 'Now that you've had your morning swim, how about we get in my car and you can introduce me to your grandmother?'

'Go? In this?' she asked, staring down at the Ferrari with incredulity.

'If you're going to go anywhere in life, why not do it in style?' he said, giving her a smile as he walked back around to the driver's door.

But she still didn't seem keen and remained hovering next to the car. 'I can walk back instead. I'm soaking wet,' she reminded him. 'I'm sure you don't want me to ruin your fancy car.'

He shrugged his shoulders. 'It's over forty years old and used to be owned by one extremely disreputable playboy,' he told her. 'I'm sure it's seen a lot worse over the years than a few drops of water.'

Not waiting for her answer, he climbed inside behind the wheel. He couldn't blame her for being a bit amazed at the car. He had been the same the first time his father had brought it home. To a six-year-old boy, it had been amazing to be driven around in a supercar on the narrow lanes of Tuscany. Now, all these years later and at the age of thirty-four, it belonged to him. Sort of.

The passenger door finally opened and Flora sat down next to him, having placed the towel on the seat first to protect the leather from her wet jeans.

The engine started with a throaty roar and he managed to complete a three-point turn, avoiding the many trees and boulders that surrounded them.

'Back up the track, I presume?' he asked, as they slowly drove through the woods.

Flora nodded, still staring around the inside of the car in amazement. 'Yes.'

'You've never been in a Ferrari before?' he said. 'It's very nice, don't you think?'

'If you like that kind of thing,' she told him, turning away to look out of the window.

He was getting the impression that Flora Barton wasn't impressed by anything, least of all him.

In a way, it was somewhat refreshing. Most of the women he came into contact with were starstruck by the association with his famous father. All the romances had been short-lived once he realised that all they wanted was a piece of fame. He had long since given up dating anyone over the last couple of years.

'And you don't like that kind of thing?' he prompted, slowly driving out of the woods.

'I don't suppose it's any good at ploughing fields,' she replied.

He glanced out of the window at the couple of fields in front of him up the hill. One appeared to have been left to run wild. The other much smaller field had rows of tiny green plants, but that was it. He wondered why it was so quiet. It was April and surely the place should be buzzing with activity?

His own family vineyard back in Tuscany had come alive in the spring. There had always been much to do at that time – preparing the vines and ensuring the coming harvest would be as good as it could be.

But it was spring now and there would be no more harvests ever again. The vineyard had gone and all that Nico had left was his name. The trouble was that his father had dishonoured the Rossi name so many times that even that was tainted.

The famous surname still held a certain appeal for some people, though. But if all people want from you is your famous name, who can you trust? Nico had decided a long time ago that he couldn't trust anyone.

As he drove up the hill, the farmhouse came into view. He couldn't help but be charmed by the sight of the sandy-coloured brick L-shaped building, with its terracotta pots of overflowing herbs by the front door all lit by the early-morning sunshine. There was a cheery charm about the place. It was a home, obviously cared for by a loving family.

For a moment, his breath caught in his throat as he thought about his own family home back in Italy. It too had been a large house overlooking their land, full of life and laughter. His grandparents had liked to entertain their friends and neighbours there, his father had liked to show off the vineyard to his many girlfriends. Nico had viewed it as a sanctuary, the only place where he had felt secure and loved for himself, not his famous name.

His father, Paolo, had been a gifted footballer who had risen to the heights of superstardom playing for Inter Milan. Alongside his footballing career, Paolo had also enjoyed a colourful love life, catalogued throughout the tabloids each and every week. The women loved his charm and good looks, as well as the substantial salary he was paid. Paolo's life was jam-packed full of fast women, fast cars and fine wine.

Nico was a result of a string of one-night affairs, with his young mother apparently leaving him on his father's doorstep at only a few weeks old. She had never wanted the child and had refused to be a part of his life.

Paolo was big on personality and charm, not so good with parenting. Unable to cope with a young baby, Nico had been dumped on his grandparents at the family home in Tuscany. They were the only other family that Nico had and thankfully they adored him. He found himself loved and mentored by them in their steady, reassuring way.

Even so, in the early days, Nico had longed for Paolo's infrequent visits. His father would bring an eclectic mix of toys and treats and – usually to his own parents' displeasure – a different girlfriend with him every time as well.

But suddenly Paolo's football career had been cut short prematurely due to a bad knee injury. Bored and listless without his beloved football to keep him occupied, he tried out various moneymaking schemes and investments, with varying degrees of success. Paolo lost his fortune as quickly as he made it, over and over. Sometimes, he got lucky and would return to Tuscany in his famous Ferrari showering gifts over everyone. Most of the time, he was absent, disappearing for months, sometimes years on end, whilst he tried to recoup the inevitable heavy losses incurred after yet another failed business venture.

But whenever he returned, Nico still let him back into his life and continued to forgive him. After all, despite everything, Paolo was his father.

For a while, Nico had even emulated his success with women. With his good looks and Rossi charm, he had dated a string of women in his twenties. But the frivolousness of endless dating and glamour had quickly palled. He didn't want to turn into his philandering father. He wanted something true, something honest, and was still searching for that woman who didn't want him just for the fame. He wanted what his grandparents had had all those years – companionship, trust and true love.

After studying business at university, he had returned to the vineyard armed with new ideas and excitement for what the future held for them all. He had poured nearly every last penny that he owned into investing for the future of the vineyard. He had put in place new eco-friendly bottling techniques, promoted customer experiences and even purchased a couple of drones to oversee the vast fields of vines.

For a while, they had all reaped the success of his hard work and the future of the vineyard was looking extremely prosperous.

But the last time Paolo had come home after his latest business venture had inevitably gone bust, everything had already begun to change. Nico's beloved grandmother had just passed away and Lorenzo was struggling in his grief to concentrate on business matters. Nico had taken control of the vineyard with his grandfather's blessing, but Paolo decided he wanted to take over the family business himself, stating that he could triple their profits in a few short months.

Lorenzo had passed away a short while later, still hoping that his family home would be passed down to his grandson. But his wishes were only ever verbal and so everything had passed to Paolo instead. Shortly after, the family home, the vineyard, all of it, was sold to the highest bidder and despite fighting the sale every inch of the way, one week ago Nico had lost his home. The only home he had ever known. Everything was gone, including his grandparents, the only people he had ever truly trusted and counted on. He was lost and heartbroken.

And angry, he realised. His father had taken everything away from him, including his future as owner of the vineyard. So it was only right and fair that Nico should take something of Paolo's as well.

Therefore, the night before the house sale was completed, Nico had stolen the car keys and driven away in his father's beloved Ferrari. He had slowly driven up through Italy and then across Europe, trying to work out what to do next with his life. His dream had always been to keep his home, with the family he so dearly cherished, and perhaps, one day, fill it with children of his own. He loved working outside, but apart from his business degree, his only experience had been at the vineyard, and now that too was lost to him.

He had no plans, except one. Whilst tidying up Lorenzo's study, Nico had come across a letter in which he had bequeathed a gift to Helen Barton and left the address for Strawberry Hill Farm. So Nico had come to England to honour his grandfather's wish. After that, he had no idea where he would go next.

The Rossi name was tainted in Tuscany thanks to his father's misdemeanours. Nico was aware that the scandals had tarred his own name with the same brush and nearly everyone that he had contacted for work or a temporary place to stay had slammed the door in his face.

And from the distrustful looks that Flora was still giving him, she looked as if she was tempted to do exactly the same.

3

Flora squirmed in the leather car seat in embarrassment, but the movement only served to remind her that her jeans were soaking wet from where she had quickly got dressed after getting out of the lake.

She was completely and utterly mortified. The one time in recent years when she had thrown caution to the wind and she had been found in only her underwear by a complete stranger! If that wasn't a reminder to live a sensible life, then she wasn't sure what was.

She glanced over at Nico Rossi as he drove up the hill. So this was Lorenzo's grandson that Grams had spoken about? The words Italian playboy certainly rang true, given the flash car she now found herself in. He drove a Ferrari, for goodness' sake! The man was a walking cliché, even down to his dishevelled dark good looks and sexy accent.

Flora's cheeks grew hot as she thought of him seeing her cheap black bra and knickers. It was just too much to bear. He had seen her at her most vulnerable and it unsettled her. Okay, he had offered her a towel and turned his back whilst she got dressed, but she was certain that being an old-fashioned gentleman was probably part of his charm routine. Hadn't Grams said something about all the men in his family being playboys?

When he parked up the supercar next to her old, battered Land Rover, the contrast couldn't have been more extreme. She leapt out of the car, desperate to put some distance between them.

Thankfully, a distraction happened in the form of Grams heading out of the door and into the courtyard to see what the unexpected noise of the throaty exhaust was.

'My word!' she exclaimed, looking on in wonder at the Ferrari. 'What a car!'

'Always happy to take a beautiful lady such as yourself out for a spin,' said Nico, as he climbed out of the driver's seat.

Grams merely looked delighted. 'Oh! You are so like Lorenzo back in the day,' she said, with a chuckle.

Flora managed not to roll her eyes and studied him instead. Not knowing anything about Lorenzo, she had no comparisons to hold him up against. Nico had wavy dark hair, a roman nose and dark eyes. His skin looked the type to go instantly bronze as soon as summer arrived. He was tall, dark and, rather annoyingly, good-looking.

She felt supremely irritated by him. She knew it was embarrassment on her part. Why hadn't she been driving her tractor feeling confident and in her comfort zone instead of dripping wet, half naked in the middle of the lake when he had found her?

Nico walked towards Grams and held out his hand. 'Mrs Barton, *buongiorno*. It's a pleasure to finally meet you. I'm Nico Rossi.'

'And I'm Helen. Let's dispense with the formalities, shall we?' said Grams, stepping forward to draw Nico into a hug.

Her tiny stature only emphasised his tall body as he gently returned the embrace.

'Let me take a look at you,' said Grams, stepping back to stare up at Nico. 'You are a chip of the old block, I must say. The splitting image of your grandfather. Dear Lorenzo. I can't believe he's gone when he was always so full of life. What a character he was.'

Nico gave her a sad smile. 'Thank you for your letter,' he said, in a soft tone. 'Your words were a great comfort to me.'

Grams gave a heavy sigh. 'I was so sad not to attend the funeral, but I'm not up to plane rides these days.' She shot a look at the Ferrari once more. 'But I'm looking forward to heading out in that gorgeous beast at some point.'

Nico laughed. 'Any time you want a spin, just say the word.'

He looked across at Flora, but she was thankful to see his laugh falter a bit as he met the glare of her eyes.

Grams too glanced over at her and gave a start. 'What happened to you?' she asked, her eyes wide. 'You're all wet.'

'I fell over,' lied Flora.

'Under water?' asked Grams, somewhat bewildered.

'I'll go change,' replied Flora, heading towards the open door.

Behind her, she could hear Grams and Nico laughing over something and she felt even more rattled. Grams wasn't friends with handsome Italian playboys. Grams was steady, secure. She was a farmer and she was sensible, just like Flora. Wasn't she?

Flora stalked through the spacious kitchen, down the narrow hallway and up the staircase. It wasn't a large farmhouse, but it was plenty big enough for the two of them. It had four bedrooms. Grams, of course, had the master bedroom and Flora was in the second largest on the other side of the corridor.

In the hope of making more money, or at least trying to stay afloat financially, Flora had given the other two bedrooms an extremely cheap makeover and they had been mildly successful for a while in renting the rooms out through Airbnb in the autumn. But a winter storm had ripped some of the tiles off the roof and now one of the bedrooms and the bathroom both leaked every time it rained. So there had been no more visitors and the money had dried up once more.

Flora went into her bedroom and shut the door, leaning back against it. What a morning and it was barely eight o'clock yet.

She looked across at the picture on her bedside cabinet. A picture of her grandparents looking happy and relaxed as they stood in the middle of the strawberry field. It had been taken many years ago when the farm had been successful and they had all been together.

She thought back to the conversation earlier with Joe and the selling of all the farm equipment. Now what? For all of his expertise, Joe didn't have any answers as to where their future lay. The majority of the fields were on a floodplain so couldn't be sold off for building purposes, nor could they be used for farming. With nothing left for them to sell except the farmhouse, Joe had been stumped for ideas and so had Flora.

They could only hang on to the farmhouse with some new type of income, but what? For a moment, Flora had a daydream of taking on a normal job and having the weekends off to lie in the warm sun and relaxing, something she rarely did. Maybe even taking up painting again. But she suddenly felt restless, unsettled by what the future held.

At the sound of laughter outside, she headed over to the window. Nico was showing Grams the inside of the Ferrari and they were both laughing along. At a crossroads in her life, the last thing Flora needed was some smooth playboy coming over and distracting Grams. Hard decisions needed to be made and they could hardly have those kinds of conversations when Nico was there.

Flora determinedly looked away at the rest of the view. Her room overlooked the strawberry field and the empty one next door. It too was now left to fallow. In fact, it had ended up making them more money than with crops the previous summer being used as a car park for the visitors to the lavender fields.

At the far end of the field and across the narrow path towards the much larger village of Cranbridge were two large fields planted with lavender. Owned by her best friend Harriet, the fields had been opened up to the public for the first time with huge success the previous summer. Harriet had been successful in love as well, having fallen for Joe, with whom she now lived in a cottage on Railway Lane.

On the opposite side of the railway tracks was the old railway station. The railway line had long since been closed, so Harriet had turned the small postroom at the far end of the station into a successful spa, using her talent as a beauty therapist to work wonders with the lavender products.

Next to the spa was the main part of the station, which had been turned into a successful coffee shop and restaurant thanks to her friend Katy, who lived and worked there with her boyfriend Ryan.

The last of her group of friends was Libby, who was Harriet's neighbour in one of the cottages just along from the station. She worked as an airline flight attendant and was often away on trips abroad, just how free-spirited Libby preferred it. But when she was home, they always met up.

Flora was pleased with her friends' success, both in their careers and in love. It seemed that only her own position was financially precarious.

She didn't really care about the lack of a love life, however. She prided herself on being sensible, practical and level-headed. Love had no place in her ordered way of life, whatever Grams might wish for her.

Hearing Nico roar with laughter once more, Flora turned away from the window to get dressed into warm, dry clothes, all the while grinding her teeth in irritation.

Grams had talked about Nico's famous father and so Flora brought out her phone to google him. There were plenty of images for Flora to gaze at in open-mouthed amazement. Paolo Rossi seemed to be always having one scandal after another in the tabloids.

Then, to her horror, she saw that his son was listed in similar stories. The photographs all seemed to be of one girlfriend or another, flashing lightbulbs and all the tabloid titillation of a euro-trash lifestyle.

Flora flung her phone down onto her bed with a howl of dismay. He certainly wasn't to be trusted whilst he was visiting them. She had to protect her grandmother. The sooner Nico Rossi left Cranfield, the better, as far as she was concerned.

4

———

Having heard so much about the summer his grandfather had spent at bustling Strawberry Hill Farm all those years ago, Nico was somewhat surprised that there was no one else around except Grams and her granddaughter.

He had been invited inside to sit in the surprisingly colourful farmhouse kitchen. It was large and clean but also full of the aroma of home cooking, with the nearby range giving out a cheery warmth.

A familiar perfume twitched his senses and he looked around until he spotted a pot of basil on the windowsill. The reminder of the sweet smell of his grandmother's Italian kitchen made him catch his breath.

Nico took a grateful sip of the hot coffee that Grams had just handed him. '*Grazie*, Helen,' he said. 'Thank you. I need this.'

'You must call me Grams,' she replied. 'After all, you're like family to me. And you should have just knocked on the door last night rather than sleeping in your car,' she added in a stern voice, having now discovered that he had fallen asleep in his car overnight.

Nico shook his head. 'I wouldn't have dreamt of disturbing you,' he replied.

After all, Grams might have the spirit and eyes of a young woman, but she was eighty years old now. Still, he could see the passion and drive that his grandfather had spoken about when they had met all those years ago.

A passion that was most definitely hidden deep inside Flora, he decided as she stalked back into the kitchen in a change of clothing. She gave him a scowl before pouring herself a mug of coffee. She was as cold as Grams was warm.

He knew what the problem was, of course. She had heard about the family name, seen the Ferrari and immediately painted him as a chip of the block. He had been experiencing this for many years and it didn't surprise him.

But whereas he had been a playboy, many years ago, that no longer ran true. Nor did the Rossi fortune have any wealth to its name either. Yes, his clothes were expensive and his jeans a designer brand, but they had been bought years ago when the money had been flowing and he had been happy to spend it. But as time had gone by, and fortunes fluctuated, he had held on to his decent clothes and stopped buying anything new. They were beautifully made and so they lasted.

Unfortunately, he had learnt too late to save enough money to buy the vineyard from his father. He had failed his grandparents and had let them down at the worst moment. And let himself down in the process.

But, of course, he wasn't going to explain any of this to his hosts.

'Thank you,' he said, as Grams placed a plate piled high with delicious-looking muffins in front of him. 'This looks great.'

'Tuck in,' she told him, putting another plate of food in front of Flora. 'There's plenty to go around.'

'Nonno never said you were such an amazing cook,' said Nico, after the first delicious mouthful.

Grams waved away his compliment with one hand. 'I probably wasn't in those days,' she said, laughing. 'After all, I was only eighteen. We were young and stupid, as everyone is at that age. But that was a very long time ago now. You know, Lorenzo always spoke about you in his letters. How are things with you these days?'

'Great,' said Nico, the muffins suddenly growing thick in his throat. 'I've been taking care of the family business until recently.'

'How is the vineyard?' asked Grams.

'Last year's harvest was one of the best yet,' replied Nico, his smile growing a little more painful on his face. 'In fact, I've got some bottles of wine in the car for you as a present.'

'How wonderful,' Grams told him. 'I shall enjoy a tipple later. Now, where are you staying whilst you're in England?'

Nico shrugged his shoulders. 'Actually, I haven't made any plans other than visiting you.'

'Then I insist that you stay for a couple of nights at least,' said Grams. 'If you have the time, of course.'

Nico was touched by her kindness. '*Grazie*. I'd enjoy that very much.'

'Excellent.' Grams looked delighted. 'And then we can have a proper chat and you can tell me all about the vineyard.'

Nico took another sip of coffee and nearly tipped it down his shirtfront, such was his shaking hand. How could he tell Grams that his father had sold the place? That the history and hard work that his family had given over the years had all been for nothing?

For a second, his heart ached with the pain of failure. He had failed his family name, his grandparents, everyone. Surely he hadn't done everything that he could have done to protect the family house? Paolo was impetuous and idiotic, but Nico was certain that some of the blame must lay at his door.

'I look forward to a glass of Rossi wine made from grapes warmed by the Italian sun,' said Grams, with a smile. 'I remember drinking it with your grandparents when my late husband and I used to visit. We sat out on the terrace, overlooking that tremendous setting over the hills.'

Nico nodded, still trying to keep his emotions at bay. 'And the hot sun was perfect for the vines,' he told her.

'Your English is much better than I was expecting,' said Grams, with a nod of approval. 'But, then again, I seem to remember that you went to school in England. Is that right?'

'My father believed that the best schools were to be found here,' Nico told her. 'So I got packed off each term to boarding school and then headed home to Italy for holidays.'

On the all-too-frequent occasions when his father's money had run out, Nico would end up back at the local school in his home town before being shipped off to the boarding school when the funds were replenished. At the time, he had been teased for his Italian accent at the boarding school, whereas the local kids in his home town teased him for the English ways he had picked up. It meant that he was now bilingual but with no real friends to rely on.

It had been a displaced childhood, confusing for a young boy to be sent so far from home, barely knowing the language. As the years went by, however, he discovered that he loved the English sense of humour and now he could talk and think in both languages.

'Shame I never got to meet you before now as we haven't visited for over thirty years. Life goes so quickly sometimes,' she added with a soft sigh. 'Of course, I know all about your famous father. How is he?'

Nico nodded, faking good humour. Everyone knew Paolo Rossi and the scandals that followed him wherever he went. 'Same as ever,' Nico told her. 'Still living the high life back in Italy.'

Still being as distant a father as ever, he reminded himself. The only contact had been an angry voicemail shouting for the return of his beloved Ferrari. Selling the family estate hadn't bothered Paolo one bit. Only the loss of his wretched supercar had caused him any grief.

'What fun,' said Grams, with a chuckle. 'I wish we lived as full a life as you Rossi men seem to do over in Italy.'

'We have a full life here,' said Flora suddenly.

'Of course we do,' replied Grams with a frown at her granddaughter.

The outburst died as quickly as it had arrived.

Nico glanced at her briefly before putting his head down and clearing his plate as an awkward silence ensued.

'That was amazing,' he said. 'Thank you.'

'You need a good breakfast to set you up for a busy day when you're a farmer,' Grams told him.

Busy day? Nico hesitated to ask the question he had been wondering about ever since arriving. 'And, er, how is Strawberry Hill Farm doing these days?' he asked.

He caught the brief glance between Flora and Grams and wondered whether he had guessed correctly that there was a problem there.

'Perhaps not as well as when your grandfather was here,' said Grams briskly. 'Anyway, I'm sure you'd like to stretch your legs and look around the place. Flora will give you the tour whilst I tidy up in here.'

Flora looked as if she wanted to do anything other than be in

Nico's company for a minute longer, but she abruptly stood up anyway.

He also stood and followed her out of the kitchen.

'Do you have wellington boots?' she asked him, as she pulled on her own boots. 'It's still quite muddy everywhere.'

'In my car,' he replied, heading over to unpack them and his coat.

In fact, he had brought nearly all of his clothes with him – a reminder his worldly possessions were in a storage unit back in Italy. He'd never been interested in material things, unlike his father. And it wasn't as if the Ferrari was big on boot space to start with. But he had everything he needed in the car.

He pulled on his wellington boots and realised Flora was staring into the back of the car with a curious look on her face.

'That's a lot of stuff considering you didn't know how long you were staying,' she told him.

Nico straightened up and gave her a broad grin. 'I always pack as much as I can. Never know what each day holds for me, from a black-tie ball to a hot date.'

'Don't think you'll be in danger of too many black-tie balls around here,' she told him before turning away.

'What about hot dates?' he asked, but she had already turned the corner of the farmhouse and had disappeared.

She was upset about him being there, that much she hadn't bothered to hide. But there was something else there. A stress, some tension perhaps? Could it be that Strawberry Hill Farm was in trouble?

Nico found himself wanting to know more, perhaps even trying to help if they needed it. His grandfather had told him that the Barton family had paid him a great kindness when he had first come to the farm all those years ago. He hadn't gone into detail and yet Nico had instantly known that it had meant a huge deal to Lorenzo. And his grandfather had always been a good judge of character.

The guilt over the loss of the vineyard and his own home still hung heavily on Nico. Perhaps if he could help repay the kindness and help out Flora and her grandmother over the next couple of days, then it might feel as if he could still achieve something in this world. That he still had something to offer people.

And maybe it would help ease the constant grief and guilt that he carried with him all the time as well.

5

Flora had heard Nico's joke about hot dates but had chosen to ignore it.

Anyway, what did she know about hot dates? Not much. Her dates the previous autumn with Tyler Smith, the farmer a few villages along, had been anything but. They had been nice but had been missing the chemistry, the thrill, the quickening pulse. All of which she'd read about but never experienced first-hand. She'd had boyfriends in her first year of art college but no one since then.

Tyler couldn't ever be described as hot, but at least he was reliable, trustworthy and steady. Everything that Nico Rossi wasn't.

And now Grams had invited him to stay! Because he had nothing in his diary, he had eagerly accepted. What kind of a person had no plans in life? she wondered.

Of course, as she reminded herself, the irony was that she was the same these days. An unknown future stretched out in front of her, and it was seriously unsettling.

She glanced at Nico as he came around the corner, his long legs emphasised in his fitted jeans and wellington boots. The thought of sitting opposite a man like him in a candlelit restaurant unnerved her. He was too suave and good-looking for her, with his glamorous background. Too much of everything, she thought with a shake of her head to dispel such thoughts.

'This is the strawberry field,' she told him, looking at the gently rolling slope in front of them as they walked through the gate. 'There's nothing to show yet, of course. But, come the summer, it'll be packed full of strawberries. Hopefully,' she added under her breath. Because without the revenue from the strawberries, the farm wouldn't have any income at all.

'Have you considered investing in a polytunnel to protect them from the wet weather?' Nico asked.

Flora turned to look at him in surprise. 'You've used them back in Italy?' she asked.

'Sometimes, if there's going to be a late frost, it helped to protect the vegetable garden,' he replied. 'The vineyard was too big to cover, though, so we would light fires amongst the vines to keep off the cold.'

'I see,' she replied. 'Well, it's never been necessary here so far.' The truth was that it had been an additional expense, one which their accounts didn't have sufficient funds for.

She watched as Nico crouched down to touch the soil bed nearest to them and rubbed it through his fingers.

'Loam,' he muttered to himself. 'Sand too for good drainage.'

She was quietly impressed. Perhaps he had a little more knowledge than she gave him credit for.

'Strawberries don't like soggy roots,' she told him. 'So the hill works well to drain away any heavy rain.'

'Then it's the perfect spot, especially being south-facing as well to maximise the sunshine,' he said, standing up once more.

She went to turn away and get the tour over with as soon as possible, but Nico remained looking at the field.

'These are the strawberries that Nonno picked,' he said, in a surprisingly wistful tone.

Flora was reminded that Nico had lost his grandad within the last year and that perhaps underneath that smooth exterior was the grief that she too felt with the loss of her own grandfather.

'Yes, it's the same field,' she replied. 'The farm was named after it. There's been strawberries here for nearly a hundred years.'

He nodded and finally turned away to walk with her along the path.

'And the other fields?' he asked. 'What do you grow there?'

'A variety of crops,' she replied. She didn't want to open up to him about how bad things actually were. It didn't matter anyway. He would be gone in a couple of days and their life would resume, although she wasn't sure what direction it would follow. 'So you seem to know a lot about soil?' she asked, hoping to change the subject away from the farm.

He nodded. 'Yes. My grandfather taught me everything. About how to take care of the vines and the best weather for the best harvest. But I also went to business college to learn about the newer techniques. Sometimes a mix of old and new is the best way forward.'

They were both quiet then. She wanted to ask more but suddenly the conversation felt awkward.

They walked to the brow of the hill before stopping to look at the view. Cranfield was close by, a tiny hamlet of around fifty houses, all built with the same sandy-coloured brick. It had come to life in the past year. The station had had a complete overhaul and Flora noticed that Katy had added a lick of green paint on the window frames to freshen them up, as well as some window boxes filled with pink and white flowers. Platform 1, the coffee shop and pizza restaurant, had opened and gradually the villagers were beginning to gather there. Some people used it as a home working office, others just wanted to chat or have a little company for a while.

She watched as Bob and Eddie, the former stationmasters, came out of the station and waved at her before they disappeared into the railway workshop. Hidden inside the large metal building was the steam locomotive which they were promising would finally be up and working by the autumn.

Flora turned slowly towards the valley where the river and Cranbridge, a much larger village, lay spread out in front of them. Before them, on the opposite side of the railway tracks were the lavender fields. Hopefully, this summer would be a repeat success with many visitors enjoying the lavender. At the moment, the rows of lavender bushes were still green, waiting for the warm sunshine to burst into their vibrant purple.

In the far distance, there were more gently rolling hills, slowly coming to life as spring took hold after the cold, wet winter.

It was one of her favourite views and Flora took a moment to savour it.

After a while, she realised that Nico was watching her and suddenly felt uncomfortable.

'So, what do you do when you're not farming?' he asked.

Flora was momentarily startled. 'There's not much time to do anything when you're a farmer,' she eventually replied. 'I'm sure you understand.'

It was the question which she had asked herself over and over in the past few months. If she didn't farm the land, then what would she do? Her artistic side had taken a back seat over the years, except for a brief glorious moment in the past winter when Katy had asked her for ideas to help decorate Platform 1.

Katy had a great business mind but had no artistic flair so had left most of the decisions up to Flora. She had revelled in choosing a colour palette, as well as finding some bargain decorations that she could embellish. For a short few days she had enjoyed herself, but once the restaurant had been decorated, then that was that.

Nico was still looking at her, so she spun the question around.

'What about you?' she asked. 'How do you relax when you're not working?'

'I find the old-fashioned way of relaxing works every time,' he joked.

Flora rolled her eyes. A few moments ago, he had been struggling in his grief and she had almost been tempted to feel sorry for him. Not any more.

'Listen,' Flora told him. 'Some of us have more serious problems than joking around and making sure your pretty car doesn't get dirty or whatever.'

'You really think that the extent of my problems is my car getting muddy?' he asked, raising his eyebrows.

'Look, you're here because you wanted to see Grams,' she told him. 'I suggest you spend the hopefully short time that you're here with her and not me.'

She stalked away, leaving him to march down the hill. She knew that she was taking out her frustrations on Nico, perhaps somewhat unfairly. But his life was so different to hers. He probably didn't spend each day with a list of tasks that needed to be completed, like she did.

Except it wasn't like that any more, she reminded herself. And she was a little lost and worried about what the future might really bring.

Whatever lay ahead, however, she was convinced it would remain a playboy-free zone!

6

Exhaustion had suddenly come over Nico late in the morning, having driven through England late into the night. So, after lunch, he lay down on the bed in the spare bedroom, still trying to catch up on the broken night's sleep he had endured in the Ferrari.

In fact, he couldn't remember the last time that he slept properly. Not since his grandfather's funeral, he thought. Ever since that, his life had been reeling from one bad decision that his father had made to another. He was exhausted from fighting the battle to save his family home. Now the fight was finally lost, he felt even more tired than before.

But the farmhouse felt familiar, despite this being his first visit. It had a relaxed feel about the place, old furniture that was comfortable to sit on and that had obviously been there for many years. The paint on the walls of the spare bedroom was fresh, but the patchwork quilt was soft and warm and obviously home-made.

Even the paintings on his wall made him relax. His particular favourite in the bedroom was a landscape one, painted at sunset when the rolling hills were bathed in golden light. He fell asleep imagining himself enjoying such a view.

He woke up late in the afternoon to the smell of a delicious dinner wafting up through the kitchen to his bedroom above.

After a quick shower and feeling much fresher, he wandered downstairs and found Grams and Flora in the kitchen.

Grams was at the stove whilst Flora was laying the table with plates and cutlery. The scene reminded him of the happier days in the vineyard when dinner was very much a family affair and for a moment he was warmed by the memory.

'Did you sleep well?' asked Grams.

Nico nodded. 'Too well,' he replied. 'I should have been down here helping you prepare dinner.'

'Nonsense,' she replied, urging him to sit down at the table. 'It's only a stew, I'm afraid. Ryan over at the railway station is the proper Italian cook. His food is wonderful. We should all eat in there whilst Nico is staying with us.'

Nico glanced across the table at Flora, who looked like she'd rather eat one of her wellington boots than have dinner with him, but she said nothing and looked down at her phone once more.

Perhaps he had come on a little strong earlier and would make an effort to apologise once more to her later. He was Italian and she was very pretty, but he wasn't his father. Or at least he hoped he wasn't.

Most women he had met in Italy adored the fact that he was the son of a famous footballer and he had even followed his father's playboy roots when the money had been flowing. The only excuse that he could tell himself all these years on was that it had been a failed attempt to gain his father's approval.

The one woman he had fallen hard for was Maria. It was only too late that he had realised that it was his famous father whom she was more interested in. Finding Maria in bed with his father had been a hard lesson taught. She had sold the story on both of them and Nico had endured the realisation that everyone was probably laughing at them both. Paolo didn't care, but Nico did. So he had kept his head down and worked the land and in his grandfather's workshop and didn't trust any stranger from that moment on.

Thankfully, he had no expectations that Flora was interested in him at all. She was quiet over the delicious dinner as he began to find out about the farm and its history. The Barton family had apparently lived at Strawberry Hill Farm all their lives, inheriting the farm from Grams' father-in-law.

After dinner, they moved to the lounge, a comfortable room full of battered but soft sofas and a large oak coffee table in front of a roaring fire. The night air was cool that evening and so the warmth from the fire was welcome.

On the coffee table, Grams pointed to a photo album. 'I got that out when you were resting,' she told him, as they sat down together on the sofa.

Flora sat down on a mismatched armchair next to them to take a look as well.

'Thought you'd like to see your grandfather back in the day,' said Grams with a smile as she handed him the album.

Nico took a deep breath, bracing himself for the inevitable grief to overwhelm him. But that was offset by the black-and-white photographs he found on the first page. The page had faded writing declaring it to be the summer of 1961. Everyone in the photographs was smiling and looking relaxed in the sunshine and he couldn't help but be charmed, instead of feeling upset.

'There's Lorenzo,' said Grams, pointing to a man at the end of a group of about half a dozen people.

Nico peered at the photograph more closely and was pleased to realise that it was a younger version of his grandfather.

'He's with my future husband Bill, Flora's grandad,' carried on Grams. 'As well as some other travellers that had turned up to help pick the strawberries that summer.'

Nico looked at his grandfather's face once more. 'I never knew why he came over here,' he said, wishing the years could fade away and that he had the time to ask the questions that he had never thought to pose. 'He spent nearly all his time at the vineyard.'

Grams looked at him. 'Apparently, he had fallen out with your great-grandfather. According to Lorenzo, he was a bully and struck him frequently.'

Nico was shocked. 'I never knew that,' he said.

Grams nodded. 'I think he had finally discovered his inner strength and had escaped out of there early in the spring when the snows melted. So he got on his motorbike and toured around Europe for a while, earning money wherever he could. He came to us in early July and ended up staying for the rest of the summer.'

'A motorbike?' Nico was stunned. 'I had no idea he ever owned one.'

Grams chuckled. 'It was a real old ropey thing,' she said, laughing in memory. 'Smoky and stuttering. It gave up on him as soon as he arrived. He had to hitchhike all the way home to Italy come the autumn!' She frowned. 'I think it's still here on the farm somewhere.'

She looked at her granddaughter, who was looking equally surprised.

'Is that where that came from?' said Flora. 'I always wondered about that. Yes, it's still in the old stables.'

Nico was amazed. 'I'd love to see it.'

Grams nodded. 'We'll go and have a look at it tomorrow.' She smiled. 'Your grandfather was charming, oh-so Italian, of course.

I'd never seen anything like it, especially here in sleepy Cranfield! Anyway, once the summer had ended, he headed home to make up with his father and then he restarted his work and life on the vineyard. Apparently, his absence had caused a shift in the relationship and he and your great-grandfather began to find some peace. And, of course, he met his darling Sofia soon afterwards. We came across to the wedding a year later, six months after they came here to celebrate ours. Do you know, it was my first ever trip abroad? And what a magnificent place it was. Your home is truly beautiful.'

Nico's smile caught in his throat at the thought of his beloved home. He could smell the hot dusty air as it swept over the rows of vines. The feel of the hot summer sun as he sat on the large patio, watching the sun turn orange and then a deep red as it sank below the hills in the far distance. The creak of the floorboards inside. The sound of the laughter as his grandmother and grandfather chatted with their friends. For a second, he could barely breathe from the loss, the thought that he would never again see and feel those reminders of his family.

Grams carried on her story and Nico tried to concentrate on the present once more. 'We exchanged frequent letters in those days and tried to visit each other once a year. Later on, as our families grew, other priorities took over. But we continued to write letters, which were full of news about you when you came along. Such a blessing for them.'

Nico looked down at the photographs once more and somehow it made his grandmother and grandfather feel closer to him once more.

He felt it was the right time to follow his grandfather's wishes and hand over the small package that he had brought with him.

'And now I have something to give you,' he said, placing the soft parcel in Grams's hands. 'Nonno requested that this was to be left to you. And as it is so very precious, I wanted to deliver it myself.'

Grams looked a little nervous as she unwrapped the tissue paper before taking a shocked breath when she discovered the material inside. 'Oh!' she said, with a little cry. 'It's my shawl.'

Flora leaned forward to view the white silk embroidered with tiny flowers. 'Is it for a wedding?'

Grams nodded, her eyes filled with tears. 'Your great-grand-mother made it for me and I loaned it to Sofia for her something borrowed. She loved it so much that I let her keep it as a present.' She stroked the material with her fingers. 'She always promised that the next time they visited she would return it to me. I wish she had been able to do so in person one last time. I wish they both had.'

There was a short silence whilst Grams seemed to need to check her emotions. Nico reached out to squeeze her hand and she grasped at it.

'Thank you for returning it to me,' she whispered, her voice a little unsteady. 'It's like having them here with us.'

'*Prego*,' he replied. 'You're welcome. There was a letter addressed to you as well.'

He held out the envelope which was written in his grandfa-ther's familiar scrawled writing.

Grams took it with a shaking hand.

Nico glanced up and saw Flora looking at her grandmother with concern.

'I'm fine,' said Grams, waving her hand at both Flora and Nico. 'Nothing that a large sherry won't sort out.'

Flora went to pour them all a drink whilst Nico stayed with Grams. She opened up the envelope and, with a deep breath, began to read. It was a couple of pages long and Nico had no idea what it said.

After she had finished reading, she carefully tucked the hand-written pages back into the envelope and took hold of his hand in hers to give it a squeeze.

'Bless you,' she told him softly. 'It's been an absolute tonic having you turn up here. Heaven knows we needed a lift.'

Nico was about to ask what she meant when Flora returned with their drinks and so he held his question, deciding to find out exactly how bad a situation Strawberry Hill Farm was in whilst he was there.

He wasn't sure why he cared so much. Perhaps it was the connection to his grandmother and grandfather. Perhaps it was just like his own family home that he was missing so much. But, either way, he felt a need to help in any way he could. And, for a moment, he wished that he too could follow in his grandfather's footsteps and stay at Strawberry Hill Farm for the summer as well.

7

'So, you've taken an instant dislike to the good-looking Italian playboy who owns a Ferrari?' asked Libby, laughing before leaning forward to take a bit of the carrot cake that she had ordered.

It was the following day and Flora had met her best friends in Platform 1 for a long-overdue catch-up.

Platform 1 was a coffee shop during the day and a pizza restaurant at night, both of which Katy and Ryan had opened to great success the previous winter. It was Tuesday morning and it was already busy with locals and walkers who were passing through on the path to Cranbridge. Held in the old waiting rooms of the station, it was a charming mix of railway memorabilia and comfy cushions and wood panelling. It helped that the coffees and cakes were delicious too.

Flora shook her head. 'I never said he was good-looking.'

'Who ever heard of an ugly Italian playboy?' asked Katy, reaching out to nibble on a biscuit. 'Anyway, I saw him this morning with Grams and he is most definitely good-looking.'

Despite their gentle teasing, as always, Flora could relax with her friends.

'I think it sounds so romantic,' said Harriet, with a happy sigh.

Libby rolled her eyes, ever the cynical one where love and romance was concerned. Her amazing long pale blonde hair, vibrant personality and pretty face made sure that she was never short of dates. However, any relationship never lasted long.

Harriet, on the other hand, viewed most things and people through rose-tinted glasses. Her long red hair swung over her face as she bent down to give a piece of her buttered scone to her golden retriever Paddington. She straightened up with a yawn. 'I'm so tired today. I need this large latte.'

'Joe keeping you up all night?' asked Libby with a sly smile.

Harriet blushed down to her redhead roots. 'Not this time,' she said, with a giggle. 'There was some bird singing away right by my window at 5 a.m. and I couldn't get back off to sleep after that.'

'It was probably the songbirds – you know, like the robins and great tits attracting their mates,' said Flora automatically. 'Now that it's spring, they've all come to life.'

Katy looked at her bemused. 'How do you know all this stuff?' she said.

'I'm a country girl at heart,' Flora told her.

'Not me,' said Katy, with a shudder, causing her blonde bob to shake around her pretty face.

But that wasn't entirely true any more, thought Flora. Since arriving from London six months ago, Katy had gradually overcome her fear and dislike for the countryside and was even known to go on long walks with her partner Ryan.

However, her city nature and style still betrayed her sometimes, such as wearing her favourite high-heeled ankle boots that day.

'So, your Italian visitor has a Ferrari? Wow!' said Harriet, wide-eyed as she finally caught up with the conversation. 'Wonder if I can trade my beaten-up old Fiesta for something more glamorous?'

'Don't bother,' snapped Flora. 'He won't be giving up his beloved supercar any time soon.'

All three of her friends turned to look at her in surprised bemusement at her sharp tone.

'My, my,' murmured Katy. 'He has rubbed you up the wrong way.'

'Chance would be a fine thing,' added Libby with a gurgle of laughter, to which the others joined in.

Flora groaned and sank back in her chair. 'Stop it,' she told them. 'Anyway, look at what I found out about him online.'

She showed them the results of googling his name and the string of glamorous dates and scandals.

Libby raised an eyebrow after reading the phone screen. 'You do realise that these photos are nearly eight years old.' She gave a shrug. 'People do grow up and change, you know.'

Perhaps there was some truth in that, mused Flora but shook off the unsettling thought that she might be wrong about Nico. 'Anyway, I don't know why he's still here,' she said. 'He's given Grams the shawl from his grandmother.'

'Who cares?' said Libby, with a wicked grin. 'You could always share a shower with him to save on hot water.'

Katy laughed, but Harriet shook her head.

'Flora's far too sensible to have a one-night stand with a playboy,' she said, smiling softly at her friend.

But Harriet's words had made Flora inwardly blanche. The sensible one. In college, she had been wild enough. But, of course, she'd been free then. The responsibility had weighed heavy on her as soon as her grandad had become ill. She owed them so much that she had forsaken everything but keeping the farm going.

Flora sighed and watched as her friends exchanged worried looks.

'Are you okay?' asked Harriet gently.

'It's just been a bit stressful,' Flora told them. 'Selling all the farm equipment. No more farming. You know.'

'We know,' said Harriet, reaching out to put an arm around Flora's shoulders. 'Joe told us everything. It must be really tough for you and Grams.'

'Actually, Grams doesn't seem as upset as I thought she would be,' said Flora with a frown.

'Maybe Nico can help with something,' suggested Harriet, ever the optimist.

'Like what? Using his Ferrari to sow some seeds?' asked Flora, with a raised eyebrow.

'I thought you weren't sowing any more grains?' asked Libby gently.

'It was a joke,' said Flora. 'Just a really bad one. It's just all so strange, especially now spring is here. Apart from the strawberry field, all the rest are empty. And what use is a bunch of empty fields?' she wondered out loud. 'No income, no farm if we don't diversify, and quickly.'

There was a short silence whilst her friends exchanged concerned glances.

'Surely we can think of something?' said Libby, biting her lip.

'Quite right,' added Harriet, in a tremulous voice. 'We can't give up and neither can you.'

'Maybe you could become something like Worthy Farm? You know, hold your very own Glastonbury-type festival,' said Katy, ever the sharp-thinking businesswoman. But she immediately gave a shudder. 'Although, personally, Glastonbury is my idea of hell. Unless I was staying in a scrupulously clean Winnebago.'

'With Harry Styles?' asked Libby, with a grin. 'I could teach him a thing or two.'

Katy shook her head. 'Ryan's the only superstar man in my life.'

They had been going out for a few months and were madly in love.

Libby made a face. 'Yuck.'

Flora smiled in memory. She had actually gone to Glastonbury with her friends from art class after the first year of university. It had been fun, chaotic and crazy. Probably the last time she had known that kind of freedom, she realised.

'I'd love to go to Glastonbury,' said Harriet wistfully.

'I'd go again given half the chance,' Flora told her.

'Well, you've got the spare fields,' said Libby laughing. 'Let's just get them to hold it here instead!'

'All those people?' said Harriet, frowning. 'As long as they're not tramping across my lavender fields.'

'As long as they all buy their coffee in Platform 1 then they're all welcome,' said Katy grinning.

'So you've changed your mind about camping,' said Flora with a nudge of her elbow.

'Absolutely not,' replied Katy, with a grimace. 'If we have our own music festival here in Cranfield, then I can go home to my own bed and bathroom.' She gave a sudden gasp and sat upright, causing her plate to turn over on the table and her cake to fall to the floor. They all watched as Paddington very gently cleared up the mess for her by eating up all the pieces of the carrot cake. Thankfully, Katy was too busy looking at Flora with blazing eyes to care about the golden retriever licking the wooden floor. 'That's it! Camping!'

'For a holiday? But you hate camping,' said Flora, not quite understanding. 'Why would we all go away camping? You'd be miserable.'

'Not that!' Katy laughed and clapped her hands. 'A glamping site on Strawberry Hill Farm! It's genius!'

There was a short pause whilst everyone digested her idea.

'It's mad,' said Libby finally. 'But you know what? I think you could have something there.'

Flora still couldn't work it out. 'But nearly all of the fields are muddy bogs,' she said.

Katy shrugged her shoulders. 'Not in the summer, they won't be. Just think. Sunset. Wildflowers in the golden haze of late sun. A glass of something cold and crisp. It's romantic. Of course, you'd have to give people a nice proper bed with clean linen. Maybe even a sunken bath or a hot tub! Oooh! Proper glamping. Even I would go for that.'

'Did you add brandy to that coffee this morning?' asked Flora, laughing.

'I think it sounds lovely,' said Harriet, in a dreamy voice. 'I'd totally have a night in something like that with Joe.'

'I think it sounds mad,' said Flora, shaking her head. 'You know I love you, Katy, and your ideas are normally spot on, but this time you're way off the mark. Besides, some of those fields won't dry out unless we have a heatwave. The only field we've got spare is on a hill. What use is that for camping?'

'My instincts are always right,' said Katy in a prim tone.

But Flora just laughed. A campsite? On muddy fields or a hill? It was totally unsuitable.

It was a shame it wouldn't work because for a brief moment there had been a tiny glimmer of hope for Strawberry Hill Farm. But the campsite was definitely a non-starter as far as Flora was concerned.

And with the list of other options worryingly non-existent, that still left the future of Strawberry Hill Farm in jeopardy.

8

Later that afternoon, Nico decided to take a look at the old stables to find his grandfather's old motorcycle. He was amazed that the Barton family had held on to it after sixty years and was intrigued to discover just how bad a state it was in.

He paused as he stood outside the farmhouse, looking across at the rolling hills. The view reminded him a little of Tuscany, with its green land spreading out for miles in front of him. The only things to remind him that he was in England were the different trees and lack of rows of vines.

With a pang at the pain still held in his heart, he went to move away but stopped when he heard someone walking up the lane.

A group of men of a similar age to himself smiled and nodded at him as they drew nearer.

'You must be Nico,' said a tall, dark-haired man walking over and holding out his hand. 'I'm Joe. Grams invited us over to introduce ourselves.'

'Hi,' said Nico.

Despite Grams explaining a few of the local names to him, he still felt a little on edge at the sight of three men who were total strangers, which always set his guard up.

'I'm Ryan,' said the other dark-haired man. 'And this is my younger brother Ethan.'

'Hey,' said the blonde man. 'I'd like to say we're here to welcome you temporarily to the village, but let's be honest, we're all just here to see the car.'

Nico laughed and led them over to the Ferrari. 'Then help yourselves,' he said, unlocking the car door and opening it up for them to see inside.

Ethan blew out a long whistle as he slipped behind the steering wheel. 'What a machine,' he said, staring around in wonder.

Joe bent down to peer inside. 'I had a replica of one of these on my shelf when I was growing up. Probably worth a fortune now.'

'Not as much as the actual car,' said Ethan, stroking the steering wheel in a loving manner.

'It's really something,' said Ryan, turning to look at Nico with a warm smile. 'How long have you owned it?'

'Only a short while,' replied Nico quickly. 'It belonged to my father.'

Instantly, he regretted his words, but Ryan nodded in a knowing fashion.

'The great Paolo Rossi. Your dad came into my restaurant when I was working in Rome,' Ryan told him. 'The man sure knows how to tip. The waitress was beside herself.'

'I'm sure if she was pretty then it was probably double the normal amount,' drawled Nico.

'Great footballer,' said Joe, coming round the car to join them. 'That second goal he scored in the World Cup against Brazil. Incredible!'

'Do you play?' asked Ethan, clambering out of the driver's seat.

Nico shook his head. 'Just enough to kick a ball around. I didn't inherit his great gift.'

Nor had he wanted to. He loved football, of course, but the attention and pressure wasn't for him. He had seen from an early age what it could do to a man's soul if he wasn't strong enough to handle the trappings of fame and fortune.

He felt his mobile in his pocket, knowing that there had been many missed calls and voicemail messages from his father that Nico had completely ignored. It was all still so painful to think that after everything, Paolo had committed the ultimate betrayal and taken the vineyard away from him. His heritage. His future. It all lay in tatters now.

'I was just heading down to see the stables,' he said, suddenly anxious to stop talking about Paolo.

'We can show you the way,' said Joe, with a congenial smile.

Normally, Nico could sense when people were fawning over his famous surname to get to his father, but this time he wasn't picking up on the vibe. And, he had to remind himself, Grams trusted these men.

'It'll be quicker if we go in the Ferrari,' said Ethan, with a gleam in his eyes.

'That's a great idea, little bro,' said Ryan, rushing to get into the passenger seat. 'We'll meet you both down there.'

Ethan scowled as he realised his missed opportunity, but Joe merely laughed and said, 'The fresh air will do us good.'

'What's the point in that?' muttered Ethan.

As the other two men watched, Nico sat in the driver's seat and started up the engine with a throaty roar.

Ryan broke into a grin. 'I feel like a kid in a sweet shop,' he said.

Nico slowly drove the car away, anxious to avoid the potholes on the track down the hill.

'Sorry if we've kind of jumped on your quiet afternoon,' said Ryan. 'We heard about the Ferrari and we had to come and see.'

'That's okay,' said Nico, slowing down to turn the corner. 'So, you mentioned your restaurant. How long were you in Rome?'

'Three years,' Ryan told him. 'I was head chef at Romano's. Then six months ago, my parents split up unexpectedly so I came back to help Dad. He was pretty broken up about the whole separation so I've stayed on and made Cranfield my forever home.'

'How is your father now?' said Nico.

'He's better, thanks,' said Ryan. 'My grandfather lives locally as well and together they're putting all their efforts into getting an old steam train up and running.'

Nico was impressed. 'Sounds interesting. How's it going?'

Ryan rolled his eyes. 'I don't know whether they'll ever get it going. But it keeps them happy. We'll have to show the train to you whilst you're staying here.'

Nico stayed silent as Ryan chatted on. He explained that he was part-owner of Platform 1, along with his girlfriend Katy. It was a coffee shop, pizzeria and restaurant, all of which appeared to be doing very well.

'And now that Katy and I are together and the station is doing well, it's nice to have the family all together again, you know?' said Ryan. 'Although Ethan still stays away a lot of the time for work. Some people prefer the buzz of the big cities. I'm guessing your father's maybe the same, given the headlines.'

'He's definitely not one for the countryside,' said Nico, parking up the car.

He got out of the car before Ryan could ask him anything else about his father. That was all most people wanted to know about. It was no wonder he didn't trust strangers. His strategy had always been to keep all conversations light and not let on anything personal. But it made for a lonely life, he had come to realise.

As they waited for the others to walk down the hill, Ryan looked across at the farm. 'So I understand you might be here for a little while?' he asked.

Nico nodded. 'For a couple of days,' he replied. 'They were very kind in asking me to stay.'

Especially because he had nowhere else to go for the time being. Once more, he realised that he had to come up with a plan as to what to do next.

'Well, heaven knows Flora and Grams need all the help they can get these days,' replied Ryan, crouching down to look at the Ferrari once more.

Nico gave a start. His initial suspicions about Strawberry Hill Farm sounded as if they were unfortunately right. But before he could ask, Joe and Ethan joined them and the moment was temporarily lost.

9

Nico was still mulling over Ryan's words as he walked over to the stables. Was the farm in trouble? Or was it just that they needed extra pairs of hands to help out? He wasn't sure.

But, for the moment, as he drew open the door, he was distracted. It was a long building, housing about four stables, he reckoned. It was somewhat dilapidated but fairly solid. The roof at least looked intact.

He went inside the first stable. It was full of hay bales and not much else apart from a few piles covered with tarpaulin sheets.

Joe, coming in behind him, nodded thoughtfully. 'I'd forgotten this was even here,' he said, going to stand in the middle. 'Don't think it's been used in a very long time.'

'I remember playing hide-and-seek with Libby and Flora in here when we were young,' said Ethan, with a smile to himself.

Ryan looked across at Nico. 'We grew up in the village with Flora and Libby. I don't know if you've met her yet.'

'She's the blonde with the permanent scowl on her face,' said Ethan, with a grimace.

'Only when she's talking to you,' said Joe, coming inside to join them. 'Ethan and Libby have one of those hate-hate relationships.'

'And Harriet just came home for the school holidays,' said Joe with a smile. 'Now we live together here permanently.'

'Katy arrived last autumn,' added Ryan. 'We live in the flat above the station.'

Ethan rolled his eyes. 'And thus all the happy couples were created,' he drawled. 'Well, this has been a nice trip down memory lane, but what's so interesting about an empty block of stables?'

'That,' said Nico, pointing to the furthest corner where a large piece of tarpaulin hopefully held another family treasure. He went over and pulled it off and there was the motorbike. '*Bellissima*,' he said with a sigh.

The other men headed over.

'Wow,' said Ethan, blowing out a long whistle of appreciation. 'Always loved a Ducati.'

'Me too,' said Nico, nodding. 'I had no idea Nonno even owned one until Grams told me about this.'

'And it's been here all this time?' asked Ryan, peering at the motorbike.

'Since it broke down in 1961,' replied Nico.

It did look in pretty bad shape, he thought. Hardly surprising when it had been stuck in a draughty, damp stable for the past sixty years. But the Ducati insignia could still be made out amongst the rust and dirt. And the shape was pure Italian style.

He had only ever thought of his grandfather as an elderly man, but, of course, he had been young once. Riding the roads of Europe in his late teens on a classic Italian motorbike. Nico wished he had heard about his grandfather's adventure when he had still been alive and added the lack of conversations about his past to the long list of regrets that he had now that his grandfather was no longer around.

'Good job this place is one that isn't on the floodplain so it wasn't submerged,' said Ethan. 'What are you going to do with it?'

'I've no idea,' said Nico truthfully.

'You could always have it shipped back to Italy when you leave,' suggested Ryan.

Nico's heart froze. The trouble was that there was nowhere to ship it to. He was effectively homeless until he found himself work and a place to live and it broke his heart to feel so adrift of life and his family. But perhaps he could store the bike somewhere until a more settled time arrived in his life.

'They've still got a decent amount of hay,' said Joe, nodding thoughtfully to himself as he glanced around. 'Perhaps Flora can do something with that.'

'Well, if anyone can it's Flora,' said Ryan. 'She's always been the sensible one.'

'She's going to need to be if they're going to stay afloat,' said Joe with a grimace. 'I'm afraid it's looking pretty bleak,' he carried on. 'You know that I was looking into the business for them?' He glanced at Nico. 'That's what I do. I help farms diversify and help turn a profit.'

'And did you?' asked Ethan. 'Help, I mean.'

Joe blew out a sigh. 'If I could, I would. But the majority of Strawberry Hill Farm sits on the floodplain.'

Nico was silent. He had been used to being beholden to the weather whilst tending the vines. A late frost in the spring could be the end of a decent crop later that summer. Too much rain and not enough sun would mean a smaller yield during harvest time. It had always been a balancing act and one completely out of his control.

'It was fine in the olden days, according to Grams, give or take the odd bad year,' carried on Joe. 'But more recently, with the climate changing, it just doesn't work for any kind of agricultural planting. They've just sold all their farm equipment to clear their debts.'

Ryan and Ethan took a sharp intake of breath. 'No!' they both said at the same time.

Joe nodded his head sadly. 'There was nothing else that could be done. If things get worse, the tractor will have to go too. I hated to be the bearer of bad news, but I just don't know what they can do. Diversify, but how?' He sighed. 'Listen, don't mention it at the birthday party tonight. They're both pretty upset.'

'I'm sure,' said Ryan, with a frown. 'Do you think they'll have to sell up?'

'I don't know,' replied Joe. 'I hope not, but hope alone is not going to keep their bank balance in the black.'

'I had no idea,' said Ryan.

'No one has,' said Joe quietly. 'They're both incredibly private people and there's a sense of embarrassment that the business might not survive.'

'To hell with being embarrassed,' snapped Ethan. 'They need our help.'

'Yes but how?' asked Joe. 'The majority of their fields are on the floodplain and so that only leaves the top couple free. That's not enough to sustain an income.'

'I can't believe they might have to sell up and leave,' said Ryan, looking dismayed.

Nico felt the same way. He had remained silent but was feeling stunned. Flora had lied to him when he'd asked about how healthy the business was. Or perhaps she'd never answered the question, he realised, when he thought back to their conversation. But there was no doubt that the farm was close to failure.

The trouble was, he wasn't sure what the failed son of a renowned playboy could offer in the way of help.

10

The last thing Flora had wanted to do after a miserable afternoon overseeing the collection of the last of their farming equipment was to go to a party. But it was Katy's birthday and perhaps a night with her friends would perk her up.

She clinked glasses with the girls and said, 'Cheers!'

The event was being held in Platform 1, which, for once, was closed to pizza takeouts for the private birthday party of friends and family.

'This is wonderful,' said Katy, looking a little teary. 'Last year, I didn't even celebrate my birthday and just worked instead.'

Katy had been a high-achieving career woman before a temporary stay in Cranfield had changed everything.

'Well, you deserve it after all your hard work,' said Harriet, giving her a hug. 'This place was empty a year ago and now look at it.'

It was true, thought Flora. All the fairy lights were switched on and the old station waiting room was filled with laughter and conversation as everyone enjoyed themselves. Ryan had provided lots of delicious food, which everyone was enjoying, especially

Paddington the dog who was sitting underneath the table and hoping for any dropped crumbs and tummy rubs.

'Here you are,' said Libby, giving Katy a hand-wrapped box. 'As requested. Although I do think it's a bit rubbish to know in advance what your present is going to be. Spoils all the fun.'

'I don't care,' said Katy, unwrapping the paper and squealing with delight at the box within. 'These are my favourites.'

She lifted the lid and instantly they were all enveloped in the sweet smell of chocolate. The tray held a number of shiny round truffles, all looking extremely tempting.

'Mmm,' said Harriet, sniffing the air. 'They smell amazing.'

'Taste good too,' added Katy, who had already popped one in her mouth.

'You're so clever to have a talent like that,' Flora told Libby who made delicious chocolates in her spare time.

'You should set up a business, you know,' urged Katy.

'It's just for friends and family.' Libby shrugged her shoulders. 'Anyway, it's all thanks to Maggie's tempering machine that she gave me.' She lifted her glass and smiled at the lady on the opposite side of the room. Maggie was one of her neighbours in Railway Lane and had cleared a lot of her cottage of clutter, including a chocolate making kit. This had elevated Libby's homemade efforts into a professional finish.

'This one's lavender,' murmured Harriet, looking delighted as she licked her lips.

'And this one's strawberry,' said Flora. It was delicious.

'All the tastes of Cranfield,' confirmed Libby, with a smile.

'Can I have one?' asked Ethan, wandering up to them.

'Of course,' said Katy.

'Absolutely not,' said Libby, her face dropping into a scowl.

She and Ethan had been mortal enemies ever since Ethan had, apparently, ruined her prom night. Although she had never gone into specific details. On the few occasions they had tried to ask more about it, Libby had given them short shrift.

'You don't deserve one,' carried on Libby, before quickly shutting the lid on the chocolate box. 'Katy, I'll hide these so you can enjoy them later. On your own,' she added in a pointed tone, throwing another scowl at Ethan before she walked away.

'Here,' muttered Katy, sliding the truffle that she had been holding into Ethan's hand. 'But keep it to yourself.'

'Thanks,' said Ethan, giving her a kiss on the cheek before walking away.

They were close as Ethan stayed with Katy and Ryan whenever he came home from his long work contracts abroad.

Libby returned and had them all in hysterics as she described her latest date which hadn't gone well.

'Finally I poured him into an Uber and sent him on his way,' she said before doing a double take across the room. 'You know,' she added in a lower tone looking directly at Flora. 'Your Italian Stallion is looking mighty fine tonight.'

Flora flicked a glance over to the fireplace where Nico was standing. Sure, he looked very smart wearing dark jeans and a shirt but didn't everyone else?

'Everyone looks good under flattering fairy lights,' said Flora.

'Are you protesting too much?' murmured Libby.

'Hey, if you're interested,' began Flora.

Libby laughed. 'Are you kidding? I've got three different dates this week. I haven't got time for a fourth.'

Katy rolled her eyes. 'Your love life is like a revolving door,' she said.

'You know me,' Libby told her. 'I get bored easily. I'll leave all the serious relationships to you and Harriet.'

Libby asked direct questions of everyone but herself. She was still a closed book, even where her friends were concerned. Flora knew that there were secrets hidden there but would wait until Libby was ready to tell them.

The party was good fun as the drinks flowed and the conversation carried on.

From time to time, Flora watched Nico as he chatted away to her friends and when she caught up with Grams as the party began to wind down, she found her and Nico talking to Bob and Eddie about the steam train.

'You'll have to come and see it,' said Bob to Nico. 'It's an absolute beauty.'

'Are you going on about that bloody train again, Dad?' asked Ethan as he passed by, rolling his eyes at Flora.

'Stop teasing them,' chuckled Grams.

'You know, maybe one day we're going to surprise you, lad,' said Eddie. 'And it'll be trundling up and down the railway tracks once more.'

'More chance of it flying, to be honest, Grandad,' said Ethan. But he softened his words with a smile before turning to Flora. 'Have you got a minute?'

Flora nodded and followed Ethan into a quiet corner, where they were joined by Ryan. 'What's up?' she asked, looking from brother to brother.

'We just wanted to make sure that you're okay,' said Ethan, his normally jokey stance replaced with a much more serious one.

'Joe told us about you having to sell the farm equipment,' added Ryan.

Flora sighed. 'Oh. Well, it'll keep us going for now,' she replied. 'Thanks for looking out for me and Grams. We'll be okay. Even more so when the Italian playboy has wandered off into the sunset, hopefully very soon.'

Ryan looked surprised. 'You don't like him?' he asked.

'He's just so fake,' said Flora, making a face. 'Just like his dad.'

To her surprise, Ryan shook his head. 'I've met Paolo Rossi and that's not the vibe I'm getting from his son,' he said.

'I agree,' said Ethan, nodding enthusiastically. 'He's been chatting about the woodwork in here, as well as his family home. He doesn't seem like a flash kind of guy to me.'

As she wandered back to join Grams, Flora found that she was surprised. All of her friends seemed to like Nico. She normally trusted their opinions, but surely they were wrong this time, weren't they?

11

The following morning after Katy's birthday party, Flora was feeling slightly delicate as she walked downstairs for breakfast.

She hadn't felt drunk the previous evening but had obviously had more alcohol than she had intended and needed one of Grams' special breakfasts to perk her back up.

However, Grams had begun to have a lie-in each morning and Flora found the kitchen empty. In fact, Grams was not even getting up at sunrise any more. Of course, there wasn't any point as the fields lay empty, and yet, it was a change of rhythm and it unsettled Flora.

She wolfed down some toast and coffee by herself and then decided to go out for some fresh air. Once outside in the sunshine of the early morning, her feet automatically led her across the courtyard and past the large barn.

Until recently, it had housed all the extra equipment needed to work the land. But now it lay empty. Exposed on one side to the elements, she had no idea what else they could use it for.

She carried on past the barn and up to the top of the hill. It was her favourite part of the whole farm. She walked through the gate and stared across the land at the back of the hill. It still looked so odd to her eyes. After all those years of hard work, the fields were now just barren earth that had been left for the winter. She thought back to all those days going up and down the ploughed lines, but now it had been left to its own devices.

Feeling guilty at the failure, she turned away to look at her preferred view down towards the woods and the river. As always, it made her feel comforted. It really was quite something. Even from the top of the hill, she could see the river glinting down at the bottom of the valley. She could see the church spire and roofs of nearby Cranbridge. She could even see where the railway track began to wind its journey far beyond Cranfield and through the countryside.

There was a piece of a large fallen tree trunk nearby that had been left there many years ago and she went over to sit down on it with a sigh. Flora looked at the view once more, but it became blurry as tears pricked at her eyes. She shook her head, but the tears began to pour down her cheeks. It was just all too awful. She had tried to stay strong and steady for Grams, but here, on her own, she could finally let her emotions bubble to the surface. She felt utterly and completely lost, without hope for her beloved Strawberry Hill Farm.

'Hello.'

She gave a start and looked up, hurriedly brushing the tears from her face. Then she saw that it was Nico who had silently come into the field.

'Oh, hello,' she said, deliberately looking away so that he couldn't see the emotion in her face.

He didn't reply and, to Flora's dismay, he walked over and sat down on the tree trunk next to her. She kept her face turned away, trying to bring her hand up surreptitiously so he couldn't see her wiping her cheeks.

She waited for the witty comment, but it didn't come. All she could feel was him turn his head towards her.

'What's the matter?' he asked softly.

'Nothing's the matter,' she told him quickly. 'Haven't you got one of your many girlfriends to call up or something?'

'I can always do that later,' he replied in a breezy tone.

Flora didn't reply and found, to her horror, that the tears were starting to fall again.

'*Cristo*,' he swore, and she knew that he could tell that she was crying. 'What's wrong?'

'Why? What does it matter?' she replied, finally turning her face.

'Because I might be able to fix it,' he told her. 'I'm not the enemy, if you can believe me this one time.'

She thought back to what her friends had been trying to tell her the previous evening about trusting him and decided that perhaps it didn't even matter any more.

'It's the farm, isn't it?' he finally asked into the silence.

She gave a shrug of her shoulders and looked away once more.

'How bad a financial mess is it in?' she heard him ask.

Her shoulders sagged. 'About ten Ferraris' worth of mess,' she replied, still looking out across the view and not at Nico. 'Maybe add in a couple of Porsches as well. Not that any of this is anyone's fault. The farm was built on a floodplain, unknown to us.' She gave a shrug. 'In the early days, we had the odd bad year of weather but never like this. Year after year of heavy rain over the winter. All the fields behind us are submerged most of the year. Can't farm the land in that state. And any dry summer doesn't last long enough to make a difference.'

'I'm sorry,' he murmured. 'That must be hard for you and Grams.'

'It's the truth, so we can't hide from it,' said Flora, trying to sound strong, but her voice cracked on the last word.

'Will you lose your home?'

It was the question that she had asked herself over and over to no avail. 'I don't know,' she told him simply.

There was a short silence before he suddenly sprang up and began to pace up and down. 'Well, there must be something!' he said, before standing in front of her and crossing his arms across his chest. 'What are your options?'

Flora looked up at him. 'Well, I thought I might go to Hawaii, maybe even Monaco for a long holiday,' she began to say.

But she was surprised to see that there was no sarcasm or derision in his expression, merely concern as he crouched down in front of her.

'Is there nothing else that you can do with the land?' he asked softly.

The tears pricked at her eyes once more as she shook her head.

'Well, it's not over yet,' he told her in a determined voice. 'We must be able to think of something?'

'We?'

He looked at her, his dark eyes unreadable. 'Yes. We,' he stated simply.

Despite her better judgement, for a second Flora felt a moment of reassurance. That she and Grams weren't alone in their struggle. That there might just be someone else to share the load with.

But that was ridiculous, right? Because Nico was a playboy with a flashy car who would be leaving soon. How could he possibly help them?

12

Flora stayed seated on the log as Nico began to pace up and down once more at the top of the wildflower meadow.

'There must be some kind of business which would bring in some income for the farm,' he said, walking back and forth. 'You've got all this land, haven't you?'

Flora shook her head. 'But it's all useless. Unless you count one incredibly ridiculous idea given to me by my friend Katy. But it'll never work.'

'Why?' he asked, stopping in front of her. 'What was it?'

'A campsite!' she told him with a teary laugh. 'Or, rather, a glamping site. You know, with trendy yurts and bunting.'

He looked confused. 'Where would you situate it?' he asked.

'Exactly!' she told him. 'Put them on the floodplain and they'd be underwater within days!'

He looked around before turning back with a smile on his face. 'Not if you situate it here.'

'Here?' She laughed. 'This is a joke, right?'

He shook his head. 'Actually, I'm not so sure.'

She stood up next to him. 'It's a crazy idea,' she told him. 'I mean, look at the slope. It's not steep by any means, but nobody wants to camp on an incline, do they? It's hardly glamorous to wake up outside of your tent because it's slid down the hill whilst you were sleeping!'

But Nico was still looking down across the land. 'Actually, it would be quite easy,' he told her. 'All you would need would be some kind of level platform for each tent. A couple of steps. It's quite simple to erect.'

'A platform?' she asked.

He nodded. 'Something like wooden decking that would keep the tent level and off the wet ground as well.'

'Handy if it rains a lot, which it seems to do around here,' joked Flora.

'You'd need some proper posts too,' he carried on. 'Concrete to secure it, but I really think it would work.'

She turned to check his face to see if he was joking. But, to her surprise, he was entirely serious. 'You're not really suggesting that this is a good idea, are you?' she asked, aghast.

'Why not? These fields don't flood, from what I've been told. The view is stupendous. The slope is only gentle and can be overcome to make it habitable.' He turned to look at her. 'Tell me why this can't happen?'

'First of all, I know nothing about running a campsite!' she replied. 'Let alone a glamping site. You know, with made-up tents, proper beds and all that added expense.'

'Sounds great,' he said. 'Don't you want to make a profit?' he asked.

'Of course I do,' Flora told him. 'But we don't have any funds to purchase any of the equipment and make the renovations required to get it up and running in the first place.'

'What about the stable block?' Nico asked.

Flora was nonplussed at the change of subject. 'What about it?'

'Your friend Ryan was telling me how much money they're getting from renting out the old railway carriages. Perhaps it would work with the stables as well.'

Flora made a face. 'I'm not sure anybody would want to stay in there.'

'They might do with a bit of work put into it. Let's go see.'

She shook her head. 'What's the point?' she asked. 'We haven't got any savings to make it habitable.'

'*Andiamo*. Let's just go take a look,' he said, turning away and beginning to walk down the hill.

Flora rolled her eyes at his back. 'This is crazy,' she told him, as she walked quickly to keep up with him.

'Sometimes a little crazy is what's needed,' he replied, over his shoulder.

They walked down the hill in silence until they reached the stable block at the bottom.

Looking at it with fresh eyes, she could see why Nico had had the idea for it to be turned into accommodation. It was large, with a high roof and, thankfully, four walls.

He went to go inside and the wooden step collapsed underneath his weight. He reached out to feel the timber of the step which had completely rotted.

'See,' said Flora with a sigh. 'It's just falling apart.'

Nico studied the space inside. 'I don't know,' he said, before taking a slow walk around the whole building. 'Yes, the timbers need replacing but it would be quite a simple job. I could easily manage it with an extra pair of hands. The joints look pretty secure, thankfully.'

'How do you know all this?' she asked, in bemused amazement.

'I had a carpenter for a grandfather,' he told her. 'Lorenzo taught me everything that he knew.' He shot her a grin. 'I'm quite an expert with my hands, I've been told.'

She rolled her eyes. 'Just when I thought you were getting serious.'

She went to walk away but he reached out and held her arm.

'I was,' he told her. 'Listen, I've got a small amount of savings which I was looking to invest into a business. Grow the nest egg, as it were. I could be your silent business partner.'

She was shocked. 'What are you saying?' she asked.

He let go of her arm. 'I'm saying that we make this a partnership. I invest the money for the work required to renovate the stables, work through the legal side of things and get the campsite up and running. Hopefully, we can get some of them rented out in time for the summer season. We could make some money, share the profits and then see where we stand in the autumn.'

She thought for a moment. 'I don't know,' she finally said. 'What about your own life and work back in Italy?'

'Actually, I was thinking of taking the summer off,' he told her. 'I needed a break after losing Nonno. I was going to do a bit of travelling, but I would be happy to stay here in Cranfield for a couple of months.'

Flora stood still for a moment. Her sensible side reminded her of all the problems that owning and running a campsite, as well as separate accommodation, might incur and how much renovation it would take. And yet, she was comforted to be able to spread the burden of the business and it shocked her. She'd never needed to depend on anyone before now and it surprised her how much she was grateful to lean on Nico. That she wasn't alone, if only briefly.

So she found herself nodding and saying, 'Okay.'

'Deal?' he asked, holding out his hand.

She hesitated before taking his warm hand in hers. 'Deal,' she said, shaking it before she changed her mind.

To save the farm, she could put up with anything over the summer, she decided. Even an unreliable, impetuous Italian playboy.

13

Nico felt almost as surprised as Flora was at his decision to stay in Cranfield for the summer. He knew that he was running away from his problems and yet he found that he couldn't stand by and not help the Barton family after they had given safe haven to his grandfather all those years ago.

And there were worse places to stay, he thought, looking around. It was the quiet of the countryside that he liked. With just the birdsong and the sound of the wind, it brought a kind of peace that he hadn't had for quite some time, he realised.

It really was an incredible view, too. A man would be happy to wake up to this every day, he found himself thinking. Which was ridiculous because this wasn't his home. And yet, for whatever reason, he felt at home in Cranfield. The people were very friendly and it seemed like a proper community. There was also the familiarity of a family-run estate, the countryside and working with the land. He wondered whether that was part of the charm.

Also, there was a link to his grandparents. They had visited often. His grandfather had found refuge here when he had fallen out with his own father. He thought back to the note that his grandfather had left him when he had found the shawl and envelope to hand over to Grams. 'Go to Strawberry Hill Farm,' Lorenzo had written. 'And find your future.' But did his grandfather mean that he had a future away from Italy? In Cranfield?

Anyway, Nico had made the impetuous decision to invest the majority of his savings into Strawberry Hill Farm and so there was no time like the present to get going.

He looked at Flora. 'It might work,' she said. 'The campsite and the separate accommodation here.' She looked at the old stable block with a sudden frown. 'The trouble is, I'm not sure Grams would like it. She's pretty precious about maintaining the history of the place. Shame, because it might be a decent idea.'

'Well, I was due one this year at least,' he drawled. 'Let's go ask her and see,' he added, turning around to walk back up the hill.

'Hey!' he heard Flora call out. 'Wait a moment!'

But Nico kept his head down and kept walking until she caught up with him and they continued up the hill with Flora beside him in resigned silence.

Nico was pleased to see Grams waiting outside for them, on the bench in front of the farmhouse. 'I wondered where you both were. I was wondering whether to steal your keys and take that car of yours out for a spin.'

'Be my guest,' Nico told her with a smile. 'But before you head off, we have something to run past you.'

'We?' Grams looked surprised but pleased as she looked between them.

'Haven't we, Flora?' prompted Nico, giving Flora a wide smile.

She shot him a pointed look before looking at her grandmother. 'We've been talking,' she began.

'Well, that's a start,' said Grams, giving Nico a wink.

Flora faltered, seemingly unsure as to what to say. So Nico took over. 'There was an idea that perhaps we could renovate the old stables together,' he told her. 'Turn it into self-contained accommodation. And then there was a further idea to create a campsite in the field over there.'

'In the new wildflower meadow,' added Flora.

Grams' eyebrows shot up in surprise. 'I see,' she said.

'But that's something that you wouldn't be keen on, right?' asked Flora quickly.

Grams was quiet as she thought. 'Actually, I think it's a good idea,' she said. 'But it all sounds quite complicated,' she carried on. 'And, unfortunately, terribly expensive.'

'I have offered to be the business partner in the renovation, putting up the funds to complete the necessary work,' said Nico. 'And I'm also a pretty decent carpenter, so I could do a lot of the work myself.'

Grams looked delighted. 'Well, that is good news! So you'll be wanting to stay for a while longer?'

'If that's all right with you both. I was thinking of staying over the summer whilst the renovations take place,' said Nico.

'Of course,' said Grams, shooting Flora a grin.

Flora merely stood as still as a statue before finally giving them a brief nod of her head.

'This is marvellous,' carried on Grams. 'And with you helping, I feel like our luck has finally turned. A fresh start for the farm and a profitable business. How exciting!'

Nico nearly choked on her words as they hit home. If he failed, the farmhouse would be lost. And he was absolutely determined that, what little money he had remaining, he would use it for some good. For some people who actually deserved it. It was the least he could do, to help one family when his own was in ruins.

He caught Flora's frown and wondered how much of an uphill battle it was going to be. But no matter, he decided. Failure couldn't happen again. He wouldn't let it happen. This time they had to succeed. Because he wasn't sure he could live with himself if it didn't.

14

'You're going to renovate the old stables?' came the chorus.

Flora looked at her friends as they exchanged wide-eyed glances before seemingly getting over their shock.

'And start up a campsite?' asked Harriet.

'Well, the railway carriage accommodation worked, didn't it?' said Katy with a small, smug smile. 'I think you're onto something.'

'Aren't the stables a bit of a mess?' asked Libby, frowning as she peered inside.

'A little,' said Flora. It was an understatement, such was the dilapidated nature of the place.

'But how are you going to afford to do them up?' asked Harriet, frowning. 'I only ask because Joe was moaning about the cost of timber the other day.'

Flora took a deep breath. 'Nico has offered to be our financial partner for the renovation,' she said through gritted teeth. 'As well as taking on the carpentry role, apparently.'

She was still struggling with the idea of being beholden to anyone, especially Nico whom she had only known for a matter of days.

All three of her friends took a shocked intake of breath.

'Oooh!' said Harriet, her eyes gleaming. 'So he's staying for the summer? This could be interesting. See what develops between you two.'

Harriet was a romantic who saw love at every opportunity.

'Nothing will develop between us,' said Flora quickly. 'The man's a playboy who can't take anything seriously.'

'But his offer is serious, isn't it?' asked Katy, with a frown.

'I think so.' Flora really wanted to trust him, but her trust was in short supply where it came to men. 'Anyway, it's all going to take ages to sort out.'

Libby shook her head. 'But don't you want to get up and running in time for the summer holidays?'

'Of course,' said Flora. 'But we need to be steady and sensible. Not rush into things until the paperwork is all signed off.'

Libby gave a shrug. 'Just get going, I reckon. Time is of the essence and all that.'

As her friends nodded, Flora felt rattled. She was still worried that it was all too impetuous. Everything needed careful consideration. But Nico was impulsive, sweeping Grams along with his recklessness and, it seemed, her friends as well.

It was down to her to keep him in check. After all, it was her home on the line, not his. He could run back to Italy and just pick up his old life. But if it all went wrong, it would be down to her and Grams to start over and that just didn't bear thinking about.

* * *

When Flora returned to the farmhouse, Nico had already looked up their options on the local council's website.

She felt slightly mollified that at least he appeared to be doing things by the book.

'So we can have a maximum of ten tents,' he told her.

'That sounds like too many anyway,' she replied. 'Especially when we've never done this before.'

'If you want to make any kind of profit, then I would definitely max out the number of tents you can have,' he said.

His phone rang and he excused himself to take the call.

Flora was still worried about Grams, who seemed to be taking the idea all too well, as far as she was concerned, not even asking any questions or raising any doubts.

'Are you sure that this is the right idea for us?' asked Flora when the two of them were alone, sitting at the kitchen table. 'For the farm?'

'If the choice is to change our path or lose the place altogether, then I think we have to go for it,' said Grams. 'I don't want to lose our home. Not after fighting this for so long.'

Flora reached out to take her hand. 'I don't want to lose it either.'

'Then go down a new path and see where it takes you,' said Grams, squeezing her hand. 'You never know. You might enjoy not only the journey but the destination.'

Flora laughed. 'Erm, why just me? Aren't you coming along for the ride too?' she said.

To her surprise, Grams looked a little sheepish. 'Dear girl, you've been utterly amazing. I love you so much. But it's time for me to retire and to pass all this down to you to do with whatever you feel is right.'

Flora took a deep intake of breath. Of course, she hadn't expected Grams to carry on working on the farm forever and yet she wasn't sure about going forward without her help. She had always been there through thick and thin and so taking a step back meant more responsibility. And Flora just wasn't sure how much more she could take.

Grams took her hand and squeezed it tight in her strong, rough one.

Flora had a terrible thought. 'You're not thinking of leaving, are you?' she asked, her throat thick with trying to imagine what life at Strawberry Hill Farm would be like without her grandmother by her side.

Grams shook her head. 'Not unless you want me out of here,' she said.

'Never,' Flora told her fiercely.

Grams smiled at her granddaughter. 'Thank goodness. I'd hate to live anywhere but with you.'

Flora leaned back in her chair. 'So what are you going to do with all the time that you're going to have on your hands.'

'Well, I'd like to help out with the campsite where I can,' Grams told her. 'It might keep me feeling young. But with my spare time, I'd like to take up ballroom dancing again.'

Flora looked at her amazed. 'Ballroom dancing?' she spluttered. 'Since when?'

'Oh, about thirty years, give or take a year,' replied Grams. 'Your grandad and I loved to dance in the early days. And then at Katy's birthday party, Eddie was telling me about a club he's joined in Aldwych where they dance the night away twice a week. And I thought, that sounds like fun.'

'I had no idea,' said Flora, shaking her head.

'I've always wanted to learn how to do the foxtrot,' said Grams. 'And, after all, I'm only eighty.'

She and Flora looked at each other and they both burst out laughing.

'Well, why not?' said Flora, still laughing.

She was pleased to see her grandmother making the most of life. After all, she had spent her life on the farm, giving it all of her time and energy.

Grams nodded. 'The farm has kept me fit and healthy despite my age and I'd like to keep exercising.'

'I think you're incredible,' said Flora in awe. 'To be starting something like that at your, er, age, is amazing.'

'You know,' said Grams in a soft tone. 'There's still time for you too, my darling girl.'

Flora laughed and shook her head. 'I don't think I'm the ballroom type, Grams. I'll stick to watching *Strictly Come Dancing* with you instead.'

'That's not what I meant,' said Grams, in a pointed tone. 'I mean, perhaps all these changes will give you a chance to pursue your own dreams as well.'

Flora was quiet for a moment. Her only dream had ever been to paint, but where on earth was she going to find time for that if she was going to be running a campsite from now onwards?

At that moment, Nico came back into the kitchen.

'So the main decision to be made seems to be how many tents we want to provide and where they would be situated,' he said, as he poured himself another mug of coffee. 'Along with the facilities we would provide. Do you want everything compostable and sustainable?'

'Absolutely,' piped up Grams. 'We've never used chemicals on our farm.'

He smiled. 'Glad to hear it. And I think that's the ethos that we should be going for. To make it as green a campsite as possible.'

His use of the word 'we' resonated around the room.

'But you're going to be a silent financial partner, isn't that what we agreed?' prompted Flora.

Nico raised an eyebrow at her in amusement. 'Actually, I was thinking of being a financial partner who is actively involved in every single decision.'

Flora was dismayed and it must have shown in her face because he burst into laughter.

'You're easy to wind up,' he told her.

Flora gnashed her teeth. 'It's just that this is important and neither of us have any experience in running a campsite.'

He shrugged his shoulders. 'Between us, I think we can make a beautiful partnership.'

Flora rolled her eyes. Everything he said sounded like something he would spout to a girlfriend. She could just imagine him all too well, with his smooth talk and whispering sweet nothings into some girl's ear.

Nico leaned back in his chair. 'Well, seeing as I'm the one with the money in the bank account, I guess the biggest decision is what kind of tents and I've already found ten that we can buy second-hand.'

Flora immediately made a face.

But Nico held up his hand. 'There's no way we have the money to buy ten brand new bell tents as well as filling them with furniture, fitting them out and anything else. But second-hand doesn't mean awful. I've seen some online and agreed with the owner that we will go and view them at the weekend.'

'Okay,' said Flora, conceding defeat. 'And where are they?'

'Scotland.' He broke into a grin. 'I've always wanted to see the Highlands.'

'Scotland!' Flora sat bolt upright. 'How are we going to get there and back in a day?' she asked.

'We won't. But I'm sure we can find a hotel somewhere en route,' said Nico, his eyes twinkling. 'Don't worry. I reckon if I lock my bedroom door, then I should be safe from your unwanted advances.'

As he and Grams laughed, Flora sat back in her chair and wondered once more just what had happened to her safe and sensible life.

15

The lorry that Flora and Nico had hired to drive up to Scotland was not particularly comfortable or quiet, so Flora was grateful that Grams had declined to come with them.

Flora spent most of the journey wishing that it were also far quicker so that she could escape the confined cab space she had to share with Nico.

'It's certainly not as sophisticated as your Ferrari,' she said, as they stretched their legs at a fuel stop somewhere just south of the Scottish border.

They had grabbed a coffee and snacks and were just getting ready to get on the road once more.

'I'm not sure where you got the idea that I'm sophisticated,' said Nico, taking a crisp before offering her the packet to help herself.

'Thanks,' she said, taking a handful. 'Well, let me see. There's the cashmere jumpers. The flash car.'

'Both of which are just stuff,' he told her, with a raised eyebrow. 'Not a personality, sophisticated or otherwise. Not the inside of a man's soul.'

She was a little surprised that he seemed almost defensive at her small joke. 'Okay. How about your private education?' she countered.

He shrugged his shoulders. 'For which I'm grateful, but, again, the upbringing doesn't maketh the man. Or did your local school teach you differently?'

'It taught me about community and helping each other out,' she told him, primly.

'Which part of us hiring a lorry and driving it up to Scotland doesn't shout that I'm not helping you and your grandmother?' he asked, rolling his eyes.

She faltered and thought for a moment. She went to speak, but he had opened up the driver's cab and climbed back inside.

Feeling a little sheepish, she got inside the passenger's side.

'I'm sorry. I guess I just need to understand why you're helping us?' she asked, holding out the crisp packet to him.

He shook his head and seemed out of sorts. 'Does it matter? You know what? You keep thinking the worst of me, Flora, if it makes you feel better. It makes no difference to me.'

He sounded irritated and perhaps even upset. He wasn't one to have a fragile ego, she didn't think.

She wanted to say more, to even apologise, but he had started up the noisy engine and once they got up to speed on the motorways, conversation was near on impossible.

It made for an awkward remainder of the journey and she was glad of the roar of the engine that prevented any more uncomfortable conversations. Perhaps she had been a little harsh in judging him, but it didn't make sense. Why help out two perfect strangers, just because his grandfather had visited their farm a very long time ago? She couldn't work it out. Surely he had somewhere far more glamorous to go to?

Once they had reached the border of Scotland, the roads

became narrower, but the view was sensational. Flora relished the mountains and views as they went along. The sun was lower now and casting a golden hue on every mountain face. It was spectacular.

The road finally stopped being a motorway and, an hour later, became only a single track.

'I hope this is the right way,' said Nico, slowly manoeuvring the truck around a sharp corner on a stony track. 'Because I'm not sure where we're going to be able to turn this thing around.'

Flora grimaced. They certainly were in the middle of absolutely nowhere, despite the stunning backdrop of mountains and lochs.

But just as they were starting to fear the worst and contemplating where to turn around, a large manor house came into view far ahead and the sign by the entrance read Loch Fyne. They had made it at last, she thought with a sigh of relief.

They had only just parked up in front of the manor house when the front door was flung open and a tall, severe-looking woman came outside to stand on the doorstep.

They climbed out of the lorry and walked over to greet her.

'Hi. I'm Nico Rossi and this is Flora Barton,' said Nico, shaking her hand. 'Nice to meet you.'

'Mrs McKinley,' snapped the woman in reply, giving them both a finger-crushing handshake. 'Glad to see you weren't later than the agreed time. I dislike tardiness. Follow me.'

Nico exchanged a surprised look with Flora at the woman's abrupt attitude as they followed her around the side of the large house.

An offer of a cup of tea was obviously not forthcoming, thought Flora. Also, on closer inspection, the beautiful manor house appeared to be crumbling and quite run-down.

They went across a courtyard and found themselves at the

entrance of a large meadow. The view was spectacular across a loch to the mountains on the other side.

'How wonderful,' said Flora, appreciating the view.

The woman nodded. 'No better place,' she snapped back. 'Well. Here you are.' She gestured at a large pile which appeared to be layers of canvas. This was obviously the tents they had come to purchase.

Flora and Nico stepped forward to inspect them. It was hard to see the state of the canvas, but it appeared to be heavy and of good quality. But who knew what holes and tears were hidden in the many layers.

'Are all the tents in equally good shape?' asked Nico, who had only managed to lift the top layer to inspect underneath.

'They most certainly are,' snapped Mrs McKinley. 'I never lie. I said that they were in good wear and I meant it.'

'Of course,' replied Nico quickly.

She was extremely prickly, but given the large amount of tents she had to sell and the extremely low price she wanted in return, they had no choice but to grin and bear her attitude.

'It was my husband's idea,' she told them. 'But he's gone now and so I can do what I like.'

'I'm sorry for your loss,' said Flora quickly.

'I'm not,' snapped Mrs McKinley. 'He ran off with his assistant and they've legged it to the Isle of Skye. Good riddance too.'

Nico coughed in his throat and Flora had the distinct impression that he was trying not to laugh.

'So, do we have an accord?' asked Mrs McKinley.

Flora exchanged a look with Nico before giving him a tentative nod. After all, the woman appeared to be quite trustworthy, even more so given her abrupt manner.

'If we find that each tent is in the same good condition as this top one as we load them into the lorry, then yes, we have an agreement,' he told her.

Mrs McKinley stuck out her hand, which he gave a firm shake. 'So that's done,' she said. 'Tea?'

As she walked away, Nico turned to look at Flora. 'Congratulations,' he said. 'You're now the proud owner of a campsite. Or, at least, the very beginnings of one.'

As he followed Mrs McKinley inside, Flora shivered in the cool air, wondering what on earth she had signed up to. And whether it would be enough to save the farm.

16

After a cup of extremely strong tea served by Mrs McKinley, Flora and Nico began the arduous task of moving the heavy tents from the courtyard into the back of the lorry.

It was a slow and back-breaking task, with only the aid of a small trolley that they had placed in the back of the lorry at the last minute.

Finally, after nearly two hours, Flora stretched her back as she stared at the pile of canvas in the lorry. 'At last,' she said, with a sigh. She felt absolutely exhausted and somewhat hungry as well. She looked at Nico. 'How about we get going and find somewhere to stay?' she said. 'I'm shattered.'

He nodded, but frowned as he looked around. 'When did this mist appear?' he asked.

Flora followed his gaze and noticed with a start that the sun had disappeared and there was now a grey gloom cast all around them. 'I hadn't noticed,' she told him.

'I'm sure it'll be fine,' he said, ever the optimist.

She hoped so. It had been a long drive after a very early start. She was hoping that there would be a hotel nearby that they could stay in for the night, preferably extremely cheap given their tight budget. But when they went to wish Mrs McKinley goodbye and check that the money had been transferred into her account for the sale of the tents, the woman merely shook her head when Flora asked about accommodation.

'There's no hotels near here,' she replied.

Nico was trying Google, but there was no signal for him to search online.

'I guess we'll just have to drive back overnight,' said Flora, with a shrug.

'I wouldn't set out now,' Mrs McKinley told her, making a face. 'Now the mist has arrived, it won't shift until morning. In some places on the track, it'll be that thick that if you don't know what you're doing, you'll end up driving over the edge of the pass.'

Flora and Nico exchanged a worried look.

'I suppose you can stay here,' said Mrs McKinley, looking as thrilled about the prospect as Flora felt.

'I guess we could always sleep in the lorry,' said Nico.

'We wouldn't want to impose,' added Flora quickly.

'Nonsense,' replied Mrs McKinley. 'Never let it be said that the McKinleys aren't a generous brood. You can use the guest suite. Not that anybody's stayed there in many a year. Dinner too, I suppose?'

After a stilted but somewhat welcome supper of soup and bread, she led them upstairs. It was an unhappy house, thought Flora, with a shiver. She thought longingly of the warm and friendly farmhouse and felt very homesick.

Mrs McKinley guided them along a long corridor at the top of the stairs before turning and opening a door. Flora followed her inside and stopped abruptly, causing Nico to clatter into the back of her.

'Hey,' she heard him say. 'Keep moving.'

But Flora was too busy staring at the small double bed in the middle of the room.

'Erm,' she began to say.

'The en suite is temperamental but should be acceptable,' said Mrs McKinley, nodding at a nearby door through which Flora could see a pink handbasin. 'I rise at 6 a.m. sharp and expect any guests to do the same. Breakfast will be porridge. Well, goodnight.'

And then she left, closing the door behind her with a sharp click.

The silence stretched out as they both stared at the double bed in the middle of the room.

'Well, this is, er, awkward,' said Flora eventually. 'Do you think I should go and tell her that we need separate rooms?'

'I should think she's already back in her tomb by now,' said Nico, with a grimace. 'Besides, this place is suitably creepy that I'm not sure I want to be by myself tonight.' He gave her a weary smile. 'Good thing I've got you to protect me from all the ghosts and ghouls.'

Flora sighed heavily. 'Maybe I can sleep in the lorry?' she wondered out loud.

'If you think you can creep past the lady of the manor's room without her hearing, I think you're mistaken,' said Nico. 'No wonder her husband legged it with his assistant. Probably the only peace he ever got.'

'We can't share a bed,' stated Flora.

'Should I be worried that you'll take advantage of me?' asked Nico with a grin. 'Because I'd be perfectly fine with that.'

Flora rolled her eyes. 'It's going to be a long night,' she said, going over to sit on the upright chair which had seen better days.

Underneath the window, a draught whistled through a gap and made the moth-eaten curtains flap.

'I guess this must be a bit of a comedown for you, eh?' she said, looking around at the tatty room. 'Your holiday destinations are probably more fake gold and synthetic, like your girlfriends, am I right?'

Expecting a witty comeback, she was surprised when Nico sank down onto the bed and looked at her. He appeared to take a deep breath. 'Why do you hate me so much?' he asked.

Flora gave a start at his serious expression. 'I, er, well, I don't hate you. As much as I would like to,' she said, adding a smile. But it wasn't returned. 'I guess I just envy you. You seem to have it all. No responsibilities. A free and easy life.'

It was true, she realised. There was a tiny part of her that envied him, the part that whispered in her ear late at night when she was lying in bed alone. The part that wondered whether to let go of her sensibilities and that a bit of romance and excitement would be fun. Fun that she was sorely missing from her life. Fun that had taken a back seat when she had a duty of care to her grandmother and to the family farm.

She was somewhat stunned when Nico laughed, but it was without humour. 'That's what you believe? That I have it all?'

She shrugged her shoulders. 'On the evidence, of course. I'm guessing you lead a charmed life.'

But he surprised her by shaking his head, a shadow crossing his dark eyes. 'You're so very wrong.' He dragged a hand through his dark hair, messing it up even more. 'You're the one with the loving family and friends, not me. I have nothing.'

Flora was shocked to realise that he was entirely serious. 'I don't understand,' she told him, confused. 'You own a vineyard and drive a Ferrari. I wouldn't exactly call that nothing.'

But the eyes that stared up at her were haunted and her smile quickly dropped as she saw the pain in his face.

'The vineyard was sold last week by my father and I stole the Ferrari. Everything is lost.' He sighed heavily. 'Don't worry about it, Flora. I already know how low your opinion is of me. The good news is that it can't possibly be lower than what I think of myself. So laugh away. It's all my fault anyway.'

But Flora had never felt less like laughing than at that moment. She felt nothing but sympathy for him as she realised that he was telling the truth. She suddenly found herself wanting to get closer to him, to find out the real Nico underneath the smooth charm and help ease his pain, as he had tried to do with her own.

17

Nico was feeling extremely cross with himself as he sank down onto the bed. Why on earth had he told Flora the truth? This wasn't a confessional. He never normally blurted out stuff about himself. Everything should be kept light and easy. He really should have kept his mouth shut.

He shivered. The bedroom really was freezing and his warm Italian blood wasn't used to it, he told himself. But that wasn't it. Why had he confessed to Flora that everything was lost? Yes, he was weary but he was mainly tired of pretending. Tired of being something that he wasn't.

He waited for her usual sarcastic comment, but it never came. Instead, she came to sit next to him, the ancient bed springs creaking and squeaking as she did so.

'So you lied to Grams when you said things were good over in Italy?' she asked.

Nico shook his head. 'No. I just omitted a few truths.'

'About the vineyard?'

He nodded mutely. His shoulders sagged at the thought of it and he pressed his eyes shut to try to blot out the pain. It didn't help. All he could see with his eyes closed was that heavy front door, the view from the balcony of the lake. The creak of the staircase and the feel of the wooden banister under his fingers.

He gulped away his emotions and tried to steady himself.

When he reopened his eyes, Flora was still watching him.

'Why couldn't you keep it?' she asked gently.

He turned to look into her deep green eyes. 'Because my father sold it without my permission.'

Flora's eyebrows shot up, but she didn't say anything. Nico was grateful. Now that he had begun to speak, he just needed to get it all out there once and for all.

'That vineyard was my family home,' he carried on. 'My legacy. My grandmother and grandfather wanted it passed down to me, but, as usual, it's all about my father and nobody else. He didn't care about the history, about any of it. About the years and years of hard work that had gone into every vine.' He dragged a hand through his hair, trying to steady his emotions once more. 'Nonno is – *was* – a great man. Steady as a rock, loyal to his family and friends. My father inherited none of this. He was always wild, always seeking something better, something grander. The trouble was that each time he failed, the family fortune dwindled. In the end, there was no money left.'

'How?' asked Flora. 'What happened?'

'One rotten business deal after another,' said Nico in a bitter tone. 'My father didn't care how much pressure or pain he was causing my grandparents. It was all about him. He is a lousy father and a lousy businessman. Pretty much the worst combination you can find.' He hung his head.

'What about your mother?' she asked.

He shook his head. 'Didn't want a baby so left me with my dad after a couple of weeks. Anyway, after Nonno passed away last summer, Dad inherited everything. I contested the will. In the end, the judge found in his favour and not in mine, despite it being my grandfather's wishes. Turned out the judge was a great fan of my father's football career!' He could hear the bitterness in his voice, and the emotions that were causing his words to be shaky as well.

Flora must have heard it too, because she reached out and covered his hand with hers. He drew strength from the reassuring warmth and softness of her skin.

'There was nothing I could do,' he carried on, staring down at her pale skin against his own hand. 'Once my father owned it outright, it was put up for auction there and then. A week ago, the vineyard was sold to the highest bidder.'

'And the car?'

He allowed himself a small smile. 'It was in the garage. My dad's favourite possession. And I was so mad at him that I took the keys and stole the car. I had nowhere else to go except Nonno's wish to hand over the shawl to Grams, so I spent the next couple of days driving to your farm and I ended up sleeping in my car on the way.'

Flora looked shocked. 'Seriously?'

'Absolutely, and I can't complain about the view of the lake when I woke up that first morning in Cranfield.'

She blushed and rolled her eyes. 'Can we focus on the serious bit for now?'

'That's a terrible word,' he told her, attempting some humour to lighten the moment. 'Serious.'

'I'm sorry.'

Nico nodded and gulped. 'Yeah, well, that's life.'

'Why didn't you tell me and Grams any of this?' she asked, a frown creased between her brows.

'Because I didn't want to think about it,' he admitted. 'Because life has been utterly dreadful these past six months and, for once,

I wanted to remember what it was like to smile. I had nothing left, you see. Nothing but Dad's old Ferrari and a promise to visit your grandmother and repay the favour that we owed her.'

'You should have said,' Flora told him.

'Would you have believed me?' he asked.

She looked away and withdrew her hand. He was shocked to feel how empty his felt without her soft skin on his.

'But I googled you and all I saw were loads of tabloid stories of you being some kind of playboy,' she told him.

'Perhaps in my twenties. But hard work and no money makes Nico a dull boy.'

'I don't think I'd ever describe you as dull,' she replied, turning to look at him.

He gave her a small smile. 'I think that's the nicest thing you've ever said to me.'

'It must be the cold,' she told him.

He shivered once more. 'You may be right. It's freezing in here. It's only mildly above the temperature of Mrs McKinley's blood, I imagine.'

Flora gave a soft laugh. 'She is a little severe,' she replied.

'Thanks for listening,' he said, after they had locked eyes. He felt as if a weight had been lifted from his shoulders. That at least someone knew the real him at last.

'Thanks for coming all this way to help out me and Grams,' she replied.

'For what it's worth, I truly believe we can do this,' he told her, suddenly anxious to reassure her about her own home. 'Between us, we can build a great campsite and help save the farm.'

'I hope so.' Flora hesitated before speaking again. 'And I'm sorry. For not giving you the benefit of the doubt when you arrived. For not believing that your intentions were well placed in helping us.'

Nico looked over at the extremely uncomfortable looking hard chair in the corner. 'You take the bed,' he told her. 'I can sleep in the chair.'

Flora looked at him and, to his surprise, shook her head. 'It's okay. We can share. Besides, there's only one set of bedding.' She hesitated before adding, 'I trust you.'

He was unable to stop himself from breaking into a wicked grin. 'Of course, there's lots of different ways to keep ourselves warm overnight.'

Flora laughed, her pretty face lighting up. 'Just when I was starting to believe you.'

'Hey, it's your mind that's one got only one track,' he told her, laughing. 'Not mine. That's not what I meant.'

'Wasn't it?'

He gave her a warm smile. 'Maybe a little. You bring out the worst in me.'

She smiled as she headed into the bathroom.

Nico lay back on the bed, thinking that for once he was doing the right thing. He was helping Flora and that felt good. He could make amends for his rotten father.

He wanted her to believe that he wasn't a playboy. He wanted her to think the best of him, not the worst. He realised that her opinion mattered to him and he wondered why.

But it was nice to have finally told someone the truth. That it was Flora surprised him even more, but he trusted her, perhaps more than anyone else in his life at that moment.

18

Early the next morning, Flora woke with a start, wondering where on earth she was.

As she turned her head, she saw Nico lying next to her and then she remembered. She was in Scotland, on a tiny double bed in the freezing-cold guest bedroom of Mrs McKinley.

The sensible part of her wanted to get up and run, but recalling her conversation with Nico the night before made her stay. His own family upbringing was as troubled as hers had been. She had seen the flash car and nice clothes and had made her assumptions about him, all of which had been wrong.

Even the playboy act wasn't quite true, she thought. He was a good person deep down who had tried to do his best. In fact, he was so good that he had offered to give them a large amount of money in honour of their grandparents' friendship when it sounded as if money was quite tight for him. He was honourable.

And handsome too, she thought, continuing to study him. Asleep, he looked younger, a little more vulnerable than she had ever considered him to be. She had assumed that he was never serious, that he had no problems. Nothing could have been further from the truth.

He suddenly stirred and Flora quickly sat up, looking away so that he wouldn't know that she was studying him.

'Good morning,' he said, with a sleepy smile. 'Did you sleep as badly as I did?'

'Probably worse,' she replied, swinging her legs around and standing up. The bed gave a creaky groan as she did also. 'The mattress was so thin, I could feel every coil on my spine.'

He sat up with a groan. 'I thought the thin pillow as hard as rock was the worst bit.'

Flora stretched and headed towards the window. Peeking outside the curtain, she could see a fine drizzle settled over the landscape.

'It looks like the fog has finally cleared,' she told him.

'Thank goodness,' he replied. 'Let's get out of here as quickly as we can.'

After a meagre and somewhat awkward breakfast on the dot of 6 a.m., they thanked Mrs McKinley for her hospitality ('some hospitality,' muttered Nico as they got into the lorry) and began the long drive home.

At the first service station on the motorway that they could find, they treated themselves to a large cooked breakfast and copious amounts of coffee.

'That's better,' said Nico, leaning back in his chair in the food court and smiling at his empty plate. 'I don't think I've ever been so hungry.'

'Me neither,' replied Flora, draining the last drops of coffee from the mug. 'Although I don't think that was quite as good a breakfast as Grams makes.'

He nodded. 'Agreed.' He studied her for a moment. 'So, I guess you know a little more about me after last night. And yet I know hardly anything about you. Did you always want to follow in your grandparents' footsteps and become a farmer?'

Flora sighed softly and shook her head. 'Actually, I went to art college. I'm a painter.'

He looked surprised. 'Oh, really? Wait a moment, did you do the artwork in my bedroom? The landscape one of the valley, I mean? I looked, but there was no signature on it.'

She nodded. 'Yes. That's one of mine.'

'Wow,' he said. 'It's really good. I'd love to have that kind of talent. So what did you do after college?'

Flora hesitated before replying. 'I never got to finish my art course or even use the skills learnt in the first year. You see, my grandad got sick. My mum passed away when I was young, Dad was never around and so Grams was struggling all by herself. So I came back to the farm to help my grandparents.'

'I see. And you never thought to go back to college and finish your studies?' he asked.

'There was never time,' she told him with a sad smile. 'Grandad became more frail and Grams was nearly in her seventies by then. I took on more and more responsibility until I ended up doing pretty much everything.' She leaned back in her chair with a heavy sigh. 'And it still failed.'

'I don't think you can blame yourself for that,' said Nico with a frown. 'Times change and the climate hasn't done you any favours either. Did you do your best?'

She nodded vehemently. 'Absolutely.'

'Then that's all you can do,' he replied. He smiled to himself. 'So, the decoration of the kitchen...?'

'That was after a summer trip to Africa when I was at college,' she told him. 'I was inspired by the colours and life over there.'

'Have you been anywhere since?' he asked.

She shook her head. 'No time and no money. Anyway, I have a farm to run. *Had*,' she added, with a frown.

'I'm sorry it didn't work out after all your hard work,' he told her.

'Looks like neither of our futures panned out the way we thought they would,' she said.

'I'm not sure I truly thought mine would ever be on a safe foundation anyway,' Nico told her with a grim smile. 'Dad lost money over and over.'

'How?' she asked.

'Wine, women and gambling,' he replied, with a roll of his eyes. 'He spent a fortune over the years. I guess it was inevitable that he would come for the vineyard eventually.' He sighed softly. 'That's why I started to put money aside in a savings account. Just in case Dad proved me right one last time.' He seemed to deliberately brighten himself up. 'But hopefully the campsite will be a better prospect than we've both been used to. And even leave you time to enjoy yourself.'

'I enjoy myself,' she told him, feeling a little defensive.

'Not from what you've just told me.'

Flora dragged a hand through her hair. 'Look, I've had all these responsibilities, as well as Grams to take care of. I have to be sensible.'

'So why did you strip down to your underwear and go into that lake?' he asked, with a knowing smile.

She choked a little, blushing furiously. 'That was a one-off,' she muttered.

'Shame.' His smile grew broader. 'I was hoping to join you in there some time.'

She laughed. 'You wouldn't have said that if you'd felt the water temperature. It was freezing cold!'

He joined in with her laughter. 'Maybe some time in the summer then,' he said.

Flora was still blushing as she picked up her mobile, as if making to leave. The thought of being in the lake with Nico in only their underwear brought up confusing thoughts. But the sensible side of her won over. Of course, she didn't think about him that way. Nor him about her, she was sure.

Something had changed between them, though. Now that she felt she could trust him, she began to relax and found herself liking him. He brought something out of her. Excitement. A tiny bit of the thrill of life. And she wasn't sure she wanted to deny herself any of that in the future, whatever her sensible head was trying to convince her otherwise.

19

Back in Cranfield, Flora woke up late the following morning, grateful to have finally fallen into bed just before dawn when she and Nico had arrived back from Scotland.

It had been a long but relatively easy journey home, with Flora feeling completely differently about Nico. So much had changed now that he had finally been honest with her. She felt sympathetic for his situation and, in many ways, grateful that he was staying on at the farm to help set up the campsite.

After a much-needed brunch, she left Grams and Nico planning to head into Cranbridge to talk through legal matters whilst she went to meet the girls for a coffee and a brainstorm.

'It sounds like you need this,' said Katy, as she placed a large coffee in front of Flora before heading over to take another customer's order.

Flora glanced at the long to-do list on her phone that she had just read out to her friends. There were the tents to inspect and hopefully erect, as well as all the administration required for the change of business on the farm. After that, they would need to get the groundwork started. There were inspections to be had from the council, as well as the main communal areas to get ready.

'So, once all the boring legal stuff is done and dusted and the tents are up, what are you going to fit them with?' asked Libby.

'Nico was talking about flat-pack furniture,' said Flora.

Harriet made a face. 'Really?' she said, raising her eyebrows.

'What's the matter with that?' asked Flora. 'It's cheap.'

'Yeah, but the point of glamping is the "glam",' said Libby.

Flora frowned. 'I know, but our budget isn't really going to stretch that far.'

Katy popped by the table. 'What did I miss?' she asked.

'Flora's talking about flat-pack furniture for the tents,' said Harriet in a pointed tone.

Katy grimaced. 'Seriously?' She shook her head. 'This is about budget, I suppose? Listen, when I was sourcing stuff for the railway carriages, I went to a couple of those second-hand furniture places in Aldwych. Plus eBay for vintage stuff.'

'Yes, but that fitted in with the vibe of the railway theme,' said Flora. Although she had to admit that she had been a little concerned about the look of the flat-pack furniture that Nico had showed her. She had hoped for something a little more pretty. And the girls seemed to agree.

'Looks are, unfortunately, everything in the hospitality business,' Katy told her. 'You want something that somebody sees online and gets excited about sleeping in. You know. Even if it is a tent!'

She went off to take another order, leaving Flora thinking. Perhaps she could stretch her artistic talent just a little bit, if she could find the right furniture.

'So when does all the hard work begin?' asked Harriet, interrupting Flora's busy thoughts.

'Today, I guess,' said Flora, stifling a yawn. She was still a little weary from the trip to Scotland.

'Tired?' murmured Libby, with a knowing smile.

'What's with the look?' asked Flora.

'Just you and the Italian stud, in a mansion house,' said Libby, her eyes gleaming. 'Overnight and in the same bed, no less.'

Flora rolled her eyes. 'I've already told you that it wasn't like that. It was more like sleeping in a haunted mansion. With Miss Haversham in charge. Nothing happened.'

'Why not?' asked Harriet.

'Because it's not like that,' said Flora. 'He's too much for me. He's so impetuous. Who buys a whole load of tents just like that?' She shook her head. Although, of course, now she didn't feel quite so disapproving of him. 'I need a quiet and steady man in my life, not someone like that.'

Libby made a face. 'Dullsville, more like. Where's the fun? The excitement?'

'What did I miss?' Katy asked again, coming to sit down with them. 'I've got a five-minute break, so hit me with the gossip.'

'Five minutes?' Libby frowned. 'Is that all Ryan will give you?'

'No, that's all I'll allow myself because we've got a delivery coming shortly. And leave Ryan alone.' Katy smiled. 'If he needs punishing, then I'll be the one to do it.' She shot them all a wink accompanied by a cheeky grin.

Harriet giggled. 'You two are so cute,' she said.

'In a sickening way,' added Libby, giving Katy a nudge with her elbow so that she knew Libby was only joking. 'Flora was just telling us that she wants a nice, dull man in her life.'

Katy looked aghast. 'Dull!' she repeated. 'Where's the fun in that?'

'Left behind, apparently,' murmured Libby.

'Look, I don't have time for all this,' Flora told them. 'There's so much to do. On top of everything else, Grams had the idea that the pond might be a good selling point as well for any campers, so I've got to make sure that looks ready for its photograph.'

'I'd forgotten about the pond,' said Harriet in a dreamy tone. 'I haven't been there in ages.'

'The what?' asked Katy, looking confused. She had only arrived the previous autumn and hadn't really explored the woods fully.

'In the middle of the woods, there's a large pond,' Flora told her.

'Like a duck pond?' asked Katy.

Libby shook her head. 'Not really!' she said, laughing. 'It's huge. It's a natural swimming pond, which I'm told is the height of fashion these days. We used to go in it all the time when we were kids.'

'It's really pretty,' said Harriet. 'Or at least it was many years ago when I saw it.'

'Is it clean?' asked Katy, with a grimace.

'The water is crystal clear,' Flora told her in a proud tone of voice. 'And the plants around the edge help with the oxygenation as well.'

'I'd forgotten it was even there, to be honest,' said Libby.

'Me too,' said Flora, nodding. 'Until last week when Nico found me skinny-dipping in it.'

The others gasped and then there was a round of shocked laughter.

'No!' said Harriet.

'God, yes!' added Libby, her eyes gleaming. 'Were you naked?'

'No!' replied Flora quickly. 'What's the matter with you? I was in my underwear.'

'Why were you in there at all?' asked Katy, looking nonplussed.

'Who cares why!' said Libby, staring at Flora in amazement. 'What happened?'

'Nothing,' replied Flora. 'I got out and we introduced ourselves.'

'And that was it?' Libby's face fell.

Katy shook her head. 'Maybe he's not the playboy after all,' she said with a sad expression. 'And I had such high hopes for you two.'

'Me too,' said Libby, with a groan.

'I don't know why,' said Flora, feeling irritated. 'I'm very happy with my life, I keep telling you all. It's not my fault you don't listen.'

She felt her friends exchange a look but ignored them. She knew that she was right. A quiet life was the best way. Wasn't it? She and Grams were better off on their own.

For a moment, though, she found that for the first time she wasn't quite so sure any more. And that perhaps she was protesting just a little too much and ignoring what she was feeling deep inside.

20

'This is doing wonders for my local street cred,' said Grams with a chuckle as Nico parked the Ferrari on the side of the road in Cranbridge that afternoon.

He got out and then went around to help Grams out of the low seat.

She straightened up and smiled. 'I do love spring,' she said.

Looking around, Nico had to agree with her. April had only just turned into May, but the trees either side of the wide river which ran through the village were now bright green and bursting with new growth. The water was clear and shallow. A goose and her four goslings were warming themselves on the grassy riverbank under the May sunshine.

Grams linked arms with Nico and led him down the pedestrian road called Riverside Lane. On the corner was a bustling shop, busy with villagers coming and going. At the far end of the lane was a tea shop, equally popular judging by the amount of customers heading inside.

'This is the place,' said Grams, in front of one of the two middle shops. The one next door appeared to be a furniture shop with some beautiful wooden pieces in the window. But Grams was leading him into a place with a sign above the door which read The Cranbridge Times. There was also a sign in the window which read The Community Hub.

Not sure what to expect, Nico followed Grams inside.

It was part meeting place, he thought, with a couple of comfortable sofas where some locals were chatting over a cup of coffee. It was part nursery, as there was a meeting room at the back which was holding a mothers and toddlers group. And then on the other side of the large room were a few hot desks, most of which were in use with people on laptops. It had a noisy, bustling feel to the place but was most definitely relaxing.

'Here is our local fountain of all knowledge,' announced Grams, as she headed over to a man with messy, dark hair who was sitting at a larger desk nearby.

He laughed upon hearing Grams' words. 'Thank you, Helen,' he said. 'I've been called worse things, to be honest.' He turned to shake Nico's hand. 'Tom Addison. Nice to meet you.'

'Nico Rossi,' replied Nico.

'Tom is the editor of the local newspaper,' Grams told him. 'He'll put you straight about what we need. I just need to go and catch up with a few old friends.'

She headed away to the sofas to begin chatting to a couple of elderly gentlemen who had just sat down.

Tom gave Nico a warm smile. 'Take a seat,' he said, swiftly removing a pile of papers from the chair on the other side of the desk before they both sat down. 'How can I help?'

'I'm a family friend staying at Strawberry Hill Farm,' Nico told him.

Tom's expression dropped a little. 'I see,' he said. 'I gather they've been having a tough time in recent years.'

Nico nodded. 'I'm afraid so. Anyway, with the fields not

yielding any profit, there was an idea that perhaps a campsite might be worth looking into. We've already sourced the tents, but I guess it's the legal stuff that we need to be sure about.'

Tom nodded enthusiastically. 'That's a great idea,' he said, before turning to his keyboard. 'Let's have a look and see what the local council say about it. From what I know, farm diversification, especially tourism, is normally encouraged under the right approach.'

They dug into the information provided on the local government website, and by the time Grams returned to join them, Nico had copious notes to follow up on.

'How's our money-spinning idea looking?' she asked.

Tom nodded. 'I'd say pretty optimistic,' he replied. 'The licensing is relatively straightforward as some small-scale camping is allowed under development rules for change of use from agricultural. I've given Nico the links to start filling in the paperwork. If you get started today, you may be lucky and be able to open by the end of the month, which is the Whitsun bank holiday weekend.'

'Sounds easy enough,' said Grams, with a shrug.

Nico laughed. 'I wish I had your optimism,' he told her, standing up. He shook Tom's hand. 'Thanks so much. You've been a huge help.'

'Always happy to answer any further questions if you get stuck on the legal side of things,' replied Tom.

Nico took one last look around the community hub before he left. It was the conversation and laughter that affected him the most. It reminded him of days long past and he realised that for too long now, he'd been really lonely. He'd missed having a family to get together. He missed having friends too. Everyone dropped away in the past few years. His dad had upset nearly everyone in the neighbourhood so that nobody trusted the Rossis now. His grandfather's good name was in the mud and undeservedly so. Nico didn't care what people thought of him, but he felt very protective of his grandfather.

He never felt more alone than at that moment and was comforted by the feel of Grams threading her hand through his arm once more as they left the hub.

As they walked slowly back up the lane, Nico was perturbed to see a young man on his knees peering underneath the car.

'Hey,' he said, worried that the lad was putting something under there. 'What are you up to?'

The teenager straightened up quickly and backed away. 'Nothing,' he said quickly. 'Just looking. Nice wheels, mister.'

'Yes, they are,' replied Nico.

'Shame about the oil leak,' said the young man.

Nico gave a start. 'What oil leak?' he asked.

'There,' said the teenager, pointing at the ground.

Nico crouched down and saw that there was indeed a tiny patch of oil underneath the engine. He straightened back up, wondering whether it had only just begun to leak.

'It's probably just the valves need cleaning,' said the lad.

Nico looked at him. 'Oh, yeah?'

'When was the last time it was serviced?' the lad asked.

Nico nearly laughed. His father had never maintained anything that he had owned and the Ferrari was likely to have been the same. Thinking about it, he was now immensely grateful that it had even made the journey from Italy to England.

'I'm not sure,' said Nico. He looked at the young man a little closer now. 'You know a lot about cars?'

The lad looked away. 'I like engines,' he said. 'How they work, how they move, how they can be fixed.'

'Well, if that's the case, any time you want to come by Strawberry Hill Farm, I've got an old motorbike you can look at,' Nico told him.

The teenager shrugged his shoulders. 'I dunno,' he muttered.

'No pressure,' said Nico, holding out his hand. 'I'm Nico, by the way.'

The lad looked at his outreached hand before turning away to climb back onto his bicycle. He put one foot on the pedal and hesitated before saying, 'Tyson,' and quickly cycling off.

Nico looked at Grams with raised eyebrows. 'I apologise. Have I just invited a local hoodlum into your home?'

She laughed and shook her head. 'The lad's all right,' she said. 'He's just having a bit of a tough time at home, that's all. His younger brother's got a long-term illness and takes up most of Mum's attention with him being in and out of hospital a lot. Dad disappeared off a long time ago. She tries her best, but Tyson has to shoulder a lot of responsibility on young shoulders.'

As Nico helped Grams back into the car, he glanced over the river to the other side and saw Tyson watching them in the distance. He gave him a small wave and saw the teenager immediately tear off into the distance and around the corner until Nico couldn't see him any more.

Tyson looked like someone in need of help and Nico found himself hoping that he turned up at Strawberry Hill Farm at some point soon.

21

Once the tents had been unpacked from the lorry, Flora and Nico needed to ensure that they were usable.

'They'll be fine,' Nico told her. 'Mrs McKinley might have been a somewhat dubious hostess, but I don't doubt her word that they are in good condition.'

Despite the incline of the hill, they decided to put the first one up in its intended site in the wildflower meadow.

After laying down a large tarpaulin sheet to protect the tent from the sodden grass, Flora and Nico used various ropes to secure it until it appeared structurally sound. Finally, after a bit of manoeuvring, the first tent was up. It was a cream-coloured bell tent, round with a pointed roof held up by a large pole which reached up to the apex. The high roof gave it a light and airy feeling which Flora hadn't expected when she went inside.

'I like it,' she said.

'Me too,' said Nico, coming to stand alongside her. 'There's plenty of space for a double bed and extra furniture.'

'I couldn't keep away,' called out Grams before stepping inside. 'My word! It's much larger than I thought it would be.'

'Which is a bonus because it means there'll be space for a large bed as well as a sofa too perhaps,' said Flora.

'A sofa?' Nico looked surprised. 'Why would there be a sofa inside a tent?'

Flora smiled at him. 'I thought we were going for a glamping vibe?'

Grams chuckled. 'Folks today want a bit of luxury, I reckon. Plus, if we had sofa beds, you could have people with families come too.'

'That's a great idea,' said Nico, nodding thoughtfully.

Flora walked around, screwing her eyes up to think. For a moment, she could see exactly how she could decorate it. The bedding would be soft and warm, in pale colours, matching the bedside lights and numerous fairy lights that would be twirled right around the pole to the top of the ceiling.

'The structure is good,' she heard Nico say as he and Grams wandered back outside. 'And we can respray them so that they remain waterproof.'

'Good job if the next month's forecast is to be believed,' said Grams.

'It's not good?' asked Nico.

'Not for the farmers, that's for sure,' Grams told him. 'A little bit of rain is always good. A lot of rain is not any good for anyone but the ducks.'

Flora headed out of the tent to join them.

'Thankfully, they don't always get the forecast right,' said Nico smoothly.

'Let's hope not,' said Grams. 'So how are you going to make these things level?'

'I'm going to build a platform for each one,' Nico told her. 'Like decking, so that also creates outside space as well as keeping the tents on even ground.'

'No soggy bottoms here then,' said Grams, with a chuckle. 'Talking of which, I must take that cake out of the oven.'

After she had left, Flora turned to look at Nico. 'I've been thinking about your flat-pack furniture suggestion,' she said.

He raised his eyebrows. 'And you hate the idea?' he prompted.

She shook her head. 'Not hate, but I just don't think they're going to suit what we're hoping to achieve here. New beds and mattresses, absolutely. But I thought perhaps we could look at a second-hand furniture shop in Aldwych. There might be a few things we could work on to give it a more glamorous vibe.'

'Okay.'

She gave a start that he would agree to such a major decision so quickly. 'Okay?' she said. 'As in...'

'As in, let's go for it,' he told her with a shrug. 'Listen, I trust you and we really don't have the luxury of time if you want to maximise the short summer season. We'll just have to jump right in with both feet. Just like you in that lake.' He grinned at her.

She shot him a look. 'Very funny,' she muttered, blushing.

He looked serious once more. 'I've been thinking. I'm going to tell your grandmother later about what happened with the vineyard,' he said in a soft tone.

Flora was surprised. 'Really?'

'I don't want any secrets between us,' he replied. 'And it's the truth and can't be changed, no matter how much I would like the outcome to have been different. Anyway, your grandmother deserves the truth, especially if I'm staying under her roof whilst the campsite gets up and running.'

She was grateful for his wanting to be honest with Grams and protecting her from any lies. 'You should have told me about what happened sooner,' said Flora. 'I believed the worst in you.'

He nodded. 'I'm just amazed I've told you any of it, to be honest.'

'I saw the Ferrari and just thought that you...' Her voice trailed off.

'Were just as bad as my father?' said Nico, finishing the sentence for her. He nodded. 'I let you think it anyway.'

'So that you could keep me at arms' length?' she guessed.

He shrugged his shoulders. 'I'm sure you can understand why I don't trust anyone.'

She nodded. She understood because she was exactly the same. 'It's a shame, though, that there was no one around to step up on your behalf to help save the vineyard,' she told him, thinking of her friends in the village who had tried to help them find a way to save the farm, and now Nico was trying to do the same. 'Listen, I don't think you're like your father. Look at what you've done for Grams. For the farm. And for me, I guess. I don't even think of you as a smooth playboy any more.'

Nico laughed. 'I don't know whether to be pleased or upset about that!' he joked. 'Perhaps I've lost my touch.'

'Maybe you're done hiding behind that smooth exterior,' she told him.

He looked at her, concern in his dark brown eyes. 'What if nobody likes what's underneath?' he asked softly.

'I do.'

She said it so quickly that they both gave a start in the silence that followed.

He looked at her with surprise on his face. 'Are you being nice to me?' he asked, with a smile.

'Don't get used to it,' she muttered, heading back inside the tent to hide her blushes.

She was just being friendly, that was all, she told herself. To make up for being so cool to Nico in the beginning when she didn't know the true story.

At least, that's what she was hoping it was.

22

Before their trip to Scotland, Nico had wondered what had made Flora so level-headed and steady, so lacking in spontaneity. Now he understood that it was the weight of responsibility of taking care of the farm. He had a new-found sympathy for her and felt that he had understood her a little more.

At least, despite her initial reservations about the campsite, it felt as if they were finally moving forward.

And it was too late to turn back now, he thought, looking at the large piles of wood for the decking that had just been delivered and were now towering in one corner of the courtyard.

'How much did you say you ordered?' asked Ryan, who had promised to help Nico that morning.

'Just enough, hopefully,' said Nico. 'Maybe I underestimated the amount we might need.'

'Looks like you've got plenty,' said Ethan.

'We can start to shift this if you're taking charge of the electrics,' said Ryan.

Ethan nodded. 'Rather leave you to all the heavy lifting

anyway,' he said with a grin. 'I'll start working out how much wiring we're going to need.'

Ethan was a qualified electrician who had also offered to help them out.

'Are you sure about this?' asked Nico, who had been over-whelmed when Ethan had announced that he would complete all the electrical work required for the campsite for free.

'I'll do anything to help save the farm,' said Ethan, with a firm nod.

Nico was touched by the villagers volunteering their time to help. Ryan and Ethan were helping him with the decking and electrics. Joe and Katy were working together on building a website and marketing the campsite. Harriet had offered them lavender soaps and hand cream and even prickly Libby had suggested that she make each guest a small box of truffles as a welcome present. It felt as if it were a tight-knit community, much like the vineyard had been in a smaller capacity. It made him feel that perhaps not everyone was like his father – selfish and not interested in anyone else's feelings or problems. Here in Cranfield, at least, the wider community cared about their own.

By the end of the week, Nico was pleased with the progress that he had made with the platforms, thanks to Ryan's help. Nearly all ten decks were now up. Thankfully, the weather had remained warm and dry, which had helped not only the work on the platforms, but also Ethan laying the hundreds of metres of electrical cable. Each tent now had its very own decking for customers to sit on, as well as electrical hook-up.

In addition, Joe had come up trumps with the website, which was looking very snazzy and would hopefully bring in their very first booking once they'd put some pictures up on it.

Nico was so grateful that he offered to buy the men a drink in return. So, on Friday night, they all headed across to the long path that led towards Cranbridge. Nico was once more charmed by the pretty village.

The group led him over a narrow pedestrian bridge to where an old pub was situated next to the river. Once inside, they all ordered drinks and fries and found a couple of tables to gather around.

The inn was certainly a pleasurable place to be, Nico thought. It had roaring fires, large oak beams and a cosy atmosphere. The restaurant was full, even though it was a drizzly night, so Nico, Ryan, Ethan and Joe sat at a table near to the large-screen television, which was showing the football.

'*Salute!*' said Nico. 'And thank you for your help. We really appreciate it.'

'Cheers,' said Ryan, before taking a sip from his pint of beer.

'You're welcome,' said Joe, who was sitting on the other side of the table.

'Anything for Grams and Flora,' added Ethan.

'Well, I've found muscles I never knew I had,' said Ryan, leaning back in his chair. 'And work is crazy busy this weekend. The restaurant is fully booked again tomorrow night.'

'You've done really well,' Joe told him.

'I think you'll find it's Katy who's done all the work,' drawled Ethan, whom Nico was beginning to realise was never serious about anything. 'You just mess around with your pizza dough a couple of nights a week.'

Ryan grinned at him. 'Katy seems to like my dough,' he replied, with a wink.

Ethan groaned. 'Ooof! Enough with the love talk, bro! I love Katy, but living with you two is like being shacked up with Romeo and Juliet.'

'Isn't that a tragedy?' asked Joe, with a frown.

'I sincerely hope not,' said Ryan before looking at his brother.

'There's always a solution if you don't want to stay with us,' he added in a pointed tone.

Ethan shot his brother a look. 'Yeah, but everywhere else doesn't have free bed and board,' he said.

Ryan rolled his eyes. 'Looking forward to you leaving for your next contract, to be honest. You're costing me a fortune in food and drink.'

Ethan raised his glass. 'I like to think of myself as free taster for your next seasonal menu,' he replied.

'Contract?' asked Nico.

Ethan nodded. 'Electrical lighting specialist for large-scale events such as concerts and theatre productions.'

'Impressive,' replied Nico.

'I hear anyone can do it,' said Ryan, shooting a grin at his younger brother. 'Now, making your own pasta? That's a real art form.'

'No, that's art,' said Ethan, nodding at the big screen as one of the football players scored an incredible goal.

They watched the game for a while. Nico had already noted that Inter Milan were playing Barcelona and had braced himself for the inevitable. Just before half-time, it came.

The camera zoomed in on his father in the stands, waving and smiling to the crowds, ever the showman. Nico thought that he looked older, a little more worn around the edges. But the charm shone through as always.

Nico felt the same way he always did on seeing his famous father. A mixture of pride for his footballing skills and a dull ache deep inside for the pain that one man could cause.

He turned away from the screen to find the other men nodding and smiling at him.

'Do you play?' asked Ethan, nodding at the footballers on the screen.

Nico shook his head. 'Not to any decent standard,' he replied. So far, the conversation between the four men had been light and friendly. But still he was wary of revealing too much about himself. Since Maria had sold his story to the papers all those years ago, he still trusted barely anyone with his innermost thoughts.

'So, no chance of a kick-around whilst you're here?' carried on Ethan.

'I always preferred a fierce card game, to be honest,' confessed Nico.

Ryan looked delighted. 'Oh, yeah, I'd forgotten,' he said. 'All those gorgeous squares in the middle of Rome where there was always a couple of guys playing cards.'

Nico nodded. 'Most likely to be briscola,' he said. 'Or poker.'

'Do you know, I haven't had a decent game of poker for ages,' said Ethan. 'We'll set one up whilst you're here.'

'Sounds good,' said Nico.

When Joe and Ethan went to the bar to order another round of drinks, Ryan looked across the table at Nico.

'Do you see much of your dad?' he asked.

Nico shook his head. 'He's pretty busy most of the time.' He knew that Ryan had spent a few years in Rome and decided to face up to the inevitable. 'You know about him? His reputation?'

'Doesn't everyone?' replied Ryan, with a sympathetic smile. 'Gotta say, the son of Paolo Rossi sounds a tough call, whatever everyone thinks.'

Nico nodded, somewhat surprised that Ryan seemed to understand. 'I'm actually the grandson of an Italian farmer at heart,' said Nico. 'You see me as the son of a famous footballer, but that's not the whole story.'

'Glad to hear it,' replied Ryan. 'And, for the record, that's not how any of us see you.'

* * *

As they walked back from the pub that evening, Nico thought
about friends and how much he'd missed out on having some.
And how lucky Flora was to have so many.

She had said that he had all the sophistication, with his nice
clothes and the Ferrari. But the truth was that she had everything
that he had ever wanted: family, friends and a home. And that was
more precious than any supercar or a famous surname.

23

'So we've had the provisional say-so from the council that we can have a temporary campsite this summer,' Flora told her friends as they all stood at the bottom of the hill looking up.

On each of the large decks, a bell tent stood. She was quite amazed at the transformation of the wild, empty field, but actually the tents looked very inviting, despite the lack of any decoration and furniture.

'That's great,' said Harriet. 'Everything's really pushing ahead now.'

'I knew you'd be okay,' said Katy. 'So what's left?'

'Each tent needs to be dressed,' explained Flora.

'Make one look like a show tent,' suggested Katy. 'I mean, the best possible one with all the trimmings. That way, we can photograph it and add it to the website. People like to see what they're sleeping in.'

Flora nodded. 'Okay. I need to look at the second-hand furniture market to see what's suitable, as well as new bedding, and we've got a whole load of fairy lights on order.'

'Excellent,' said Libby. 'When in doubt, cover everything in fairy lights is my motto.'

Flora turned around to look at the old stable block. 'We haven't done anything to this yet,' she said, with a sigh. 'Nico says we should concentrate on the campsite this summer and this could be a longer-term project.'

Libby went over to study the Ducati motorbike, which Flora had just wheeled out of the stable block to place on the back of the trailer connected to the tractor. She was going to take it up to the main farmhouse for safekeeping.

'What a machine,' cooed Libby. 'Sexy bike for a sexy Italian.'

Flora shook her head. 'We're just business partners,' she replied.

'So take his money and anything else on offer,' said Libby with a wicked grin, her eyes gleaming as she touched the handlebar. 'There are worse ways to get through the summer than with a hot Italian stallion.'

Flora rolled her eyes. 'It would be a disaster.'

'No, *that* is a disaster,' said Libby, looking over her shoulder with a grimace.

Flora turned around to see Dodgy Del walking towards them and gave a soft groan, which everyone else joined in with.

Dodgy Del was the local coach driver and was a nice guy whose heart was in the right place. Unfortunately, his way of trying to help, and earn himself a bit of extra money at the same time, normally meant disaster for anyone within a one-mile radius. Trouble followed Del everywhere he went, despite his generous nature.

'Good afternoon, lovely ladies,' said Del, with a beaming smile.

'Afternoon, Del,' said Flora. 'What are you doing here?'

'More like, what are you up to now?' asked Libby, putting her hands on her hips.

'Ladies!' said Del, shaking his head. 'Is that any way to greet an old friend?'

Flora groaned. If Del was putting on the smooth patter, then a favour was definitely about to be requested.

'Old friend?' repeated Harriet, with a wry smile.

Each of them had been on the receiving end of a few of Del's disasters and were now prepared for the worst.

'Spill it, Del,' snapped Libby, always straight to the point. 'We're busy.'

His grin faded quickly. 'All right. Keep your hair on.' He looked at Flora. 'Got a shipment of sheds, haven't I? Or, rather, I'm hoping to sell them as those luxury home office things.' He gave her a wink, which made Flora wonder just how 'luxurious' the sheds actually were. 'Trouble is, the guys that delivered them have just dumped the whole lot in the middle of my yard. Can't get my coach round there now and I can't shift 'em by myself. So I was wondering whether I could borrow your tractor and trailer to move them.'

'Have you ever driven a tractor?' asked Flora, glancing nervously at the only remaining farm vehicle they had left.

'Oh, yeah,' said Del quickly.

A little too quickly as far as Flora was concerned.

Before she could say anything else, he had launched himself at the tractor door and wrenched it open.

'I'll prove it!' he called out.

'Del,' said Flora in a warning tone, coming to stand by one of the enormous wheels. 'Wait a moment! The steering is a bit temperamental and needs gentle care.'

He waved away her concerns with his hand. 'I'm just getting a feel for it,' he told her. 'Now, what does this do?'

Suddenly, the tractor roared into life. Del had obviously turned the ignition key on! Through the driver's window, Flora could see him pulling on various levers and switches.

'Del, get out of there,' warned Flora, stepping forward to drag him out of the cabin.

But before she could get there, the tractor jolted forward and Flora jumped out of the way before it ran her over!

'Where are you going?' she shouted, running alongside, but not too near in case her feet were crushed under the huge wheels.

'I don't know!' came Del's shouted reply. Even he looked nervous now. 'How do you stop this thing?'

Before she could answer, the tractor swerved alarmingly before turning at a right angle straight for the Ducati.

'Turn the wheel!' she shouted, running to keep up with him.

Suddenly, the tractor turned and Flora's shoulder sagged in relief, anxious that Lorenzo's precious motorbike wasn't harmed.

But then Flora realised something and stared in horror as Del seemed to be aiming right for the stables in front of him. Once more, the tractor swerved. However, the trailer tied on at the back took out a large corner of the stables. The tractor kept going for a few more seconds before thankfully Del found the off switch.

But as Flora ran over to take the keys before Del could do any more harm, something else was moving. It wasn't the tractor this time, it was the stable block itself!

The corner Del had run into was beginning to disintegrate in front of their eyes, swiftly followed by an increasing amount of roof tiles all sliding down the now lopsided wooden structure.

At the sound of splintering wood and smashing tiles, Flora and Del abruptly ran in the opposite direction, following the girls as they all dashed away from the collapsing stables.

Finally, Flora stopped and spun around, just in time to see the whole roof plunge to the ground, swiftly followed by two of the walls.

She stared open-mouthed, trying to find the words – any words – but nothing would come. She could only look at the stables, which were pretty much destroyed. There was no point worrying about Nico helping to renovate it now. There was nothing left to be worked on. It was just two walls standing upright.

Dodgy Del came to stand next to her, just as one of the remaining walls folded in on itself and crumpled to the ground. 'Sorry about that. You haven't used them stables for years though, have you?' said Del, with an apologetic smile. 'Don't suppose I could still borrow the tractor, could I?'

24

Nico had come running down the hill upon hearing the sound of the stables collapsing and now stood alongside Flora and her friends, who thankfully seemed unharmed.

He stared at the mess in wide-eyed horror. Everyone was standing around looking shocked and stunned.

'So this Del is a friend of yours?' he asked in a shocked tone, turning to look at Flora.

'More like a one-man wrecking ball,' said Flora with a heavy sigh.

Nico looked back at the abandoned tractor and the back of Dodgy Del, who was retreating from the scene of the crime at a fast pace, after profusely apologising.

'He means well,' interjected Harriet, in an optimistic tone. 'Despite things always seeming to go wrong around him.'

'Who is he?' asked Nico, looking back at the stables, which was now mostly matchsticks. Earlier that day, it had been an actual building and something that he had been wanting to invest in. That dream now seemed dead in the water before it had even begun to take any kind of form.

Ryan had come down the hill with Grams and was also staring around him at the destroyed stable block. 'My cousin, I'm afraid. There's one in every family, yeah?'

'Except Del counts as two,' said Libby, rolling her eyes.

Nico began to walk over to survey the damage, but Flora stopped him with her hand. 'You can't,' she told him. 'It's not safe.'

He dragged a hand through his hair. 'You seem remarkably calm about all this,' he said.

He, on the other hand, was severely rattled. What if someone had been hurt? What if Dodgy Del had destroyed the campsite instead?

'I think I'm still in shock,' said Katy, with wide eyes as she joined them. 'I can't believe there's nothing left of the stable block.'

Grams gave her a grim smile. 'Well, my husband built those stables many years ago. He was a fine farmer but not so skilled as a builder, unfortunately.'

Libby rolled her eyes. 'Nothing short of a nuclear bunker would be able to stand up to Dodgy Del. What an idiot!'

But Flora's steady nature appeared to be working in her favour as she turned to give Nico a wide smile. 'I guess we'd better make the campsite as much of a success as we can,' she told him.

He smiled back at her and nodded. 'Yes, we better had.'

* * *

The following day, Ethan came over to the farm to present the electrical certificates to prove to the authorities that all the wiring had been up to the right specification.

'Thanks,' said Nico, shaking his hand. 'We're really grateful.'

'My pleasure,' said Ethan before looking over Nico's shoulder with a frown. 'Unfortunately, there are some people only bent on destruction.'

Nico turned around and took a deep intake of breath as Dodgy Del clambered out of his battered coach to wander over.

'Good morning, all,' he said, with a wide grin.

'It will be if you don't destroy any more buildings,' said Ethan, with a frown. 'What are you doing here? Don't you think you've done enough damage?'

'Well, I wanted to make amends for that,' said Del.

'Do you?' asked Nico.

'Of course,' Del told him. 'I feel really bad for the ladies here on the farm. So what can I do to help?'

'You can stay away from the tractor,' said Nico quickly.

'And from my electrical wiring as well,' added Ethan, narrowing his eyes. 'I don't need you causing any unexpected shocks to any future guests.'

'Humph,' said Del, making a face before turning to look at the spare decking. 'What about this lot?'

'It's all in hand,' said Nico.

'I must be able to do something to help!' Del told them.

'Well, that would prove that there's a first time for everything,' drawled Ethan.

'Good morning, Del,' said Flora as she came out of the back door and walked across the courtyard. 'What are you doing here?'

'Offering up my services to you all,' he told her, with a winning smile. 'Still feel bad about what happened yesterday. So what can I do to help around here?' he repeated, looking between them all.

'I think we're okay, thanks,' she replied quickly.

'We're really okay for everything,' added Nico, as he and Flora exchanged alarmed looks.

'You've got the tents?' asked Del.

Nico nodded. 'Yup.'

'Lights?'

'I've sourced them,' said Ethan.

'Listen, it's not that we don't appreciate the offer,' began Flora.

'Where are the campers going to wash and, you know, do their business?' asked Del, screwing his face up in thought.

Nico suddenly found himself hesitating. It was the last big decision and cost that they needed to make. The easiest solution would be portable washrooms with toilets attached. But their investigations online had garnered some eye-watering prices for even the most basic of models. 'We'll figure something out,' he blurted out.

It was exactly what Del appeared to want to hear. 'So you haven't got anything sorted yet?' he asked, suddenly looking delighted. 'Well, don't fret. I can certainly help you there.'

'It's fine,' Nico told him, his words coming out in a rush.

But Del was holding up his hand and shaking his head. 'Nah, I know a guy, you see? Got some top-quality items. I'll have a word and see if he's got something with a shower as well. Yeah?'

Flora looked panicky. 'Del, you don't need to make anything up to us. It was just an accident, that was all.'

'Happy to help,' said Del, nodding enthusiastically. 'Listen, I'll be in touch, but you should have something within the week. You're opening for the bank holiday weekend, right? Let me go and have a word with my contact.'

'Del!' called out Flora, but he had already turned his back and was climbing aboard his coach.

Flora turned to look at Nico with wide eyes. 'Oh no,' she muttered. 'What now?'

Ethan came over to place a hand on her shoulder, giving her a sympathetic smile. 'Just be grateful that he isn't anywhere near your tractor again.'

'Yes, but what will he turn up with?' she replied, still biting her lip in worry.

'I always think you should expect the worst and hope for the best where my cousin is concerned,' said Ethan before walking over to the pile of decking to inspect it.

Nico looked at her. 'Maybe it will turn out all right,' he said, trying to remain optimistic despite the overwhelming evidence so far to the contrary.

Flora made a face. 'Or not,' she said. 'Whatever he brings, it won't be eco-friendly or in keeping with the rest of the site. Knowing Del, he'll probably turn up with a bucket and a watering can.'

And with the opening date fast approaching, there wasn't the luxury of time if they didn't want to miss the start of the holiday season. Strawberry Hill Farm campsite would have to open, ready or not. And with whatever facilities Dodgy Del was going to bring them.

25

'Well, this all looks wonderful,' said Grams, gazing around at the tents all set up in the field.

Flora was pleased that her grandmother approved. She too was starting to think that the field looked quite cheerful with the ten tents standing proudly on the side of the hill on their platforms.

'The decking is much larger than I thought it would be,' carried on Grams. 'But in a good way. Plenty of space for people to sit and watch the sunset.'

'That was your idea, apparently,' said Flora as they both stepped up to peer inside the nearest tent.

'The new beds look good,' said Grams.

Flora nodded. It was the only piece of furniture in each tent so far, but she was pleased. The bed was off the ground and she had chosen a whitewashed frame which would hopefully match the shabby-chic décor that she was planning on. 'I've seen some second-hand furniture online that I can paint to match the bed,' Flora told her. 'And there's brand new rugs and bedding on order.'

'You've both done so well,' said Grams. 'I might even book

myself in here one night for a treat.' She gave her granddaughter a smile before they stepped back out into the afternoon sunshine.

There was so much to do, but when Grams perched on the edge of the decking, Flora joined her and sighed as she sat down.

'What's up?' asked Grams.

'Nothing,' said Flora quickly.

Grams looked at her. 'Flora Barton, I love you, but you are no great actress.'

'I just hope it works,' she said. 'With the stable block gone, there isn't too much else we can do.'

'I'm sure it'll be fine,' said Grams. 'Nico assures me that it will be, and I trust him.'

Flora was quiet.

'Don't you trust him?' asked Grams softly.

Flora hesitated. She did trust him as a person. It was just the idea that she didn't know about. That none of them had any experience in dealing with a campsite. How would it work? Would it even work? And what would they do if it didn't?

She sighed. 'I do trust him,' she finally replied. 'I just worry that it's all going too fast and we don't know what we're doing.'

Grams smiled to herself. 'I know,' she said, reaching out to squeeze her granddaughter's hand. 'You like to consider everything through properly, think it over, mull over the positives and negatives. The trouble is, life doesn't always allow you that luxury. And perhaps a bit of spontaneity will do us all some good.'

Flora looked at Grams. 'A bit like your first dance class?'

Grams smiled. 'I can't wait,' she said, with a giggle. 'Isn't that mad? Me on a dance floor again after all these years.' She sighed softly and looked across the field where the long grass wafted in the gentle breeze as it drifted across the valley. 'You know, I like the way this field ran wild.'

'So do I,' replied Flora.

Grams nodded. 'We're just lucky to be in charge of this land for a short period in our lifetimes. We're the caretakers, so it'll be good to give something back to the land that's given us so much. In fact, it'll be just like it was in the early days here.' Her eyes misted over. 'I think your grandfather would love it. He was an organic farmer earlier than anyone else in the area. Using chemicals never sat well with him, so he decided not to. You know, we only ever worked half the fields in the early days. The ones at the bottom were always wild until we made the decision to plough those fields as well. So perhaps nature and the farm have gone full circle. With a few people missing, of course.'

Flora knew that she was thinking of her late husband and squeezed her hand.

'I miss him so much,' Grams said softly.

'I know you do,' said Flora. 'So do I.'

'I think that's why I enjoy having Nico here,' said Grams. 'It feels as if a small part of Lorenzo is here and that in turn takes me back to happier times when we were all together.'

'But he's not Lorenzo,' said Flora.

'And he's not his father either,' said Grams in a pointed tone.

'I know that,' replied Flora quickly.

'Then why don't you let him in?' asked Grams.

Flora let go of her grandmother's hand and looked away. 'We're friends now.'

'Nothing more?'

Flora shook her head.

'He's got a good heart underneath that handsome exterior,' said Grams. 'I know that he told you about what happened to his family home.'

'He's told you as well?' she asked.

Grams nodded. 'Terrible. Must be heart-breaking for him. After all, we know what it's like to have the loss of our family home hanging over us. Imagine if we had lost it altogether, not having our friends around us to help.'

Flora couldn't even conceive how much pain that would cause her.

'So the fact that he's here fighting for our family home makes it even more extraordinary, don't you think?' said Grams. 'You can't help but think the best of him because of that.'

'I do,' Flora told her.

And she realised that she was speaking the truth. Nico was generous of spirit, to help them so much when he could have just walked away. She admired him for that. And so much more.

For a moment, she thought back to the paparazzi photos that she had googled when he had first arrived. At the time, she had been concentrating on him, but last night she had looked again at the photographs and studied the women instead. They were all glamorous and fashionable, super polished women that Flora hadn't a hope of ever being. She wondered why that mattered to her. She didn't want Nico to think of her as a potential girlfriend, did she?

26

Flora had received assurances from the local council that the application would be approved and so was able to forge ahead with getting everything ready on the campsite for inspection.

She had sourced all the furniture for one of the tents and so, with the photographs being taken the following day for the website, the tent needed prettying up.

Ethan had been a huge help in setting up the electric supply to each tent and the fairy lights were already installed. Although not everyone approved when she said so at their girls' night in at the farm that evening.

'He's infuriating,' muttered Libby.

'He's free which makes him our new best friend,' said Nico, who had wandered into the farmhouse kitchen to make himself a drink. 'Ethan seems like a really nice bloke. Why don't you like him?'

'He ruined my prom, so I will never forgive him,' said Libby, with a sniff.

Her friends all exchanged a knowing smile as it was the same excuse that she had always given. There had never been full details from Libby and Flora was pretty certain that she was hiding something from them all, even after all these years. But Libby's hard shell, despite being the most generous and supportive of friends, was still pretty tough to get through.

Nico merely raised his eyebrows at Flora, who shook her head to warn him from digging any further.

'Well, I'll leave you all to your exciting evening,' he told them, nodding at the pile of materials on the table.

'You can always help,' said Harriet in a hopeful tone.

Nico laughed. 'These hands are made for hammering in nails, not sewing, I'm afraid,' he said, leaving the kitchen.

'Shame,' said Libby, after he had gone. 'I can think of a couple of other things that his hands might be good for.'

'Libby!' hissed Katy, flicking a glance at Flora.

'Don't mind me,' said Flora, even though she could feel a blush spreading across her cheeks. 'I don't think of him in that way at all.'

'She's still protesting too much,' muttered Harriet.

'Definitely,' added Katy, nodding in agreement.

'So why am I wasting good gin-drinking time by cutting up triangles of material?' asked Libby, with a groan.

'Because I haven't got the time to make all the bunting by myself and I thought you could help,' replied Flora.

'Not sure how much help I can be, to be honest,' said Katy, making a face. 'I can't sew to save my life.'

'Then you can be in charge of cutting up the triangles,' Harriet told her.

'What about me?' asked Libby. 'I can't sew either.'

'Well, you can be responsible for making sure our gin glasses never run dry,' said Katy.

Libby shot her a grin. 'That is definitely my kind of job.'

'But I can't drink too much tonight,' said Flora in a warning tone. 'I've got so much to do tomorrow. The bed needs making, the outdoor furniture is arriving and I still want to set the scene for the photographs.'

'Definitely,' said Katy with a grin.

'So I'll need that bunting tomorrow as we want to take the photos when the sun's out in the morning.'

'Yes, ma'am,' said Libby, with a grin as she held up her scissors snapping the blades together. 'We're on it.'

'Can't Nico help?' asked Harriet.

'He's already got a long list of stuff to do,' Flora told her.

It was all getting close enough to be able to open up to the public. However, the decorating part was her favourite bit. She and Grams had gone through a whole load of leftover unwanted material and decided to use it for proper bunting that could be machine washed if it got too grubby over the summer season. Flora was hoping the only thing that would happen would be that the pretty material would fade in the hot summer sun. Although she could hear the rain hammering against the window that evening. It had been on and off all week, making working outside difficult. But at least it highlighted which paths could get a bit slippery and she and Nico had decided to put down some stone chips to stop people falling over when it got a bit wet.

'The weather's terrible at the moment,' said Katy, with a frown as she too heard the rain against the window.

'Good for the lavender plants,' replied Harriet, smiling. 'They need watering before all those lovely hot summer months. Hopefully.'

'Not sure how much water you want them to get,' said Libby, making a face. 'I read that this unsettled weather is here to stay for the foreseeable future.'

'Let's hope not,' said Katy quickly, flicking a concerned look at Flora.

Flora had read the same thing but stayed quiet, merely sending up a prayer that as soon as the campsite opened at the end of May the weather would change and summer could truly begin. And that if they managed to get open in time, people would actually want to stay at Strawberry Hill Farm campsite. All she could do was keep everything crossed that all their hard work would be worth it to help save the farm.

27

Nico stood back to look at the photographs that he had just taken on his mobile.

'What do you think?' he asked Joe who was standing next to him.

Joe peered at his phone and nodding approvingly. 'Looks great,' he said.

They both looked back up at the tent in front of them. Flora had done an amazing job with the decoration, thought Nico in admiration.

The bell tent had arrived in a crumpled pile, but thanks to Flora's vision, it was now welcoming, homely and, he even had to admit, a little bit glamorous as well.

The oak decking he and Ryan had built would weather over the years, but it brought a touch of sophistication. The front large V opening had been bordered by pretty bunting in pastel colours, entwined with fairy lights to give it an enchanted glow as darkness fell. On the deck were a couple of deckchairs, which too had been re-covered with leftover material. It gave the whole place a bohemian but comfortable vibe.

Between the deckchairs was a table made from a tree stump and placed on the top was a storm lantern. The rope along each side of the decking was also entwined with fake flowers in pastel colours as well as more fairy lights. Nico had initially thought it was too much, but he had to concede that it looked pretty amazing.

Inside, there was a large double bed, dressed with rich cotton sheets, duvet and squishy pillows and cushions. Either side were two more tree stumps on which lamps had been placed. On the floor were a couple of colourful rugs which made for a comfortable feel and nearby there was a battered leather sofa, decorated with soft cushions and an old cupboard which had been sanded and painted. There was a hat stand for coats, as well as an old wardrobe for guests to place their clothes.

Nico looked around and admitted that he would be quite happy to spend a night in there and was hoping that, by showing off the photographs on the internet, paying customers would be as well.

The outlay had not been as much as he had feared as Flora had repurposed anything and everything that she could lay her hands on. Apparently, she had even sent out a begging post on the local website which had brought in lots of deliveries over the past couple of days. They even now had a couple of sofa beds, which meant that some of the tents would be able to sleep families of four.

She had worked hard on the look and feel of the place, but Nico knew that her artistic skills were what had really brought the place to life.

'I'll get this put on the website asap,' said Joe as they headed back to the courtyard.

Joe and Katy had built the website for the campsite as they had experience and Nico was thankful, not only for their help but

Ryan and Ethan too. Everyone had contributed something to the effort of keeping Strawberry Hill Farm going and he knew how grateful Flora and Grams were.

As they reached the courtyard, Nico peered at what appeared to be a pair of feet sticking out from underneath his Ferrari.

'Hey, Tyson,' he said, crouching down, having already guessed whose feet they were. 'What are you doing under there?'

The teenage boy crawled out from underneath the car and stood up quickly. 'Just proving that I was right. You've got a small hole under the radiator too. It's rust.'

'I see.' Nico looked at the car. 'Well, I'm glad you came over. There's not many mechanics around here, from what I've seen. You were saying something about it needing a service. Don't suppose you could recommend anyone?'

'I could do it,' said Tyson, looking down at the ground. 'I've done my grandad's car and that works fine. You can ask him, if you like.'

'No, that's okay,' said Nico. 'How about this weekend?'

'You mean it?' The lad's face lit up. 'I can really service the car? This car?'

'Sure. And I'll pay you the going rate as well.' Nico held out his hand. 'Do we have a deal?'

Tyson hesitated for a moment before taking Nico's hand and shaking it. It wasn't a firm grip, thought Nico, reminding him of the boy's age and lack of confidence. 'Deal,' said Tyson.

'Excellent,' said Nico. 'Do you want to come in for a drink?'

Tyson shook his head. 'Only came over after school. Gotta get home.' Then he grabbed his bicycle which had been abandoned on the ground, before quickly mounting it. 'Which day at the weekend?' asked Tyson.

'Doesn't matter,' said Nico.

'I'll come after football practice on Sunday,' said Tyson before he cycled away.

'I'm not sure I'd be letting my precious supercar in the hands of a teenage tearaway,' said Joe, laughing before he headed indoors to talk to Grams.

But left alone in the courtyard, Nico merely shrugged his shoulders. He had no love for the car. It had been about making a point. To say to his father that because he had taken away his future and the vineyard, he would take away something precious that belonged to him. And if it gave a young lad whose family was going through a tough time a lift in sprits as well, then he really didn't care whether it worked or not afterwards.

After all, he thought, looking up as Flora came out of the back door, some things were more important, he was beginning to realise.

'The first tent looks amazing,' he said to Flora. 'Joe's going to upload the photographs now, so fingers crossed we get some bookings.'

'That's the least of our problems,' Flora told him. 'We need to furnish and decorate each tent!'

'That's your domain,' said Nico, laughing. 'I'm not getting involved in any of that!'

'Regarding the rest of the furniture, how low is our budget?' she asked.

Nico grimaced. 'Pretty low considering how much all the wood for the decking cost,' he said. 'Sorry.'

He was concerned how quickly they were going through his savings account. The campsite bookings were going to be much-needed by them all.

'That's okay,' said Flora. 'I'll have a look and see if we can upcycle a lot of it. Apart from the mattresses and bedding, of course.'

'Thanks,' said Nico.

'I don't know why you're thanking me,' said Flora. 'This is all on you,' she said, looking around. 'I guess I owe you a drink or two when all this is over,' she told him.

He looked pleased. 'Sounds good to me,' he said.

'I might even be able to stretch funds to a piece of cake as well,' she told him.

She gave him a winning smile and Nico's heart missed a beat. She really was quite beautiful, he decided. Even more so when she relaxed and smiled.

'Of course, that might have to wait a while,' said Flora, her smile dropping into a frown. 'There's still so much more to do.'

'And to decide on,' said Nico, looking at his to-do list. 'Most importantly, once we get all the licences, then there's the website and marketing to get on top of.'

'As well as the promised Portaloos from Dodgy Del,' said Flora with a grimace.

'I'm trying not to think about those,' replied Nico.

'Also, I was thinking that perhaps we should have a trial run,' Flora told him. 'After all, neither of us has ever run a campsite before and there's probably loads of little things that we haven't thought of. I was thinking that perhaps someone could spend the night here and give us some feedback.'

'Good idea,' he replied. 'Do you have anyone in mind?'

Flora nodded before breaking into a wide smile. 'The most unlikely person to ever use a campsite!' she said.

28

'Me?' Katy looked at Flora wide-eyed with shock. 'Camping?'

'Think of it more as a research trip,' Flora told her quickly. 'And it would only be for one night.'

She knew that Katy had no love for the countryside, despite falling in love with both Ryan and Cranfield.

Katy sank back against the wall in the courtyard and looked across at Ryan. 'I don't know why you're smiling,' she told him. 'If I'm camping, there's no way I'm being out in all this fresh air on my own.'

'Just think,' he told her, slipping an arm around her shoulders. 'The night sky, you and I tucked up in what I hope would be a large double bed.' He looked at Flora, who nodded, despite there being absolutely no furniture yet in most of the tents.

'I could be persuaded,' murmured Katy, leaning forward to brush her lips against his.

Ryan turned to look at Flora. 'You might need to include a bottle of wine with that tent,' he told her, with a grin. 'I'm not sure my girlfriend will be able to face a night in the fresh air sober!'

'Hey!' said Katy, pretending to look affronted. 'I've made huge strides forward in my, er, love of the countryside. I even own my own wellies now, although they're bright pink! And I know the difference between an oak tree and a holly tree.'

'That's really not saying much,' said Ryan, laughing.

'Well, as long as you think it'll be all right,' said Katy, biting her bottom lip in a nervous gesture.

'You know, this was all your crazy idea anyway,' Flora told her.

'But a good one, right?' said Katy, with a grin.

'It would be great to get your feedback,' replied Flora.

Katy nodded. 'I understand.'

Ryan looked around. 'Of course, if you haven't got any bathroom facilities, we might have a long walk to our flat in the morning.'

Flora rolled her eyes. 'Apparently, bathroom facilities will be provided in time,' she said, through gritted teeth.

Katy looked at her suspiciously. 'If it's out in the open or using the stream, then forget it,' she said. 'I love you but not that much.'

Flora laughed. 'It's not that. We're waiting on delivery. It's a portable thing, you see, on wheels.'

'That all sounds very vague,' said Katy.

'That's because it's being donated by Dodgy Del,' said Flora, with a gulp.

'Oh no!' said Katy, beginning to shake her head. 'It'll be a bucket and a sponge!'

'The sponge will cost them extra,' added Ryan, also shaking his head. 'I can't believe you trusted my cousin.'

'We couldn't say no,' Flora told him. 'He felt bad about knocking down the stable block and so promised us a Portaloo or some such in return.'

'And you believed him?' Ryan threw his hands up in despair.

Flora found herself agreeing with her friend's pessimism, still fearing the worst.

* * *

The following day, and with great uncertainty, Flora waited in the courtyard for Dodgy Del to arrive.

'What if it's really bad?' murmured Nico.

'Then we hide it in that empty barn and he'll never know,' Flora told him, looking up at the sound of a large vehicle making its way down the potholed lane towards the farmhouse.

She took a deep breath as she saw Dodgy Del's battered truck coming around the corner. But what was being trailed behind it came as a huge shock.

It appeared to be an extremely upmarket portacabin. Painted in a dark green on the outside, with gold fleur-de-lis accents, it looked surprisingly classy. When Del parked up and they were allowed to peer inside, they were even more shocked to see the walls and furnishings decorated in deep purple, with both the toilet cubicles, washbasins and shower cubicle all having gold taps and fittings as well.

'There's another one arriving later for the ladies,' said Del.

'It's even got a chandelier,' said Flora, wondering if she was seeing things as she glanced upwards.

They both turned to look at Del in shock.

'It's incredible,' said Nico, in a stunned tone.

Del gave them a winning smile. 'Told you, didn't I?'

'Where did you get it from?' asked Nico.

Del touched the side of his nose. 'Can't say any more,' he said, with a wink. 'But let's just say it's almost majestic, innit?'

Nico and Flora looked back at the gold toilets once more.

'A royal throne indeed,' muttered Nico, before he burst out laughing.

And Flora couldn't help but join in.

29

Now that one of the tents was fully set up and Dodgy Del had provided the bathroom facilities, it was ready for the trial run. Flora just hoped it would run smoothly.

'So that's the drinking water labelled,' she said, finishing securing a sign next to the tap on the outside wall of the old stables. 'It's fresh water from an underground source and safe to drink, as well as use for washing up.'

Nico made a note on his checklist. 'I think we're about there,' he told her. 'So all that's left is to double-check Tent No 1 for tonight's guests.'

Flora smiled to herself. Despite her nerves, she had good reason to be thankful for her friends that evening as Katy and Ryan had promised to spend the night in the tent to check everything worked.

'The kettle's set up, the bed's made and I've just got to double-check the fairy lights,' she replied.

'Definitely the glamping side of camping,' said Nico with a grin. 'I remember sleeping outside years ago and it was just me, a tent and a sleeping bag.'

'That will never do for Katy,' said Flora, laughing.

Katy's love-hate relationship with the countryside was well-known to her friends. But if the trial went successfully, then they would be all set for when the campsite officially opened to the public in a fortnight's time. If the licences came through on time.

'Why have we asked that particular couple again?' asked Nico, frowning. 'Isn't she the worst person to ask?'

Flora shook her head. 'On the contrary, she fits the bill perfectly. Because she is the least outdoorsy person I know, she's our perfect guinea pig.'

There was still much to worry about, but she felt herself relax a little later that evening as she showed Katy and Ryan around the site as if they hadn't already seen it all.

'I've never seen anything like it,' said Katy, shaking her head in wonder as they stood outside Dodgy Del's extremely glamorous washing facilities. 'Have you seen the inside? It's like a stately home.'

Flora smiled. 'It's a bit over the top for the country vibe we were going for but they're free so they'll absolutely have to do. And I'll probably put some bunting outside as well, just to soften it up.'

'So Dodgy Del finally came through with a winner?' said Katy, still looking amazed.

'Well, he was probably due at least one helpful suggestion after so many failures,' said Ryan.

Flora didn't mind. She was just grateful that they now had working toilets and showers for their customers.

'So there's spare blankets in that box over there,' she told them as they returned to the tent. 'And there's a spare plug for chargers or whatever in the drawer of the table, as well as a list of emergency contacts and numbers for local services.'

'This looks great,' said Ryan, beaming. 'And as we've bought our own pizza, we can relax and just chill out.'

Katy was nodding but still looking a little worried. 'Will there be bugs?' she asked, glancing nervously at the floor.

'You're off the actual ground, remember,' Flora told her. 'Thanks to the decking. Then there's the ground sheet of the tent, plus a fluffy rug as well. And the bed is on a proper divan too.'

'Okay.' Katy bit her lip, causing Ryan to laugh and put his arm around her.

'I'll be with you, if you get frightened,' he told her, before leaning forward to whisper something in her ear that made her blush.

Flora was smiling as well, happy to see her friends so in love, but also finding herself wishing that she too could have that special a partnership. She was surprised, not sure where that particular thought had come from and tried to concentrate on her friends instead.

'Well, if you're happy that you've got everything you need, I'll leave you to it,' she told them.

'Thank you,' said Katy, stepping forward to give her friend a hug. 'I'm sure it'll be fine.'

'I just hope you enjoy your stay,' Flora told her. 'You've got my number if you need anything.'

As she walked away, she mentally checked through her list but couldn't think of anything else that they might require. She glanced up at the sky as she walked back to the farmhouse and was thankful to see that there were no clouds. A clear night would mean a colder one, but hopefully the extra bedding would make them comfortable.

But it did also mean that it would be a beautiful sky to enjoy their pizza on the decking and watch the view.

When she stepped into the kitchen, she realised that she

wasn't the only one that was obviously a bit nervous about their friends' feedback. Nico was pacing up and down and only stopped when he saw her step over the threshold.

'Is it all okay?' he asked, for once his smooth mask of calm and confidence completely at odds with the nerves in his words.

'It's fine,' she told him.

'Did you show them the switches for the bedside lights?' he asked.

She found that she was smiling at him. 'I'm sure they'll be able to figure that out,' she replied. She sniffed the air appreciatively as she realised that Grams had left a delicious chicken pie in the oven for them before heading out to her dance class. 'How about some wine with dinner?'

Nico nodded. 'I think I need one.' He gave her a sheepish smile. 'I didn't think I'd be this nervous. But if the trial run doesn't go well...' His voice trailed off as Flora poured them both a glass of wine.

'Here,' she said, handing him one of the glasses.

'Thanks,' he replied, taking a large sip before sinking down at the kitchen table. 'So I have some good news. We've had our very first booking for the bank holiday weekend. And it's a family booking, meaning that four of the tents are already booked.'

'They are?' said Flora, shocked.

Nico nodded. 'I know, right? I mean, it helps that it's half-term week so some people are off school and work, but I had no idea that it would be this popular so early on.'

'Then let's hope our trial run tonight is successful,' said Flora, now feeling even more nervous.

But, as it turned out, there was no need.

The following morning after breakfast, Katy and Ryan were beaming from ear to ear when Flora and Nico went to check on them.

'How did you sleep?' asked Flora.

Katy and Ryan exchanged a look and Flora smiled to herself. 'Let me rephrase that question,' she said. 'Was the bed comfortable?'

'It's lovely,' Katy told her. 'Far more luxurious than I was expecting. The lighting was just right. We were toasty warm in bed. And the kettle was very welcome this morning. Those vintage teacups and teapot are a beautiful touch.'

'Plus the view from the deck last night with our dinner was incredible,' added Ryan.

Katy nodded. 'It really was.'

'Anything that we can change or add?' asked Nico.

Katy sat on the step and pulled on a pink wellington boot. 'I guess it was just the question of breakfast,' she finally said.

Ryan nodded in agreement. 'That's right. I mean, we're heading home now to our apartment and, of course, we'd be more than happy if people wandered over to grab a pastry from our shop. But we don't open until nine o'clock so what if there are any early risers?'

Nico tapped his chin in thought. 'You know, I camped in France a long time ago and each morning the local boulangerie would drive around the campsite in a little van with freshly made baguettes and croissants.'

'Sounds great,' said Ryan. 'Maybe between us, we could provide something the night before or even for early in the morning?'

'So everyone benefits,' said Nico.

'Absolutely,' replied Ryan with a grin.

'I can't believe I actually enjoyed camping,' said Katy, reaching out for her other wellington boot. But just as she was about to put her foot inside, something leapt out and she dropped the boot with a loud scream. 'It's a frog!' she shouted, looking absolutely terrified.

Flora rolled her eyes. 'It's a toad,' she replied. 'Nothing to be frightened of!'

'Ha! That's easy for you to say,' said Katy, rushing to stand behind Ryan.

It turned out that Katy still had a way to go before she completely embraced the countryside, thought Flora, laughing.

30

As Flora headed back to the farmhouse, she heard excited voices in the kitchen and went in to find Grams chatting and laughing with Eddie.

'Good morning!' said Grams, who was standing at the Aga. 'Who's for eggs?'

'Good morning to both of you as well,' said Flora. 'And yes please.'

'Morning,' replied Eddie. 'Thanks, Helen. I think I need the energy today.'

'How was your dance class last night?' asked Flora, suppressing a yawn as she poured herself a coffee.

'Fabulous,' said Grams, cracking some eggs into a pan.

'We learnt the samba last night,' added Eddie, with a laugh. 'I'd like to say we mastered it perfectly.'

'But we were the worst ones there,' said Grams, also laughing. 'It's much harder than it looks.'

'We'll master it,' said Eddie, nodding his head as if to convince himself.

Grams flipped the eggs over. 'Of course we will. We managed the cha cha cha, didn't we?'

Flora smiled to herself. Eddie was Grams' oldest friend and it was nice to see them so upbeat after so many years of widowhood between them.

'What about the foxtrot?' she asked.

Grams grimaced as she spooned the eggs onto a couple of thick slices of bread and placed the plate in front of Flora.

'We're working up to that,' she said, with a smile.

Flora thanked her for the food and dug in, her stomach now rumbling in anticipation. She wondered about asking Grams if she would mind making up a breakfast basket for the campsite guests when they were up and running.

'You can always join us,' said Eddie, waggling his grey eyebrows at her as he made a perfect spin on the kitchen floor tiles.

Flora shook her head, thankful that her mouth was full and couldn't reply.

'I'll get her to a class one of these days,' said Grams. 'If she ever has a spare moment.'

'I'm not sure Flora's going to have any of those in the next two weeks,' said Nico, heading into the kitchen. '*Buongiorno*, everyone.'

After the chorus of good mornings, Nico came to stand next to Flora. She looked up at him with raised eyebrows. 'Am I allowed time for breakfast?' she asked.

His brown eyes twinkled back at her. 'Of course,' he replied. 'And you're going to need the energy because we received an email from the council overnight. We're now officially a summer campsite.'

Flora put down her knife and fork with a clatter and reached out for the mobile that he was holding out in front of her. She swiftly read the email and couldn't believe it. 'Wow,' she said, leaning back in her chair. 'I didn't think it would happen that quickly.'

'Too late now because there's more good news,' he said, sitting down next to her at the table. 'We are now fully booked for our very first opening weekend.'

'We're actually full?' Flora looked at Nico in amazement.

He nodded, seemingly a little dumbstruck as well. 'I don't know how or why, but yes, two weeks today, every one of the tents will be filled with hopefully happy customers.'

Flora blew out a long breath. 'That's two weeks to fill every tent with furniture and dress it.'

'Two weeks to ensure that the Wi-Fi covers each tent, that all the health and safety measures are met,' he added. 'Signs and lighting. And that the swimming pond is safe too.'

'Then I suggest you both better eat up,' said Grams, placing a plate of eggs on toast in front of Nico.

* * *

With the days quickly ticking by towards the grand opening, Flora was rushed off her feet from sunrise to sunset.

In between applying coats of paint to all the second-hand furniture she had bought, she began to add little touches to each of the tents to make them unique.

Each day, she relaxed more and more and let her imagination take over and was thrilled with the results.

So too was Nico, it appeared.

'This looks incredible,' he said, looking in one of the tents that she had just completed.

It was one of the larger ones meant for a family. There were a couple of soft rugs on the floor, and mismatched cushions on the sofa and the bed. A blanket was draped over the back of the sofa as well as the end of the bed. She had even found a blanket box which she had varnished and polished that could be used as a table next to the sofa.

But it was the extra touches Flora was pleased with. Tarnished silver candlesticks, an old birdcage, tea light holders made out of old jam jars to give the place a romantic feel. She had even sourced some cheap little blackboard signs to place next to each tent with the names of the visiting family written on it.

'It's romantic,' said Nico.

Flora nodded. 'I agree. Especially at sunset and then, at night, you've got the vast expanse of sky. The stars.'

'A big bed,' he added with a smile.

'Be serious,' she told him, giving him a nudge with her elbow.

But in a way, she was getting used to his flirty nature. It was just an Italian thing, according to Grams.

'Just like his grandfather,' said Grams, as she was making dinner later. 'They're all charming.' She looked at her grand-daughter. 'Does this mean that you've changed your opinion of him?'

'I guess so,' replied Flora.

'Well, he's handsome, funny and smart. Is it possible that you don't want to be attracted to him when it's perfectly obvious to me that you are?'

Flora baulked at her grandmother's words and glanced around the kitchen to make sure that no one was around to overhear. 'No, it's not that,' she said, shaking her head vehemently.

Grams smiled to herself and busied herself with the dinner.

'Besides, I'm certainly not his type and he's the complete opposite of mine,' said Flora, getting up quickly. 'He's not remotely sensible!'

'Thank goodness for that, because otherwise there'd be no campsite and we'd be struggling to hang on to this place,' said

Grams, bringing out the cutlery. 'Now, don't get upset. We were just chatting. If you're not attracted to him, then that's fine.'

But as Flora laid the kitchen table for dinner, she had to face up to why she had been so desperate to dissuade Grams from thinking that she was attracted to Nico.

Because Flora was beginning to think that she might just be and desperately hoped that it was just a small crush that would disappear.

31

'So that's that. Tomorrow we open and we're officially a campsite,' said Flora, giving Grams a tremulous smile.

'Then I reckon we'd better enjoy ourselves tonight at our celebration,' said Grams. 'You've both worked so hard, you deserve a break before it gets even busier tomorrow.'

It was her birthday and they had decided to celebrate with all their friends as a way of saying thank you for the hard work that they had all contributed to the campsite. So Katy and Ryan had closed the pizza restaurant that evening to host a private party.

* * *

'Staying over wasn't really that much hard work,' said Katy, with a wide smile later that evening. 'I got to sleep in the most luxurious tent I've ever been in.'

'It's the only tent you've ever been in,' said Libby, stretching out like a cat on one of the sofas. 'And likely to be the only one as well.'

'It's still the best one,' said Katy, giving Flora a nudge with her arm.

Katy was looking very relaxed and Flora couldn't help but feel the same way. Libby had concocted one of her infamous gin cocktail mixes and anyone who drank one was feeling no pain.

'I need another slice,' said Harriet, leaning forward to help herself to the pizza that had been placed on the table. 'I think I'm seeing two Paddingtons.'

Paddington the golden retriever was sitting next to the table, his tongue lolling out in anticipation that the strong gin cocktail might just help a piece or two of pizza accidentally fall to the floor.

'So now what happens?' asked Libby.

'A large glass of water and some painkillers in the morning, I should think,' said Katy, glancing at her cocktail.

Libby shook her head. 'I meant, now that the campsite is about to open. What happens between you and your silent partner?'

Flora looked across to where Nico was sitting and laughing with Joe, Bob and Eddie. 'I guess we'll split the duties in half,' said Flora, trying not to concentrate on how good he looked that evening. 'I'm happy to take on the cleaning of the washrooms as I don't care about that kind of thing.'

Libby shook her head. 'No, no, no,' she moaned.

'It's true,' said Flora. 'I mean, once you've taken care of cows, mess and muck doesn't really affect you.'

'Please!' said Katy, with a grimace. 'You'll put me off my pizza.'

'I didn't mean that, but thanks for the disgusting heads-up,' said Libby, making a face. 'I meant what happens now between you two.'

'Nothing happens,' said Flora. 'We've got a job to do.'

'Flora, you know how much we love you,' said Harriet,

lowering her voice. 'But you've been all work and no play for a very long time.'

Katy nodded. 'I agree.'

'See?' said Libby. 'Katy's a complete workaholic and even she takes time off once in a while.'

'In a tent,' added Katy, with a giggle. 'Wow, that was some sexy night, I tell you.'

'Please don't,' said Libby. 'He's like my adopted big brother and some images I don't need to even imagine, thanks.'

'Quite right,' said Harriet, nodding furiously.

'I think you're all being a bit unfair,' said Flora, feeling a little hurt. 'I've been trying to save the farm and we're still not out of the woods yet.'

'Yes, but you've been trying to save it for ten years. Or, rather, using that excuse to hide yourself away,' said Harriet.

Libby and Katy nodded along in agreement.

Flora frowned. 'I haven't been hiding,' she told them. 'Anyway, I took a chance. Opening a campsite is a long way from farming for me and Grams.'

'Good,' Libby told her. 'It's great to see you taking a bit of risk with your life. Otherwise it was all a bit dull.'

Flora took a big gulp of her drink. Perhaps everyone did see her as dull. That her life needed shaking up. 'I can be fun and exciting when I want to be,' she said hotly.

'Of course you can,' said Libby, not sounding the least bit convincing.

Flora blew out a sigh. 'I can,' she said, looking down and finding Paddington's adoring face looking back up at her. She finished her drink and reached across to the jug to pour herself out another.

'Steady,' said Katy. 'Another one of those drinks and you won't be able to stand in the morning.'

'I can handle my drink,' said Flora. 'I went to college, didn't I?'

'Of course,' said Katy quickly.

Flora could feel her friends exchange glances. She knew that she was acting a little strange that evening, but she felt out of sorts. Restless. She needed to blow off steam. It was that 'jump in the lake' feeling, that had caused her no end of embarrassment when she had first met Nico all those weeks ago.

Now, of course, she was beyond embarrassment. They were friends. Colleagues. Partners in a business.

She looked across the room at him. He really was quite lovely, she decided. Handsome, of course. A playboy? She wasn't sure that was quite so true. Exciting? Definitely. Her heart raced and it wasn't just the gin cocktail. He'd mixed her up inside and she wasn't sure what she felt any more. She'd tried so hard to resist her feelings for him. But she had to admit to herself that she had a crush. A bad one.

Well, if she was going to throw caution to the wind and be spontaneous, there were worse people to fall for.

She made her mind up to talk to him when they got home. It was time for Flora Barton to have a bit of fun, she decided.

And with a smile to herself, she took another gulp of her strong gin cocktail.

32

Nico had taken one sip of Libby's extremely strong gin cocktail and had decided to stick with beer for that evening.

He enjoyed the party and talked quite a bit with Harriet, Katy and Libby. They were all lively, chatty, attractive women. And yet he couldn't stop his eyes being drawn to Flora.

She had certainly enjoyed herself that evening. It wasn't until he walked her and Grams home that he realised quite how many gin cocktails she had drunk. Flora was singing a song and giggling as they went.

'My dear girl,' said Grams, laughing, as they walked with linked arms down the dark, potholed track. 'What has got into you this evening?'

'Four of Libby's gin cocktails,' said Flora, laughing.

As she tripped on a pothole, Nico reached out to take her arm to steady her. 'Easy,' he told her.

'I'm fine,' she said, her words slurring ever so slightly as she shook off his hold. 'I'm super Flora. Super sensible. Super reliable. Super steady.'

'Super drunk,' muttered Grams, giving Nico a smile.

He smiled back at her but kept his eye on Flora all the way back to the farmhouse. It seemed really quite out of character for her to be so drunk. She was always in control, always so balanced and cautious.

But then he thought back to that first moment when he had seen her stripping off to wade into the lake. He felt as if Flora was the same as the farmhouse. All quiet beauty on the outside but full of vibrancy and excitement hidden underneath its walls.

He found himself wanting to know her, the real Flora behind the mask she always wore. And wanting to know why she felt the need to control herself so tightly all the time.

Except that evening, he thought, as she tripped over the small step leading into the kitchen.

'Shall I make a pot of coffee?' asked Grams, suppressing a yawn.

'Don't worry,' Nico told her, giving her a kiss on the cheek. 'You go to bed and I'll make sure she's okay.'

'Thank you,' Grams said, patting him on the cheek. She turned to Flora who was standing and swaying nearby. 'Dear girl, you go to bed soon. You hear me?'

'Yes, Grams,' said Flora, with a giggle.

Grams shook her head but was smiling to herself as she headed out of the kitchen.

'How about a glass of water? Or a black coffee?' asked Nico.

Flora shook her head. 'That all sounds far too sensible and I've decided not to be sensible any more.'

Nico smiled at her. 'Really? What are you going to be instead?'

She walked around the table with a smile on her lips that made him gulp involuntarily. She had a certain look in her eyes and he wasn't sure if he was imagining it.

She walked right up to him so that their bodies were touching.

Her green eyes were gleaming as she wrapped her hands around the back of his neck.

Nico couldn't believe it. He definitely wasn't imagining it.

'Say something in Italian to me,' she whispered.

'Why?' he asked, realising that his words were coming out a little bit croaky.

'Because it would sound sexy,' she told him.

'Flora,' he said, trying to take a step backwards.

But she pulled him even closer until he could see every freckle on her nose, every fleck of emerald in her eyes.

'I think you could be good for me,' she said.

'How?' His heart was beating very fast in his chest. It was a wonder that she couldn't feel it against her own.

'I think I should have a fling with an Italian playboy,' she said. 'Kiss me and find out how good we would be together.'

He swore in Italian to himself. He couldn't help but glance at her lips and had to force himself to do the right thing and unwrap her hands from behind his neck.

'This isn't going to happen,' he told her.

She took another step forward. 'Why not?'

'Because you're drunk and not thinking straight,' he replied. 'Trust me, you'll regret this in the morning.'

She made an impatient sound. 'I'm thinking straight for the first time in a very long time,' she said, before inclining her head to stare at him. 'Is your head moving?'

'No.'

'Is the whole room moving?' she asked, suddenly reaching out to hold on to the back of a nearby chair.

'It might be,' he said. 'How about that glass of water?'

'Make it stop,' she groaned, closing her eyes but still swaying.

'I can't,' he told her. 'But some black coffee might help.'

'I need to lie down,' she said, moving from clutching one chair to the next until she was almost out of the kitchen.

Nico had thought she would go upstairs but she only made it as far as the lounge, where she fell onto the sofa and pretty much had passed out before he had even had a chance to cover her with the blanket that was on the back of the chair.

He stared down at her for a moment. For a second in the kitchen, he had been sorely tempted to kiss her.

Despite his every inclination, it appeared that he had real feelings for Flora. He was just grateful that she had been too drunk to realise it.

33

The following morning, Flora woke up on the sofa with a bad headache and a sense that something had gone awry.

'Good morning,' said a cheery voice nearby.

Flora peeked through narrow eyes and saw Grams sitting with a mug of tea on the armchair, looking at her phone.

'Is it?' mumbled Flora. 'I'm not so sure what's good about it.'

'I think Libby should patent her gin cocktails,' said Grams, with a smile. 'Perhaps the military could use it as some kind of weapon against the enemy.'

Flora groaned. 'Why did I drink so many?' she said, rubbing her aching forehead.

'I don't know,' Grams answered. 'You obviously needed to let off steam.'

Flora frowned. 'Why?'

'You tell me, darling girl,' replied Grams, getting up. 'Anyway, I'll make you a nice strong coffee and some of my pancakes.'

'I don't think I could eat a thing,' said Flora, her head and stomach churning in unison.

'Nonsense,' said Grams. 'You'll feel much better afterwards.

Besides, you've got a busy day ahead with the campsite opening today! Nico's already gone to make some final checks.'

Nico! Flora sat bolt upright, her eyes wide as she remembered asking him to kiss her. She groaned and fell back against the sofa. Of all the dumb things to have done!

What had happened to her? Sensible Flora, who always contained herself and never put a foot out of place, had asked Nico to kiss her!

Well, she needed to put an end to that immediately. So as soon as she'd had a very cold shower and two coffees and a large pile of Grams' pancakes, she decided to face the day. And Nico.

'Good morning,' she said, when she found him in the court-yard a while later.

'Good morning,' he replied.

He was looking hot and sweaty, having already shifted a large pile of decking. Her pulse picked up on seeing him.

'So where is this all going?' she asked, deliberately keeping her voice strong and steady. After all, she was a grown-up. And grown-ups sometimes made mistakes, got a little drunk and forgot themselves. That was all. It happened all the time. Not to her, admittedly, but to everyone else, it seemed.

'I was hoping to use the tractor to take it down to the pond,' he said. 'Unless you wanted to drive?'

'No, that's okay.' She gave him a broad smile. 'I'm probably a little bit drunk still after last night. I can barely remember anything. Those gin cocktails were lethal!'

She desperately hoped that he would believe her and that it would explain her actions.

He gave her a long look before replying, 'Yes, they were. Right, I'd better get these moved out of the way before our first guests arrive.'

Then he returned to his work and Flora was able to breathe again once more.

Anyway, there wouldn't be time to think about Nico and her embarrassment that day. It was the grand opening of the campsite at last and Flora was nervous. She was about as far out of her comfort zone as she could be, she realised.

But a tiny, surprising part of her was excited too. It was something different, something other than farming. And maybe, just maybe, it might even succeed beyond her wildest dreams.

She was keeping everything crossed as she stepped out to greet the first paying customers when they arrived early that afternoon.

'Welcome to Strawberry Hill Farm,' she said, with a smile.

It was a young family with a toddler who had been the first to book one of the family tents a few weeks ago.

'I can't believe we're finally here,' said the woman, jiggling the young girl on her hip. 'The journey was awful.'

'Then you've come to the right place to relax,' Nico told them with a warm smile as he joined them.

Flora led them to their tent, showing them the Portaloo block as they went. She felt proud as the couple ooohed and aahed when they saw the inside of the tent.

'It's bigger than our first flat,' said the man, laughing.

His partner joined in. 'And more luxurious than our bedroom now,' she said, her eyes gleaming. 'Is that really a kettle in here?'

Flora nodded. 'There's a jar of coffee and teabags over there. There's a water tap on the side of the farmhouse. Let me see, what else? There's extra blankets, if you feel the cold. Did you bring your own travel cot?'

The man nodded. 'We did, but she'll probably end up snuggling in with us as well.'

The little one was currently wandering around the tent, giggling as she went.

'Be careful and don't touch anything,' warned her mother.

'There's nothing breakable in here,' Flora told her. 'Or, at least, please don't worry. It's all upcycled, so there's nothing fancy.'

'It's wonderful,' said the woman, with a satisfied sigh as she looked at the view. 'We live in the middle of a city so never get to see anything like this.'

* * *

It seemed to be a recurring theme as the day progressed and the other customers arrived.

'They all said it was wonderful and brilliant,' Flora told Grams later on.

'One lady said that it was the most beautiful bedroom she'd ever get to sleep in,' added Nico, with a proud look on his face.

Grams smiled. 'Oh, you two are so clever to have worked all this out between you. What a team!'

Flora blushed whilst Nico smiled in return.

'Let me give you both a hug,' said Grams, pulling them both forward into a group hug. 'You've done the farm proud with all your hard work.'

Flora gave her grandmother a squeeze, accidentally squeezing Nico's hand at the same time. She quickly stepped backwards.

'Well, I'll do one last walk around before leaving them to it this evening,' she said.

'I'll join you,' said Grams.

They left Nico to walk across the courtyard. But once at the gate, Flora stopped at the sound of laughter and conversation drifting past the open gate.

It was such a happy scene, she thought. Some people were

sitting outside their tents, with a glass of wine enjoying the warmth of the sun before it began to sank down behind the hills. The view across the valley that evening was stunning, lit from the golden rays of the sun.

People with young families were enjoying the wildflower meadows, the children letting off steam. There were even a few spirited card games going on. Some people had takeaway pizza boxes from Platform 1 and Flora was glad that everyone was benefitting from the good fortunes of Strawberry Hill Farm.

And hopefully it was good fortune, she thought. Hopefully, this was a good omen because didn't they deserve a bit of luck after so much misfortune? Surely even the weather would hold for them this time?

She suddenly felt a hand come into hers and turned her head to see Grams looking a little tearful.

'Are you okay?' Flora asked, aghast. 'What's the matter?'

'Absolutely nothing, my darling girl,' said Grams, reaching up with her other weathered hand to stroke her granddaughter's cheek. 'Just that you did it.'

'With a lot of help from Nico,' Flora added.

Grams nodded. 'Yes, he helped. But I was thinking back to before he came. All that hardship. All those wet, muddy days, weeks and months. All that worry. And now?' She turned her head to look over the campsite. 'Now, life has finally returned to the farm. It almost feels like it did years and years ago. When everyone used to come and help us pick the strawberries.'

'You know, we could start that up again,' said Flora, suddenly thinking of an idea.

'What? Pick your own?' said Grams, looking delighted.

'Why not?' Flora looked at the field full of happy campers. 'I think the campers would enjoy it. It'll save us some of the back-breaking work. And perhaps the old ways will help us get through all these new days.'

'Sometimes change isn't as bad as you think,' said Grams. 'It might even be good.'

'I think you're right,' conceded Flora, laughing as she drew her grandmother into a hug.

And maybe Grams was right. Maybe she needed to embrace change and learn to let go a bit. For all of their sakes.

34

Nico was feeling immensely relieved that all the campers seemed to be enjoying themselves.

Still, he waited for Flora and Grams to return to ask if there were any problems.

'Not at all,' said Flora, with a relieved smile when they arrived back at the farmhouse.

'Can I ask you something?' he asked Flora, as Grams headed inside. 'Do you think there's enough for people to do here?'

'What do you mean?'

'Should we provide games or something else?' he suggested. 'I know we've got the view and all that, and people come here to relax, but isn't that going to be a bit boring for some people?'

'There's enough in the local area to keep them busy,' Flora told him. 'There's a nice walk into Cranbridge. Food and drink nearby. Maybe people just want to sit and do nothing but read a book or whatever. Sounds like bliss to me.'

He was surprised to see her smile to herself. 'I would have thought you'd hate just sitting around doing nothing,' he told her.

'Chance would be a fine thing,' she replied. 'Imagine having the time to do absolutely nothing but watch the clouds go by.'

They both glanced up at the sky, but Nico guessed that she was thinking exactly the same as he was.

'I'm sure it won't rain tomorrow,' said Flora.

Nico nodded. 'I agree,' he replied.

'We're right on the edge of that weather system that's going to be sweeping the country,' she carried on. 'I should think we'll get a tiny bit of drizzle and that will be it.'

'Absolutely.' Nico glanced back at the campsite. 'That waterproof spray we bought was top-notch, so they should stay dry inside.'

'And warm too, if the temperature dips a little,' said Flora. 'There's a nice thick duvet and numerous blankets. There's even a hot-water bottle if they need one.'

'You've kitted each tent out so well,' he told her.

Flora blushed and shrugged her shoulders. 'It was mainly down to Katy's feedback. I pretty much copied her checklist for the train carriage accommodation.'

'Yes, but the tents are better,' he replied.

Flora laughed. 'It's not a competition,' she told him.

'I know,' he said. 'And I want them to succeed too. But we also need to do well.'

'We will.'

As she headed indoors, Nico remained outside, staring up at the early evening sky. There was still the threat of heavy rain over the next few days and although they were keeping everything crossed that the weather forecasters were right and that the storms would miss them, he just wanted to make sure everything was secure.

At that moment, under a clear blue sky, he had to agree with Flora that the forecasters probably had it wrong. It wasn't about the money, for him. He had invested pretty much all of his savings into Strawberry Hill Farm. But he hoped that one family home would remain in the same family and not be sold, unlike his own.

They had done the best they could. The tents looked phenomenal. He glanced at the portacabin that Dodgy Del had provided and smiled when he saw Flora's artistic efforts had even covered that as well. She had placed flowerpots and bunting around the outside and it now fitted in with the overall feel of the campsite.

He headed around the corner of the farmhouse and saw a familiar bicycle leant up against the side. Further along, Tyson was crouching down and tinkering with the motorbike engine.

'You're here late,' said Nico.

Tyson jumped up at the sound of the voice and looked around, a guilty look on his face. 'I didn't do nothing,' he said, his words coming out in a rush. 'I was just looking.'

Nico held his hands up. 'Woah,' he told him. 'No worries. I told you that I was happy for you to look at the engine. Especially as you fixed the oil leak on the Ferrari.'

The teenager had turned up on the promised date and got on with the job, keeping himself to himself. He didn't say much but his love of engines certainly shone through.

Tyson nodded. 'That was easy. This is a little more complicated because it's so old.'

'Old doesn't mean bad,' said Nico.

'I didn't mean it like that,' said Tyson, turning to stare at the motorbike with an appreciative stare. 'It's a classic.'

'It certainly is,' said Nico, looking down at it with a smile. 'Do you think it'll ever work?'

Tyson nodded. 'One hundred per cent,' he replied, crouching down once more.

It was then that Nico noticed the small pile of tools that were next to him. 'We've got other tools up at the farm if want to borrow them.'

'Okay.'

He leant against the wall and watched Tyson for a while, nodding in wonder as to how carefully the teenager studied each and every cog and screw.

'I'd have thought you'd have wanted to do something else with your spare time,' said Nico. 'Like play a computer game or something.'

'Nah.' Tyson gave a shrug. 'We don't have the latest ones, and anyway, if I'm at home then I've got chores to do. No time to play games.'

'I see.'

Nico didn't press the lad, merely waiting to see if he opened up to him. To his surprise, and pleasure, Tyson spoke again.

'My younger brother's ill, so Mum has to give him a lot of attention.'

'And your dad?' asked Nico.

'Dunno where he is,' replied Tyson.

'Mine's the same,' said Nico.

Tyson looked at him in surprise. 'Seriously?'

'Oh yeah,' said Nico. 'He's actually a famous footballer but completely hopeless at being a dad. Trouble was, my mum didn't want to know either.'

Tyson frowned. 'So who looked after you?' he asked.

'My grandparents.'

Tyson nodded. 'You were lucky then, if you had two people taking care of you. Mum has to work two jobs to pay the bills, so I have to do everything else.'

'Like what?' asked Nico, interested to learn more.

'Shopping, cooking, cleaning.'

Nico thought that it sounded quite a lonely life without much time to play at being a teenager.

'I don't mind, though,' he went on. 'When Kevin goes into hospital, it's worrying because you don't know what will happen. So Mum gets stressed and I like to make sure everything's okay at home.'

'Well, good on you,' said Nico, feeling impressed. 'I'm sure your mum is very grateful.'

It was a lesson not to misjudge other people's appearances, he thought. On first impression, Tyson had appeared to be a sulky teenager. But that was far from the truth given the responsibilities that he was given.

It was also a reminder of how grateful Nico was for his own upbringing. Without steady and loving parents, his grandparents had instead provided support love and a home without the additional burdens that Tyson needed to carry by himself.

'I like it here, though,' said Tyson, looking around. 'You've got loads of different stuff, like your car and motorbike. I'd love a go on that tractor.'

'You've always liked engineering and machines?' asked Nico.

Tyson nodded enthusiastically. 'Yeah,' he said, his eyes gleaming. 'When I work on an engine, it's like I can forget about what's going on at home. I feel better, not so stressed.'

Nico's heart cried out to the teenager and he found himself wanting to help him.

'Well, you'd be doing me a huge favour by trying to get the motorbike going,' he said. 'So any time you want to work on it, it's all yours.'

'Cheers.' Tyson suddenly stood up. 'I've gotta get back.'

He quickly swung his leg over the bicycle and rode off without looking back.

Nico recognised all the signs. How isolated the boy must feel.

The sense of chaos that an absent parent could cause. The responsibility to make sure everything else ran smoothly.

Helping the lad on his own journey, giving back and feeling like he could make a difference, Nico felt a little lighter as he walked away from the barn.

35

Flora woke up after a really good night's sleep and stretched out lazily in her bed.

She sighed happily as she listened to the sound of heavy rain against the window. As a farmer, she both loved and feared hearing the rain. Too much flooded everything. Too little and nothing grew.

But, of course, those worries were behind her now. After all, she now ran a campsite instead. How life had changed so quickly.

She sat bolt upright in her bed, her heart thumping. The campsite! Oh no! Heavy rain!

She sprang out of bed and rushed to the window, throwing open the curtains. It was a grey, dismal day, dark and overcast with the rain coming down in steel rods all around them. It looked more like an October day than the last weekend in May.

The forecasters had got it completely wrong. It turned out that they were being hit by the weather system that had been forecast for other parts of the country instead.

Groaning, Flora quickly got dressed and rushed out of the

bedroom, almost bumping into Nico as he ran out of his own room.

'Rain!' he said, pulling a T-shirt over his bare chest.

'I know!' cried Flora, following him downstairs.

They grabbed their coats and rushed out of the back door, heading towards the camping field. Not only was it extremely wet, Flora realised that without the sunshine, the temperature had dropped significantly overnight and it was now much cooler.

She and Nico went around each tent to say good morning to their guests. Some were sanguine about the rain and happily reported that the kettle was a wonderful addition and that the tents were dry inside, to Flora's relief.

Others, however, were unhappy and a little upset about the change in the weather.

'Maybe we should have booked that hotel after all,' mumbled one husband to his wife.

'Hopefully it'll clear up later,' said Nico, applying his smooth charm. But this time, it didn't seem to win anyone over and he and Flora walked away with worried expressions.

'Perhaps it will clear up later,' said Flora, glancing at the sky.

The trouble was that the particularly awful weather system they were now under looked set to stay for a couple of days.

'Well, the tents are dry,' said Nico. 'I don't know what else we can do for the unhappy customers. It's not as if we have any control over the weather.'

'I know, but these are our first customers and if they leave unhappy reviews, then what will we do?' asked Flora.

Nico turned to look at her. 'The only unhappy reviews we shall receive will be about the weather. Most people will understand that it's something we can do nothing about.' He gave her a smile. 'So let's keep everything crossed that it does clear up later.

Besides, I'm sure Grams' wonderful breakfast hamper will do wonders for the spirits.'

It had been an inspired idea of Flora's that Grams could provide everything from home-made pastries to warm bacon butties and the campers certainly relished the delicious food.

However, the weather worsened as the day went on. The wind got up, meaning that they had to ensure every tent was pegged down properly and their waterproofing was intact.

Most of the customers had chosen to shelter in Platform 1, where Katy was serving them all hot chocolates and cakes.

'It's so cold, I was thinking about lighting the fire,' she said to Flora when she went to check on how everyone was doing. 'I can't believe it's supposed to be summer next week!'

They were talking quietly in the tiny kitchen just off the waiting room.

'Is everyone okay?' asked Flora.

Katy hesitated before reaching out to give her friend's arm a reassuring squeeze. 'A couple of them are talking about heading off. Maybe even tonight.'

Flora was horrified. 'But they only arrived last night,' she said, feeling terribly upset.

'I know,' said Katy. 'But I think they're all a bit shocked by the weather and were imagining blue skies and warm sunshine. And there's not much to do when it's like this.'

They both glanced at the nearby window where the rain was lashing up against the glass.

Flora sighed. 'This is a disaster,' she muttered. 'We've only been open for a day!'

'You'll be fine,' said Katy, giving her a hug. 'Anyway, I'm sure they'll change their minds. After all, a holiday is a holiday, right?'

But her friend's optimism for once was misplaced.

With the rain getting worse, about half of the campers were

happy to sit it out in their tents, playing games and enjoying a glass or two of wine. A couple of others had headed to the Black Swan Inn in Cranbridge to shelter in the pub and enjoy the hospitality there. But four of the camping couples had decided to leave.

'I'm sorry,' said one lady, looking upset. 'But the weather doesn't look like it's going to improve for a couple of days. This wasn't what we had in mind when we booked. We just want to go home.'

'Of course,' said Flora, feeling upset but trying her best to hide it from the customer. 'We understand and, of course, we'll refund you the difference in your stay.'

'How kind,' replied the lady.

The other people weren't quite so upbeat and merely began to pack up without even telling Flora and Nico. However, they had been keeping an eye on the campsite from the large open barn and had watched as a couple of people began to take their bags to their cars.

They rushed out as one lady slipped over on the wet grass. She laughed and rolled her eyes at her clumsiness. 'Good job we're going,' she said, brushing off the grass from her knees.

Flora didn't feel like laughing, however. They had had to refund at least four couples for their short stay. They knew that they could do nothing about the weather and technically it wasn't in the contract, but she didn't want to make a bad situation even worse. They had barely made a profit on the weekend, let alone Nico getting anywhere near a return on his money for all the outlay of the tents and materials.

Flora was grateful for the remaining families that had stayed who were determined to stick it out whatever the weather, but she had never felt more miserable. It was an utterly disastrous start to running a campsite. And if that wasn't a success, then they had nothing left to lose but the farm.

36

After it had grown dark that evening, Flora sat slumped at the kitchen table. She had had such high hopes for the opening of the campsite and had figured in every possible problem, every potential thing that could trip them up. Apart from the weather, that was.

Nico muttered something in Italian as he sat next to her with an equally miserable expression.

'What was that?' asked Flora.

'*Piove sempre sul bagnato,*' he replied. 'When it rains, it pours.'

'Well, it's certainly doing that,' murmured Flora.

'Who wants a cup of tea?' asked Grams, in a bright tone.

'How about something stronger?' suggested Nico. 'I've got just the thing in my car.'

After a short while, he came back in carrying a couple of boxes of yellow liquid in glass bottles.

'What's that?' asked Grams.

'Home-made limoncello,' he told her.

'You made this?' asked Flora, amazed.

He nodded and smiled at her, although she noticed it didn't

reach his eyes. He was as tired and shocked as she was by the terrible start to their business. 'I do have quite a few hidden talents,' he said. 'Although changing the weather pattern isn't one of them.'

'Let's get some glasses,' said Grams, reaching up to the shelf above the worktop.

Flora watched as Grams suddenly peered out of the window. 'What is it?' she asked, wondering if it were the remaining guests on the campsite also deciding to leave.

Grams turned around smiling. 'Our friends,' she told them, just as the back door opened.

A flurry of activity followed as Harriet, Katy and Libby came inside in a rush of damp raincoats and excited babble of conversation. They were followed by Joe, Ryan, Ethan, Bob and Eddie.

'What are you all doing here?' asked Flora in amazement.

'Support,' Harriet told her, with a soft smile.

'I sent out an SOS,' said Grams.

They all shed their sodden coats and boots before everyone found a spare chair or cabinet to lean up against. Nico poured them all out a generous-sized glass of limoncello before sitting back down next to Flora.

'*Salute*,' he said, holding up his glass. 'Cheers.'

'What shall we drink to?' asked Flora, still feeling depressed.

'New beginnings,' said Grams, giving her granddaughter a wink.

Flora took a sip of the delicious drink. She hadn't eaten yet and on an empty stomach, it warmed up her insides a treat. But she still felt cold.

'Cheer up,' said Libby, sitting down at the table. 'It's only rain.'

Flora looked at her friend and even Libby's vitality seemed a little dented.

'So, how can we help?' asked Ethan.

'I don't think anyone can,' said Flora, shrugging her shoulders. 'It's raining on a campsite. What can we do?'

'Well, you can't change the weather,' Eddie told her.

'But perhaps you can give them something to take their minds off the weather,' suggested Ethan, looking thoughtful.

'This stuff will do the trick,' said Bob, his eyes watering a little at the strength of the limoncello.

'Not very family-friendly, though, Dad, is it?' said Ryan, laughing.

'So let me ask you this,' said Nico, who had been sitting quietly and staring down into his limoncello. 'What can people do in the wet? What would they want to do on holiday?'

There was a lull in the conversation as everyone thought hard.

Suddenly, Bob spoke. 'Well, I know what I would do,' he said. 'I'd want to go and see a steam train!'

Everyone laughed, except Ryan and Ethan, who had been putting up with their dad's obsession for some considerable time.

'Dad, you and Grandad see a steam train every single day!' said Ethan, rolling his eyes.

Bob shrugged his shoulders. 'So? Anyway, I reckon there's some folk who would be interested in a full-size train.'

Nico turned to look at him. 'I agree,' he said, nodding carefully. 'How do you feel about giving the families a tour tomorrow and showing them what you've done so far with the train?'

Bob's face lit up. 'That's a smashing idea,' he said.

'And those that haven't seen it so far can come and look at the old station as well,' said Katy. 'After all, we've got all the old memorabilia from when it was working.'

Ryan nodded. 'That's not a bad idea. And they might want a warm cup of coffee whilst they're there.'

'They're welcome to come and have a look at the lavender spa,' said Harriet, before reaching out for her phone. 'You know,

I've got a couple of free slots over the next few days. How about they all have a lovely hand massage with some relaxing lavender cream for free?'

'You'd do that?' asked Flora.

Harriet nodded. 'Of course. It won't take long, but it'll still feel like a treat.'

'They're welcome to have a tour of the lavender fields as well,' added Joe. 'And if they're going that way, then they could always carry on into Cranbridge, see the river and have a pint in the Black Swan Inn.'

'And there's the lovely corner shop there as well,' said Grams.

'As well as the pretty church,' added Eddie.

'If there's a let-up in the weather, we could even show them the swimming pond or they could go fishing by the river,' said Nico.

But Ethan's face was still wrinkled up in thought. 'Yeah, that's all well and good, but they might not want to go too far if it's raining. The tents are lovely, but they need somewhere outside to use.'

'What about the barn?' said Flora. 'I mean, it's got a roof but only three slatted walls so it's a bit exposed, but it might do. There's nothing in it these days except the tractor and we can move that out of there.'

'That's a great idea,' said Nico, turning to look at her. 'Perhaps we could put those leftover tables and chairs we had for people to have dinner under cover in there.'

'Talking of dinner, what about my old camp stove?' said Grams. 'They're welcome to use that.'

'And we've got a barbeque people can use as well,' said Joe.

'What about that old dartboard that we had?' asked Ryan, looking at his brother.

Ethan nodded. 'Yeah, I think it's hidden in my old room somewhere. And we've got some board games too.'

'This sounds wonderful,' said Grams, smiling. 'Shall we have another drink to celebrate?'

She held up her empty glass and everyone laughed.

Flora turned to look at Nico. 'What do you think?' she murmured.

'I think that we don't give up without a fight,' he told her in a soft tone. 'And thanks to our friends, we might just scrape through.'

She nodded, unable to look away from his dark eyes. 'Me too,' she replied.

She wasn't sure if it was the limoncello or the way Nico was looking at her, but the positivity and enthusiasm of her friends was making her feel warmer than she had felt all day.

37

Nico woke up the following morning feeing much more positive now that they had some sort of plan in place to resolve the issue of the weather.

He threw open the curtains in his bedroom and was a little upset to see that it was still raining heavily, but he felt more optimistic than he had done the previous day.

So he rushed through a very early breakfast with Flora before they both headed out to start setting up things before the campers began to rise.

First off was setting up the barn. They moved the leftover chairs and tables into place and then Nico rigged up some lighting so that it was a more enjoyable setting to spend time in. Flora strung up some fairy lights and bunting to ensure that it was in keeping with the rest of the site and gave the area a bit of ambience.

Ryan dropped off some board games early before he started work in the coffee shop. Flora was amazed at the number of different ones he had provided, including a giant Jenga, as well as a tabletop football game.

They hooked up the dartboard on one side of the barn away from the seating area. They also brought up the last of the spare bales of hay that Flora had saved for people to sit on.

Flora had some spare blackboards from when she had been using them for the tents and wrote on them the various outing options for people to choose from.

The first was a tour of the old steam train that Bob and Eddie were working on. There was also the offer of a free hand massage in the lavender spa with Harriet, as well as a tour of the lavender fields.

There was a surprise visit from Dodgy Del which made both Flora and Nico instantly tense up.

'Ethan text me and said that you needed something to keep the campers happy,' he said.

'Er, yes,' said Flora, dread hitting her stomach.

'So I've brought you this. My nephews are just bringing it in for me.'

Flora exchanged a worried look with Nico but was pleased and immensely relieved to see that it was a table tennis table.

'*Bene!* This is great!' said Nico, relief flooding his voice.

'I know a bloke whose pub has just shut down,' said Del, with a smile. 'Thought it might keep the troops happy, yeah?'

'Thank you, Del,' said Flora, so relieved that she stepped forward to give him a peck on the cheek.

Del looked very pleased at that and left with a grin on his face. Nico was feeling less pleased. Surely Flora wouldn't feel anything romantic towards someone like Del, would she?

But there was no time to contemplate that unsettling thought as Flora shuffled the table into position and began to wipe it down, ready to be used.

'This is all looking great,' she told him, a smile lighting up her pretty face. 'And just in time for the campers!'

He followed her gaze to where the campers were beginning to come out of their tents and make a break for Grams' breakfast hamper.

'Perhaps we could set up an honesty box in here as well,' she said, tapping her chin in thought. 'You know, for a few bits and pieces so that they don't need to go too far.'

'That's a good idea,' he told her.

The campers were delighted when they discovered the barn. The table tennis was immediately in use and people seemed pleased to be able to take a break from their tents, even to chat to the other campers. Grams had placed a couple of magazines and books in a box as well and people were beginning to relax and enjoy themselves. There was even space for a spirited boules competition.

The outing to the steam train workshop late in the morning proved to be hugely popular, especially with the young children, who took great delight in pulling the train whistle. Nico could hear it ring out every half-hour or so.

Some of the ladies took up Harriet's kind offer and the smell of lavender was in the air when they returned, the sweet aroma wafting around the barn.

Thankfully, the wind had died down, but the rain still carried on and on. But people were smiling more and chatting to their camping neighbours.

Nico was just walking back to the farmhouse when he saw Tyson cycling in the opposite direction.

'Hey,' he said. 'What are you doing out in this weather?'

'Was bored at home, so thought I'd look at the motorbike,' replied Tyson.

Suddenly, a cheer went up from the barn.

'What's that?' asked the teenager.

'We've set up a games room,' Nico told him. 'Come and take a look.'

Tyson hesitated but finally nodded and followed Nico back into the barn.

The cheer had been a game of darts that had just finished. Everyone was chatting and looking far happier.

Tyson looked around in amazement. 'When did you do all this?' he asked.

'Earlier today,' Nico told him. 'The campers were a bit bored being stuck inside their tents, so we thought we'd set up a few things for them to use.'

Tyson looked mesmerised by the table tennis table and was startled when a younger boy came up to him.

'Wanna play?' he asked.

Tyson looked at Nico, who merely nodded. 'Go for it,' he said. 'Stay as long as you want.'

So both boys picked up the rackets and began to play. Nico sat down on a nearby hay bale and watched, pleased, as a smile began to form on Tyson's face. It was a shame that those people had left as soon as the rain started, he thought. He could see the pleasure that Tyson was getting from playing with other children and relaxing.

With those tents now empty, he began to form an idea as to how they might fill them.

'Shame about the weather,' he said to Tyson when there was a break a little later in between games.

Tyson gave a shrug. 'Who cares? We wouldn't. We haven't had a holiday in years.'

Nico looked at him. 'Well, there's some empty tents here if you'd like for your family to stay for a few days. Free of charge. I know it's half-term but your mum has to work, I guess.'

The boy's face lit up. 'Seriously? She's got tomorrow off for the bank holiday weekend.'

Nico smiled at him. 'Brilliant. Well, please let her know. Tell her from me that if you and your family need a break, then, of course, you're all welcome to come here.'

As he said the words, he knew it was the right thing to do. He thought about Flora talking about giving back to the land. Perhaps it was right that he started to give back to people less fortunate than him as well.

38

Flora had been amazed by Nico's suggestion that they give the three empty tents to families in the community that might not otherwise be able to afford a holiday.

'I absolutely agree with the idea,' she told him, that afternoon. 'But are you sure they're going to want to be camping with this weather?' She gestured at the kitchen window, out of which she could see that the rain was still falling in a heavy downpour. The long-range forecast had given hope that it might dry up by the bank holiday Monday, but that was two days away yet.

'According to Tyson, he says any change will be like a holiday for them.'

'Well, here's hoping you're right,' she said, glancing through the window once more. 'Because I think that's Tyson and his family arriving now.'

They put on their coats and headed outside.

Tyson mum's wound down the driver's window of her car and smiled at them nervously. 'Hi,' she said. 'Listen, if you've changed your mind, I totally understand.'

She looked pale and weary, thought Flora. As if the woman had the weight of the world on her shoulders.

'We'd love to have you here,' Flora told her. 'If you can put up with the weather!'

'Oh, we don't care about that, do we, boys?' She looked in her mirror and Flora saw a boy of around ten years old sitting in the back seat. He looked pale and wide-eyed as he stared out of the car window at the farm.

However, his big brother Tyson in the front passenger seat was looking excited enough for them all. 'It's gonna be epic, Kevin,' he said. 'You should see the games area. They've even got a football table.'

The younger boy raised his eyebrows. 'I love those,' he said.

'I know,' said Tyson, giving Nico a nod through the window.

'Right,' said Nico. 'We'll show you where to park and then which tent is all yours.'

However, when they began to walk through the gate into the field, Tyson's mum stopped Flora once more. 'Are you sure?' she asked once more. 'I mean, what about the cost?'

'You'd actually be doing us a favour,' said Flora. 'We need the campsite at full capacity to make sure that everything works properly as we've only just opened up. So it's a trial run and it'll really help us out. So don't worry. There's no expense on you at all. Just your food and drink.'

'Oh, I've got a packed car boot full of our usual stuff, so that's no worries,' said the woman before frowning. 'Of course, I don't know where we'll cook it.'

'We've actually just set up a cooking area,' Flora told her. 'There's a barbeque and a stove too. So you can use those.'

Their friends' idea had been inspired. Everyone didn't want to venture too far in the bad weather but had had to leave the campsite to get some hot food. So Joe had brought over the barbeque.

Nico had bought some charcoal and left the barbeque under a gazebo just outside the barn so that hopefully it would give some shelter from the elements but also not be too smoky inside the barn. Grams had brought down the camping stove that they used during the frequent power cuts during the winter storms. That had got a proper clean-up and was left on the side in the barn for people to use.

Grams had also left out a large Victoria sponge for people to enjoy, as well as some home-made biscuits.

'This is amazing,' said Tyson's mum when they went inside the tent for the first time. She looked around with wide eyes. 'It's about the prettiest place we've ever stayed in.'

'It's magical,' said Kevin, looking up to the high peak of the ceiling, dotted with fairy lights which Flora had already switched on in the dark gloom of the day.

'The sofa is a bed as well,' Flora told them. 'So you can all sleep wherever you like.'

Tyson's mum was stroking the soft bedding on the bed. 'How wonderful,' she said. 'This is going to be so different to our normal weekends.'

'Well, there's going to be a tennis table tournament later,' Nico told them. 'The big barn is the place to be. There are other families there so you'll be amongst friends. Join us whenever you want.'

* * *

Later that evening, Flora was pleased to see both the boys playing with some new friends they had met on the campsite. The table tennis competition was hotting up whilst everyone else relaxed and chatted, drinking and eating their dinner under the cover of the barn.

Tyson's mum was already booked in for a hand massage at the lavender spa the following day and Flora had assured her the boys would be in safe hands in the meantime with Ryan and Bob showing them the steam engine.

Someone had even found a football somewhere and as the rain had temporarily eased off, some of the boys and dads were kicking the ball around outside in the field.

Flora found Nico watching them with a wistful smile on his face.

'Did you ever want to be a footballer when you grew up?' she asked.

'Every Italian boy wants to be a footballer,' he said, with a small smile. 'I even tried out for the Roma football team, but I didn't make the grade. Good thing too. My grandmother and grandfather needed me and I was happy to help. I worked the land and tended the vines. Did maintenance on the house. It was a better life for me.'

'Did you see your dad very much back then?' she asked gently.

He looked at her. 'Sometimes he rocked up and dragged me away somewhere on holiday until he got bored with me.'

Flora took a sharp intake of breath. There was real pain there behind his words and she felt terribly sorry for his sad childhood.

'But when I was older, sometimes I could take the time off and head off somewhere by myself.' He smiled at her. 'I'm still impulsive, I'm my father's son, for better or worse. Spur of the moment, go with the flow, that kind of thing. Go to the seaside for the day? Sure.'

'Steal a Ferrari?'

He smiled back at her. 'Why not? The only thing stopping you from doing the same is you.'

She shook her head. 'There's no Ferrari for me to borrow around here.'

'Where would you go if you could head off?' he asked.

She shrugged her shoulders. 'That's the thing, I truly love it here. It's home. It just wasn't my dream.'

'What was?'

'Painting. But it's not exactly a stable career choice, is it?' She laughed.

He looked at her. 'When was the last time that you painted anything like that canvas in my bedroom?' he asked.

She shook her head. 'I honestly can't remember. Years, I think.'

'Maybe you should start painting again when you have some time spare,' he told her, studying her with deep brown eyes.

'Maybe.'

'Well, you've made this barn and the tents look amazing,' he said. 'You should be proud of your talent.'

She blushed. 'Thanks.'

He looked at her for a long time and she had a feeling that he was going to say something else when the ball bounced over near to them and he gave it a mighty kick back to the others, causing them to persuade him to join in their game.

The conversation made her think, though. So when she finally went to bed later that evening, she pulled out her old art set. But it had been so long that the watercolours had dried up and were completely unusable. She stared down at the paints in dismay.

At a sound in the corridor, she looked up, realising that she had left the bedroom door open.

Nico was just passing by and looked in the open doorway. He was about to say goodnight when he saw what she was holding. 'Are you thinking about painting again? That's great!' he said, nodding his approval.

Flora shook her head. 'They're not much use now,' she told

him with a small smile, showing him the state of the dried-up palette.

'Maybe you should buy some new ones for yourself,' he said softly.

'Maybe.' She stood up from the bed. 'Well, goodnight.'

'Goodnight.'

After she had closed the door, she went back to the bed and looked at the palette for a long time before closing it with a decisive snap and placing it in the small bin next to her dressing table.

Maybe it was better this way, she thought.

But still, her heart yearned to paint once more.

39

Finally, the rain stopped on Sunday morning and there was a break in the clouds.

'Blue sky at last,' murmured Flora, somewhat relieved as she stared up at the sky.

Actually, the rainy weekend hadn't been as bad as she had feared when the first customers had left almost immediately. It had encouraged her and Nico to think about extra activities and thus the barn had become a gathering place for people to cook, play games and socialise. Everyone had been kept busy with all the extra activities, such as the lavender farm and spa and the railway workshop, all excitedly discussing the steam locomotive, which there was still hope of getting working later that year.

That afternoon, Flora came across one of the guests sitting on her deck and painting a scene.

'That's lovely,' she said, nodding her admiration.

The woman thanked her and Flora left her to her peace and quiet, anxious not to intrude.

'What's she painting?' asked Nico, who had been watching her nearby.

'The landscape,' Flora told him as they began to walk back towards the farmhouse.

He nodded. 'It's a nice day,' he said as they crossed the courtyard. 'Why don't you give yourself some time off and do a bit of painting yourself?'

Flora shook her head. 'No paints even if I wanted to,' she reminded him. 'Ah well. It was a nice dream anyway.'

'Doesn't have to be just that,' said Nico, drawing out his car keys from his pocket.

Flora watched as he opened up the car door and fumbled around on the passenger seat before bringing out a paper bag. He walked back over to her and handed her the package.

'What's this for?' she asked.

'Your birthday.'

'My birthday was at the beginning of March,' she said, nonplussed.

He smiled at her. 'Well, it's a very belated present then, isn't it?'

Somewhat bewildered, she opened the bag and drew out a large tin palette of watercolour paints. She looked up at him with wide eyes. 'I can't accept this,' she automatically replied.

'Of course you can,' he told her. 'Besides, I can't do anything with them. I was useless even with painting by numbers.'

She looked down at the palette once more.

'I don't know if they're any good or even the right colours,' she heard him say. 'I saw them when I went to the corner shop yesterday and just thought you could use them until you got some better ones. There's some brushes in the bag as well.'

Flora couldn't believe it. 'I don't know what to say,' she murmured before looking back up at him at last. 'Thank you.'

'*Prego*. You're welcome,' he replied. 'Now go and get painting. I've studied the artwork on my bedroom wall for many hours these past few weeks and it's amazing. You've got a real talent.'

'What about everything else?' she asked, glancing around the campsite.

He shook his head. 'It's pretty quiet this afternoon. Anyway, I can handle any problems. Go,' he told her softly. 'And relax.'

Still feeling stunned, she thanked him once more before going into the farmhouse to retrieve her painting pad from her bedroom. Then she headed outside once more and settled herself down on the wooden bench along the far wall of the farmhouse, out of view of anyone else but from where she could see all the way down past the strawberry field and across to the hills in the distance.

She was all ready to go when she found herself hesitating. What if she couldn't paint any more? What if she had lost her talent? What if she didn't enjoy herself?

But as soon as her brush hit the canvas for the first time, she was lost in her love of painting. The peace and serenity she had always found in creating her landscapes rushed back to her immediately and she wasn't sure how much time passed until she had completed her new painting.

When she blinked back to life and set the painting down next to her to dry, she looked up to find Grams watching her with a smile.

'I thought you might like a cup of tea,' said Grams, coming to join her on the bench.

'Thanks,' replied Flora. 'What time is it?'

'It doesn't matter,' said Grams, handing over the cup to her granddaughter. 'It's so good to see you painting again.'

Flora nodded. 'I've really enjoyed it,' she admitted.

'Are the paints new?' asked Grams.

'Nico bought them for me,' Flora told her.

Grams looked surprised but pleased. 'How kind,' she said. 'What a breath of fresh air he's been around here.'

'He has,' agreed Flora.

'I'm glad to hear you say so,' said Grams. 'There was a time back there when I thought you might push him down the hill.'

Flora laughed. 'I admit I didn't give him the warmest of welcomes. But he's grown on me. He's a friend now.'

'A friend?' Grams nodded thoughtfully before patting her granddaughter on the knee. 'Well, that's always a good foundation for anything else.'

'What else is there?' asked Flora.

'Love,' said Grams softly. 'You know, when we exchanged letters all those years, Lorenzo and I often chatted about how wonderful it would be for our families to be joined. You were sort of intended for each other.'

'Despite having never met!' Flora reminded her, laughing.

'I know,' said Grams, standing up. 'It was an old dream, that was all. But I'm just happy to see you two getting along.'

'Me too,' Flora told her.

Left alone once more, Flora looked out across the landscape to where she could see Nico in the bottom field, showing some of the campers where the swimming pond was.

Fancy her and Nico being intended for one another, she thought dreamily. They were from different countries, different lifestyles, different pasts. And yet there was a connection there, if she was being honest with herself.

Her dream for her sensible future was looking more muddled. In the early days, her dreams had been about keeping the farm and nothing else. But she was starting to think that perhaps sharing her life with someone might not be a bad thing after all.

40

Flora was thankful to see the sunshine on bank holiday Monday.

Now that the weather had brightened, there was the opportunity to pick some strawberries from the fields which had begun to ripen but thankfully weren't soggy yet.

'The mushy ones can be made into jam,' said Grams, giving a nearby group a cheerful smile. 'We can have some on my homemade scones later.'

'How do you make jam?' asked one child, peering at the strawberry she was holding.

'I can show you if you like,' replied Grams, and thus another activity could be added to the information blackboard in the barn.

The warm sunshine was the perfect finish to a successful weekend, thought Flora. And, of course, it made everyone smile and feel better.

Suddenly the lush, green grass became dry and people were able to sit out on their decks and admire the view, which cleared so that the hills across the valley were finally visible.

Some children were rolling down the hill and making daisy

chains. Others were playing games or dozing in the warm sunshine.

There was nature to be enjoyed and so Nico had also shown them the wild swimming pond which quite a few people ventured into, oohing and aahing at the chilly temperature of the water.

'Is it natural?' asked one woman.

'Absolutely,' Flora told her. 'It's just river water that's been cleaned by the stones as it filters in, as well as all the plants. See how healthy it is?' She pointed at the waterlilies from which the dragonflies were flitting from pad to pad.

'Hopefully it should have warmed up by the time we come back at the end of August,' replied the lady.

This was an added bonus that Flora hadn't been expecting. The weekend, despite the weather, had been so successful that a few people had already rebooked for later on in the summer.

'I can't believe it,' said Flora at lunchtime.

'It gets better,' said Nico, checking his phone with wide eyes. 'Have you seen this?'

She took his phone and stared at the headline on the *Cranbridge Times* website.

'When did Tom come and visit?' she asked, looking at the editorial piece by Tom Addison, the Editor.

'Yesterday morning,' said Grams. 'I think you were at the cash and carry getting the barbeque bits. He'd bumped into Eddie at the community hub and Eddie had told him all about the campsite and what you were doing for the local families that needed a break this weekend. Tom thought it was a smashing idea and so came to take a few photos and have a little chat.'

'Well, his little chat has gone viral,' said Nico, now checking on his laptop. 'Look at all these emails we've had enquiring about future bookings.'

Flora went to look over his shoulder and could see dozens of unread emails in the Inbox. 'I don't believe it,' she said.

'I do,' said Grams, with a firm nod. 'We've got a success on our hands!'

'We have!' Flora was delighted, stepping forward to give her grandmother a hug.

Nico looked at them both. 'I think we might just make a profit this summer, if things carry on like this.'

Flora held up her fingers which were crossed.

But in a way, some things were even more important than profits, she thought. She had enjoyed interacting with the families that had camped with them. Helping them enjoy their holiday whatever the weather, watching them relax away from the normal nine-to-five grind. Most had made friends and learnt something new, either about swimming ponds, farms, steam locomotives and even how to make strawberry jam.

Grams had made them all a pot of jam to say thank you when they all began to leave on Monday afternoon.

'This is so lovely,' said one woman, giving Flora a spontaneous hug. 'We've had the best time. Can't believe the weather was so awful, but it was one of the best holidays we've ever had!'

'I'm so glad,' Flora told her.

It was a familiar story with each couple and family as they left, all promising to leave glowing reviews too, which would also help the business.

But some things were even better than positive feedback, reviews and profits, she thought, as she helped Tyson's mum carry a large bag back to her car. Some things could only be measured by the length of someone's neck as the weight of their worries were temporarily left behind.

'This has been amazing,' said Tyson's mum, placing the bag in the car boot. 'An absolute tonic, to be honest. We all needed this.'

Flora and Nico looked over at the boys, who were smiling and saying goodbye to another family.

'I'm so glad you came,' said Nico. He gave Flora a quick look before adding, 'And, if you wanted, we'd like to do a similar scheme for local families at the end of summer before the schools go back.'

'You would?' She looked amazed and Flora knew just how she felt. They hadn't discussed this between them, but she instantly knew in her heart that Nico was right.

'We were thinking that from the Friday to the bank holiday Monday would be a great time for everyone to come and have a break. Maybe the sun will come out again too!' Nico laughed.

'Oh, that's wonderful,' said Tyson's mum, looking a little teary. 'I'm so grateful to you both and for all you've done for Tyson as well. He's so much happier these days.'

'Our pleasure,' Flora told her.

'Actually, he's been a huge help around her, helping fix my car, amongst other things,' added Nico.

Tyson's mum looked proud. 'I'm sure he's an engineer in the making.'

'I don't doubt it,' replied Nico. 'He's always welcome here.'

After another round of hugs, Flora was left standing with Nico alone in the courtyard as they drove off.

He gave her a sheepish grin. 'Sorry,' he told her. 'I should have checked with you first about repeating the local families thing.'

'No need,' she replied. 'After all, it's your business.'

He shook his head. 'It's your business,' he said. 'I'm the silent partner, remember?'

She laughed. 'Definitely not so silent,' she told him. 'But you're also a good man. Don't ever let anyone tell you otherwise.'

To both of their surprises, she leant up to place a kiss on his cheek.

There was a moment as she drew away that their faces hovered close. She could feel his breath as she looked up into his dark eyes.

They were just starting to lean forward as if their lips might actually meet when a car came through the gates, heralding the next round of campers and they both stepped back, the moment lost.

41

As June began, Flora was thankful that the weather had finally improved and the rain subsided at last. With clearing skies, both the campsite and its owners were given a chance to breathe and take stock after a monumental first week.

The bookings for Strawberry Hill Farm campsite remained steady, thanks to a glowing write-up in the *Cranbridge Times* going viral beyond the county. Suddenly, lots of people wanted to come and stay. So despite it still being in school term time, they were inundated with couples and friends, all of whom wanted their little slice of countryside heaven.

'We've even had a booking for a hen party who want the whole site to themselves for three nights!' Flora told Nico, laughing.

'I might hide that weekend,' he replied, with a shudder.

Flora glanced down at her checklist once more. Everything was set up for the next group of campers, including fresh linen and all the little extras, such as the tea and coffee. 'I think that's everything,' she said, looking up at Nico.

'*Bene*,' he said, with a firm nod. 'So now we can relax before the really hard work begins.'

'The really hard work?' she asked.

'We're getting more and more bookings for the summer holidays,' Nico told her. 'Those will be busy days. So now we rest.'

'We haven't got time for that,' Flora told him, laughing.

'Of course we do,' he replied. 'So be ready at seven this evening.'

'Where are we going?' she asked, bemused.

'Humour me.'

* * *

At seven o'clock on the dot, Flora found Nico waiting for her outside the farmhouse with a picnic basket. She raised her eyebrows at him in question, but he shook his head.

'Secret location,' he told her.

She shrugged her shoulders and let him lead the way down the hill. It was too beautiful an evening to worry, she decided. It had been a warm, sunny day and with midsummer almost upon them, the sun was still high in the sky.

She glanced over at the strawberry field as they went, noting the ruby-coloured fruits all ready for picking. But that was a job for the following day. She then looked to her left at the empty field. 'Looks like if it stays dry, it can be used as the car park for the lavender fields again.'

'When do the fields open to the public?' he asked.

'At the end of this month,' she told him.

She looked beyond the empty field and across the path to where the rows of lavender plants were beginning to come into bud, a faint purple hue colouring the top of each rounded bush. It wouldn't be too much longer before they would burst into colour.

Nico led her into the woods and Flora soon realised what their destination was. They stepped out into the leafy glade next to the pond and the first thing she saw was a brand-new platform made out of the remnants of the spare wood they had used for the decking.

'When did you build this?' she asked, stepping onto the wooden floor.

'Yesterday,' he told her.

'It's great,' she replied. 'It really sets the scene, doesn't it?'

The sun shone down on the water, lighting up the turquoise dragonflies as they flitted around the edge. Water lilies like pink and crimson bowls floated across the water, and on the other side, a group of sparrows were taking a bath in the shallows.

Flora turned around from the incredible view to find Nico laying out a rug and placing a couple of glasses and a chilled bottle of wine on top. She laughed. 'Since when did we plan to have a picnic?' she asked.

'When I decided to,' he told her. 'And why not? It's a beautiful evening with a beautiful view. And I'm spending it with a beautiful woman.'

Flora blushed and almost tripped over her feet as she went to sit down on the rug.

As he poured out a glass of wine, she checked her phone. 'Do you think the campers will be okay?' she asked, glancing up the hill, but they were totally hidden from sight and she couldn't see anyone else.

'They'll be fine,' he told her. 'Grams has said she will call us if there's any problems, but there won't be. Just relax.'

She sighed. 'I guess I've been keeping busy for so long, trying so hard to keep everything going, that I've never had time for myself. Now I'm not even sure I know how to relax.'

He put down the glass of wine in front of her and held her still by the shoulders, the warmth of his hands seeping into her skin. 'There,' he said softly. 'You've stopped.'

She smiled at him, locked eyes with his. 'Thanks. I guess I have.'

He handed her the glass of wine and they clinked their glasses. '*Salute*,' he said.

'Cheers,' she replied. She leant back on her elbow and let the surroundings ease the tension in her shoulders.

He raised his face to the sun and for a moment she was able to study his handsome features. His skin was already turning golden now that the days had grown sunnier.

He suddenly opened his eyes and looked at her, causing her to take a large swig of wine to stop him thinking that she had been studying him.

'This deck is brilliant,' she said, looking across the intricately interlocked pieces of wood.

'I was lucky enough to inherit my carpentry skills from Nonno,' he told her. 'I can carve as well.'

'Really?' she replied. 'You'll have to show me.'

'It's been many years since I last carved anything,' he said.

'Well, I picked up painting again after all this time,' she reminded him.

'You have a real skill. Was it always your dream job?'

She smiled to herself. 'I guess it was. Then it was just keeping the farm afloat. Now? I guess I'm enjoying life and I want to continue with that.' As she said the words, she realised it was true. 'What about you? What was your dream?'

He gave a shrug of his wide shoulders. 'It was only ever to work on the vineyard.'

'What did you like about it?' she asked, suddenly wanting to know.

'Working with family,' he replied. 'Working on the land. Being outside. I'd hate to be stuck in an office all the time.'

'Me too.'

'Then it looks like we've both chosen the right path to follow this summer,' he told her. He raised his glass once. 'Here's to taking a chance at the next crossroads.'

She smiled and raised her glass at him in return. She felt comfortable in his company these days. She had opened up to him in a way that she only did with her friends and Grams. And maybe not even that much with them either. They were becoming friends.

But as Flora drank her wine, right at that moment, the only thing that she wanted to take a chance on was becoming more than just friends with Nico. But that was impossible, wasn't it?

42

Nico was feeling glad that he had persuaded Flora to head out with him that evening. Grams' idea of a picnic by the pond was perfect.

He had, of course, invited Grams to join them, but she had told him that she wanted to perfect a certain dance move and she couldn't do that by the pond without falling into the water.

Now, he brought out the two small pizza boxes that he had packed into the picnic basket a short time ago.

'Pizza?' Flora's green eyes gleamed. 'From Platform 1?'

'Where else?' he replied, handing her a plate and one of the boxes.

She opened up the lid and sniffed appreciatively.

'No mushrooms,' he told her.

She looked up at him surprised. 'How do you know I don't like mushrooms?' she asked.

He shrugged. 'I remembered from dinner the other week,' he told her, as he helped himself to his own pizza.

One bite told him how excellent a chef Ryan was. '*Deliziosa*,' he murmured. It was incredible. The cheese and dough ratio was spot on and the tomato base had precisely the correct amount of onion, garlic and oregano. Even the basil tasted Italian.

'Isn't it amazing?' Flora told him between mouthfuls.

Nico nodded. 'This is proper pizza,' he said.

Flora smiled. 'Well, Ryan did work for three years in Rome. Apparently the restaurant was very fashionable and popular, according to Ethan.'

'I will have to take up his offer to go to his Italian-themed dinner one evening in Platform 1,' he said.

'I think they hold it once a month,' she told him.

'Have you been?' he asked.

'To the restaurant? No,' she replied. 'Never enough funds, unfortunately.'

'And what about Italy?'

She shook her head. 'No funds or time for that either.'

'You should go,' he told her. 'Especially to Tuscany. The light there is incredible on a summer's evening like this. You adore the countryside, so I'm certain you would like it there too.'

'Do you miss it?' she asked gently.

'A little,' he confessed.

'What will you do when you leave at the end of summer?' she asked.

He took a sharp intake of breath. He had been asking himself the same question, with no answer as of yet. 'I guess I'll try to build my life up once more in Italy,' he said slowly.

But Cranfield felt like his home already. He would be sad to leave it. And even sadder to leave Flora.

His investment was in safe hands at Strawberry Hill Farm. But it wasn't about that. It was about the people that lived there.

'I guess what I really miss is my family,' he confessed.

'I'm sure.' She looked at him with concern in her eyes. 'Have you talked to your father since, er, you borrowed his car?'

He shook his head. 'No. Anyway, I can't feel much guilt about that. My father has always been monumentally selfish.'

'Snap.'

He looked at her, interested. 'Really? In what way?'

'He was all encompassed in his grief for my mum,' she told him. 'But I needed him too. I was still here, still alive, but it's like I died as well as far he was concerned. He was supposed to take all this on,' she waved her hand at the land around them. 'But instead the responsibility passed to me. I was only nineteen. It was a lot to handle.'

Nico nodded. 'I'm sure.' He had a sudden urge to keep supporting her, to help ease her pain, but he kept his emotions in check.

'Anyway, it's been nice to have you here helping,' she told him.

Nico was surprised and pleased. 'You weren't so sure in the early days.'

She laughed. 'No. I wasn't. I'm sorry. When you're used to taking on all the responsibility yourself, it's hard to admit that you're struggling.'

Her words hit home and he realised that he'd been alone in his struggle as well.

'You're lucky that you have your friends and Grams here,' he told her.

'You've got friends here as well,' she said softly.

For a moment, he felt a rush of happiness that she thought of them as friends.

'And they're good guys,' she carried on.

He gave a momentary start. Of course, she was talking about Ryan, Ethan and Joe. Not herself.

'I think I can trust them,' he said.

She looked surprised. 'Of course you can. You don't have many friends back in Italy?'

'Dad broke a lot of promises to many people over the years.' He sighed. 'A lot of people gave up on us.'

'What about girlfriends?'

The question hung in the air and he looked at her with raised eyebrows.

'I was just wondering,' she muttered, before picking up another slice of pizza and biting into it.

After all that talk of trust, he knew that he had faith that Flora no longer judged him as she had in the early days.

'That's a bit more difficult,' he told her. 'I got swept away with my father's glamorous life in my early twenties and thought I could emulate him but I quickly got fed up. People see you as just a name when it's as famous as mine.'

'I don't.'

The words were said so quietly that he almost missed them before he looked up at her pleased.

'You did,' he reminded her.

'But I've learnt that now you're more than that. Better than your name.'

'*Grazie.*' He looked into her soft green eyes and almost lost himself. They were the exact shade of green when the setting sun touched the Tuscan hills. Was that what he was feeling? Homesick?

He knew deep down that wasn't it. It was about his feelings for Flora and how they were growing stronger by the day. He just wasn't sure that she felt the same way and so for now he would have to be grateful for her friendship. Even though he wanted so much more.

43

'I don't know why we didn't think about strawberry daiquiris before now,' said Libby, holding up her bright red drink in a glass.

'Me neither,' said Flora, licking her lips at the sweet but definitely alcoholic taste.

'They're really delicious,' said Katy, nodding.

'And they've only travelled about ten metres,' added Harriet with a giggle.

The four of them looked down the hill to the strawberry field which was now full of ripened fruit.

They were sitting on deckchairs outside the farmhouse on the patio, enjoying the evening of the summer solstice. Paddington the dog was sprawled at Harriet's feet enjoying a crunchy ice cube.

Flora found that the month of June had slipped by in a whirl of activity. The campsite had been at least half full on every day of the month so far and the busiest months of July and August were just around the corner.

The hours were long: from breakfast time until after dinner they were on call in case of any problems or queries. But Flora and Nico had quickly learnt how to solve various problems and they began to have a little more free time, even allowing Flora time to paint at least two or three times a week.

The painting was instant relaxation and a couple of hours could quite easily slip by whilst she was lost in the canvas. Her love of painting had hurtled back to her so quickly that she wondered how she had been able to live without it for so many years. Now it was like oxygen to her and she knew that she would never deny herself that pleasure ever again.

'Where's Grams tonight?' asked Libby. 'I'm sure she'd love one of these special drinks.'

'There was an extra dance class added due to a tango teacher coming for a show dance,' Flora told her.

'I think she's amazing,' said Katy, nodding enthusiastically. 'Eighty years old and learning all those new dances.'

Flora couldn't help but agree. It was lucky that Grams had kept her overall fitness thanks to the farming all those years, but, in addition, it was her mental state that had vastly improved. At her weekly classes, she was meeting new people and always came home full of stories and gossip.

'You must come along soon,' Grams had urged her grand-daughter again that evening before she left.

But it wasn't just her enthusiasm for the dance classes that had perked up Grams. She loved getting up to make her special break-fast baskets to place in the barn and certainly, judging by the takings, everyone was enjoying the delicious range of food she provided.

In the spare time she now had, she was pleased to be able to restart her quilting. She had already sold a couple of quilts after some campers enquired and was keen to make more.

'It's a shame we don't have an alcohol licence for the lavender fields,' said Harriet, looking at her strawberry cocktail. 'These would be hugely popular.'

'I think they should remain exclusively for us,' said Libby, reaching out to top everyone else's glasses up from the cocktail jug.

'Too right,' said Katy, licking her lips. 'Mmm. They're too good to share with the masses.'

'This had better be my last one tonight in any case,' said Harriet, with a pout. 'With the grand opening in two days' time, things are going to get crazy busy from tomorrow.'

They all looked across to where the rows of lavender were now a blur of faint purple. Any day, the flowers would burst from their buds and would be a glorious kaleidoscope of lilacs and amethysts.

The gazebos were already set up in the field for refreshments and at the entrance to take the customers' small fee to visit. But it was the lavender that was the star turn.

Flora turned her head to look across at the campsite, which she could just make out in the next field. The tops of the tents could be seen with their bunting fluttering in the warm breeze as it drifted across the green valley. The wildflower meadow surrounding the tents was now alive with bees and butterflies, flitting amongst the flowers. Nico had cut the grass to make paths through the meadow but kept everything else as nature intended.

According to the campers, it felt like their very own patch of heaven. Flora would watch as the campers would arrive in a blur of activity and then gradually relax, wind down and begin to enjoy the glorious countryside.

They had already added a few more touches to the campsite. Nico had bought a second-hand firepit and the marshmallow toasting was becoming very popular. In turn, Flora had added bunting, fairy lights and a few old lanterns to the barn to give it the same feel as the rest of the site. She had even bought lavender pouches from the previous year's harvest from Harriet to give the tents a delicious aroma, as well as the latest product – lavender wax melts.

'You know what I'm going to do with these next time?' said Libby, holding up the cocktail jug. 'Strawberry margaritas!'

'Not gin?' asked Harriet.

'Change is as good as a rest,' replied Libby, stretching out in her deckchair like a cat.

Flora sat still for a moment, mulling over her friend's words. Change had come to Strawberry Hill Farm. She had pushed and pushed against it, but it had come anyway. She had dreaded it, and yet, she felt renewed. Refreshed. Awakened.

'You okay?' asked Katy, who had been studying her for a while.

Flora nodded and looked down the hill at the campsite. She could see the sun slowly beginning to sink behind the horizon. Everything was peaceful and calm.

A warm breeze wafted over her and Flora finally felt at peace too.

44

'I'm not sure we have time for this,' said Flora, looking across the dance floor of the village hall in Aldwych on Monday evening.

'Of course you have,' Grams told her, tapping her feet in time to the music.

It was still a shock to see Grams in her finest clothes, a skirt and sparkly top, looking so glamorous. A vast difference to the farmer that Flora had grown up with.

But Grams was certainly looking much happier these days, she thought. More relaxed.

'This is great,' said Nico, standing next to Flora, tapping his feet in time to the rhythm.

They had both intended just to pick up some cleaning materials from the cash and carry, but Grams and Eddie had persuaded them to pop in and see the senior dance class before they left Aldwych and headed back to Cranfield.

Despite the advanced age of the people dancing, there was still a vibrancy about the place, thought Flora as she looked around. Most of the women were dressed in either sequins or bright colours and she felt almost drab in her T-shirt and shorts.

She looked at Nico and wondered whether he felt the same, but he never seemed to worry about his appearance, she thought. Although even when he was dressed down, he still looked pretty impressive.

He turned his head suddenly to catch her looking at him and raised his eyebrows. 'What?'

She smiled. 'I didn't think this was your kind of place at all,' she told him.

He shook his head and leaned forward to whisper in her ear. 'Let me tell you, Italy not only has its art, heritage and food, but it's also always full of music. My country loves to dance. And this all feels very familiar. We call it *ballo liscio*. Ballroom dancing.'

'You know how to do this?' she asked, gesturing at the packed dance floor.

'Oh yes,' he said, nodding and straightening up once more. 'Nonna's favourite dance was the waltz. She taught me when I was growing up.'

'Then I insist on a dance,' said Grams, who had been listening into the last part of their conversation.

Nico looked delighted. 'I'd be honoured,' he said, with a small bow.

Then he took Grams' hand and led her onto the dance floor.

Flora watched in amazement as they both danced perfectly in time. She wasn't sure who she was more surprised at. Her grandmother gliding across the dance floor, or Nico's perfectly straight back and hold as he spun her around in time to the music.

When they had finished, the dance teacher who had been standing nearby, clapped her hands. 'Oh, well done!' she said, as Nico and Grams returned from the dance floor. 'That was quite marvellous.'

'What a dancer!' said Grams, grinning from ear to ear.

'*Prego*,' replied Nico with a smile. 'I had a good teacher.'

Eddie nodded in agreement. 'I gotta say, respect, lad. I wish I could dance like that.'

'Of course you can,' said Grams, holding out her hand for Eddie. 'Come on. Let's show the youngsters how it's done.'

The pensioners headed into the middle of the dance floor and began to twirl around, leaving Flora alone with Nico.

'That was pretty impressive,' she told him, laughing. 'Maybe we should put on dance classes at the campsite.'

'Maybe we both should,' he replied, with a gleam in his eye and holding out his hand for her take. 'Your turn.'

'Oh, I can't do that,' said Flora immediately, shaking her head. 'I've got two left feet.'

But he wasn't listening to her protestations.

'*Andiamo*,' he said, putting his arm around her. 'Come on. Let's go.'

She felt his hand on the small of her back, guiding her through the crowd. His touch burned through the T-shirt and onto her skin and she didn't know what she was more nervous about – getting the right dance moves or having Nico so close to her.

Once on the dance floor, he came to stand in front of her and held out his arms. But the music had changed from a waltz to a swaying, rhythmic samba beat that was blaring out from the speakers.

The dancers around them changed their moves and were suddenly swaying close with every part of their bodies touching as they moved back and forth to the music.

Flora couldn't stop staring at them. It was mesmerising, breathtaking in its sheer joy and she had a sudden urge to join in. To let go of all of her inhibitions and sway along to the rhythm. To be free to enjoy herself. To dance.

But that would mean dancing close to a man. And not just any man.

She slowly lifted her eyes up to Nico and felt a jolt as she found him staring at her with an intensity in his dark brown eyes.

His voice interrupted her rampant thoughts. 'Don't you ever want to break free of whatever it is that's holding you back all the time?'

He drew his hands around her and pulled her gently in so that they were close now. She couldn't tear her eyes away from his, suddenly robbed of breath.

He was right. She was so sick of being bound up by her own invisible ties. She was sick of not being herself. She wanted so badly to be a part of life, to be living like everyone else seemed to do. So she reached out to slip her hands around to his back and draw him up against her so that there was no part of their bodies that weren't touching.

She found Nico staring open-mouthed at her in amazement. She was pleased to have finally caught him off guard. She would prove him wrong for the rest of the dance. She could be free. Right here, on this dance floor, she would be herself for one glorious moment in time.

Unable to fight the rhythm of the music any longer, Flora finally let it in and began to sway in time.

Suddenly, the main lights were switched off so the room was only lit by the faintest of lights around the outside.

Rather than a shocked gasp, there was a flutter of applause and approval around the room.

'Dancing in the dark time!' came an announcement over the microphone. 'Hold on tight to your partner now!'

And as the music carried on, the only person Flora could see and feel was Nico.

45

Nico was aware of no one else but Flora as she moved her hips under his hold. Then he too began to sway in time to the all-encompassing samba beat.

The music was wonderful and it felt so good to dance after so many years. How many had it been since he had last danced with any woman? Perhaps not since his grandmother?

But his thrill at moving to the music was nothing compared to the sight of Flora in front of him right now. He could just about see her in the dim light. She seemed to have suddenly come alive, he thought as he watched her sway. Despite her T-shirt and shorts, she was incredibly sexy and his senses were overwhelmed as he tried to rein in his thoughts.

The music was incessant. It was a constant sultry beat that pounded his ears and heart. Nico found he was having trouble breathing, but even that sense was overwhelmed by the soft floral perfume Flora always wore.

As he watched her, he could see those incredible green eyes were closed briefly as Flora swayed to the rhythm. He wondered if she looked that content when she slept.

He glanced across to the makeshift bar in the corner but knew it wasn't alcohol he was craving. The magnetic appeal of Flora was too much for him to resist. He caressed her back with his hand and watched as she opened her eyes at his touch and stared up at him.

She was breathless from dancing, her mouth slightly open and panting. Her hair hung in huge waves around her face, her cheeks flushed. Those stunning eyes sparkled with excitement. He could feel the heat emanating from her whole body.

He had never seen a more beautiful woman.

Despite the music carrying on, they both slowed down until they had stopped dancing. They stood in the middle of the dance floor, staring at each other, unable to break eye contact, their faces almost touching.

Then the lights suddenly came on, making Nico blink at the sudden harsh light.

'There we are,' said a voice. 'All finished.'

'All finished,' Nico repeated, still feeling dazed.

'That was amazing,' said Grams, coming to stand next to them. 'I had no idea you could dance like that.'

'Nor did I,' said Flora, looking up at Nico before letting her grandmother lead her away to get them all a drink.

Nico watched Flora walk away, his arms feeling emptier than they had ever felt.

* * *

Later on, back at the farm, Flora stood in her bedroom and recalled the feel of his hands on her. She wondered why Nico had such an effect on her.

But even as she thought it, she knew why. Because she liked him.

She knew that he was entirely unsuitable for her and that he didn't think of her that way. She knew that he was leaving after the summer.

And yet she did like him.

She liked his ridiculous flirty comments. She liked his dark brown eyes which would grow soft when looking at her sometimes. She liked his Italian accent and the way he had gone above and beyond to help out her and Grams.

Was it possible that he liked her too? And then she decided, of course not. A full-blooded Italian stallion would have kissed her on the dance floor that evening. He hadn't kissed her all those weeks ago when she had asked him to either.

They were just friends and that was that. A dull ache came over her and she felt desperately lonely.

She had a sudden thought and brought out her mobile.

'Hi,' she said, when Tyler finally picked up. 'How are you?'

'Long time, no hear,' he replied. 'I'm good, thanks.'

She took a deep breath and said, 'You know, we never got round to having that second drink, did we?'

'No. We didn't. I'm at a farm show this weekend, so how about the following Saturday night?' he asked, sounding pleased.

'Sounds good,' she replied. 'Seven o'clock in the Black Swan?'

'I'll see you there.'

After she had hung up, Flora waited for the thrill of anticipation of a date with Tyler. And yet it never came.

It didn't matter, she reminded herself.

She heard her grandmother's words describing him as dull. She gulped. Tyler was steady, like her. That was all.

But she needed to date and move on with her life. She had missed out on so much because of the sacrifices she had made. She was bored. Frustrated even.

And Nico? He only thought of her as a friend. Perhaps he even thought that she was a bit dull, a tiny bit boring?

But suddenly she decided that she didn't want to be dull Flora any more. She liked Flora who stripped off and went into the lake and propositioned entirely unsuitable men when she'd had too much to drink.

The trouble was that the only unsuitable man she really wanted was Nico.

46

July arrived and brought with it a heatwave.

'It's perfect weather for the lavender,' said Harriet with a happy sigh as she sank into a chair underneath the gazebo on one side of the lavender fields. 'They don't like too much rain.'

'Neither do I,' said Katy, leaning against the table. 'Wow, you sold a lot of tickets today,' she added, checking the receipts.

Harriet nodded and yawned at the same time. 'If this keeps up, we're going to have a record summer,' she told her friends. 'Joe's had to rush out and buy some more till receipts because we didn't order enough. There'll be no time this weekend with even more visitors.' She held up her crossed fingers.

'They'll come,' said Libby in a confident tone. 'Why wouldn't they? Look at it!'

Flora joined her friends in looking up at the long rows of lavender plants. They had bloomed just in time for the opening of the lavender fields for public visitors. The whole field was alive with bees and butterflies and the scent was incredibly beautiful and relaxing.

Flora glanced down at Paddington, who was lying underneath

the table, exhausted from his role as top greeter to all the children who had visited that day.

'There were definitely more people here than I remember last year,' said Libby.

Flora had to agree, as the empty field which she gave to Harriet to use as a car park had been full by the afternoon.

Now that the visitors were all gone for the day, however, peace had returned and it was just them and the warm summer evening.

'The strawberry field was busy when I looked over,' said Harriet.

Flora nodded. Because it was only over the other side of the path to Cranbridge, she had placed a 'Pick Your Own' sign and most visitors had wandered over after visiting the lavender fields.

'It's a big win for all of us,' said Katy. 'Because everyone's coming into Platform 1 for lunch and to cool off. We've been rushed off our feet today. And both railway carriages have had plenty of enquiries for the rest of the year!'

'Even my boxes of chocolates have sold out,' said Libby. 'I only put them next to the counter in the coffee shop a couple of days ago.'

Flora was so pleased. It seemed as if everyone in Cranfield was getting a boost. The tiny village was coming back to life after so many years lying quiet.

'And Bob and Eddie have had plenty of visitors to see the steam train as well!' added Katy, laughing as she massaged her feet. 'Gotta say, though. I'm absolutely beat!'

Flora knew how she felt. The campsite was now three-quarters full. Not that she minded. Life on the site had slowed down in the heat. People wandered down to the swimming pond to cool off or dropped some pennies in the honesty box so that they could help themselves to Grams' home-made lemonade. Others just lazed on their sundecks and enjoyed the glorious weather.

She looked over to the strawberry field once more and saw Nico walking down the hill. She was enjoying his company more and more. There was lively conversation over dinner and then quiet nights watching the sunset with him when Grams was out dancing.

As he drew nearer, however, she realised that he was walking quite fast and looked serious. Her heart automatically beat faster as she prepared herself for some kind of bad news.

'Hello, Nico!' called out Harriet when she too spotted him coming towards them.

'*Scusi*,' he said, almost out of breath when he arrived. 'I don't mean to interrupt.'

He looked so serious that Flora was instantly worried.

'What is it?' she asked, clutching her heart in fear. 'Is it Grams?'

He swore in Italian and shook his head. 'No, no,' he told her, taking her by the arms. 'It's good news, I promise.' He took a deep breath. 'We're full. The campsite is completely full until the summer bank holiday at the end of next month!'

Flora was amazed. 'I don't believe it!' she cried. 'Seriously?'

'Definitely!' he replied, laughing and picking her up to spin her around.

She was once more reminded of his impetuousness and how much she liked being swept up in his excitement. She also liked the feeling of being in his arms, but all too quickly it was over.

He placed her carefully back on the ground. 'I couldn't believe it!' he told her, his words coming out at a rush. 'There has been a mad rush these past few days. And now we're full!'

'Wow,' said Flora.

'Congratulations!' said Katy. 'That's fantastic news!'

Flora suddenly remembered her friends were standing next to them.

'Isn't it?' said Nico, beaming from ear to ear. Then he looked between them all. 'I apologise,' he carried on. 'I've interrupted your conversation. I just had to tell Flora, but I'll go now.'

Despite their protests, he gave them all a wave and began to walk away back up the hill.

Flora watched him, still amazed that the campsite had become such a success. She turned to her friends with a wide smile on her face, which faltered somewhat when she found them all smiling at her with the same goofy expression. 'What?' she asked.

'Nothing,' cooed Libby, with a wink.

Flora realised that her friends had completely misread the situation between her and Nico and she needed to put them right. 'I'm going out on a date this weekend,' she told them.

'At last!' Harriet clapped her hands excitedly.

'With Tyler,' added Flora.

Harriet's face immediately dropped. 'Tyler?' she spluttered. She looked across at Libby, who merely shook her head as if in disbelief.

'What?' asked Flora.

'Nothing,' said Katy quickly. 'That's, er, marvellous. Well, it really is good news all round tonight, isn't it, girls?'

But their smiles didn't quite meet their eyes and Flora was left wondering whether she had made some kind of mistake in telling them.

Or was the real mistake her agreeing to go out with Tyler again?

47

Saturday night arrived and Nico announced at dinner that he was meeting the guys for a game or two of poker afterwards.

'Sounds marvellous,' said Grams. 'Make sure you win.'

'I will,' he told her, with a wink.

Flora stood up from the kitchen table. 'Well, I'd better get ready too. I'm, er, going out tonight.'

Grams looked surprised. 'Is it time for another girls' night already?' she asked.

Flora seemed a bit nervous, he thought, shuffling from foot to foot. 'Actually, I'm meeting someone,' she finally said.

'Business?' he asked. But in the pit of his stomach, he knew the answer before she even replied.

'Actually, it's a friend,' she told him. 'A local farmer.'

'What's her name?' he said, still hoping for the best.

'It's a man actually,' she replied. 'Tyler.'

Grams gave a start. 'Tyler Smith?' she asked, flicking a glance at Nico before looking back at her granddaughter.

Flora nodded. 'Yes. I've known him for years,' she told Nico. Her words were coming out in a rush and he could barely keep up as she was speaking so quickly. 'Anyway, we're meeting at the Black Swan.'

'Sounds good,' he said, trying to inject some positivity into his voice. 'What time are you heading out?'

'In about an hour,' she told him. 'So I'd better get going.'

He nodded. 'Of course. Have a great time.'

He watched her leave, her long legs striding out as she headed away from him. Her ponytail swinging from side to side.

She had a date! He couldn't believe it. Didn't want to believe it.

But of course she did. Flora was attractive, personable and single. Why wouldn't other men be interested in her?

He sighed. He had backed right off after Flora's drunken come-on. He was a gentleman and hadn't wanted to embarrass her. So he had stopped with the witty remarks and teasing, thinking that it had been the right thing to do. Even though they had had this amazing connection when they had danced together the other week. Even when the best times of each day for him was when they shared the evenings together and watched the sunsets. Despite all of that, he was still determined not to turn into his father.

He felt Grams give his shoulder a squeeze before walking out of the kitchen. Then he decided that perhaps it was for the best that he kept busy that evening.

Nico had been invited to a boys' night in by Ryan. It was up in the apartment above the station as, according to Ethan, everyone was broke. Despite that, plans had been made to play poker.

'For only pennies, right?' asked Ryan, looking concerned as the cards were dealt. 'I'm not exactly rolling in money at the moment.'

'Who is?' said Joe, with a shrug. 'Although, hopefully we'll have even more visitors to the lavender fields than last year and make a profit to see us through the winter.'

'Isn't Harriet's lavender spa doing well?' asked Ryan.

Joe nodded. 'Oh yeah, it's just the constant worry about money, you know?'

'Oh I know,' said Ryan. 'We're working every hour we can to maximise our profits.'

'Then it's a good thing that Nico and I are successful wealthy bachelors,' drawled Ethan. 'Right?'

'Right,' said Nico, a little too quickly. 'Although I'm not so sure about the wealthy these days.'

'What about being a bachelor or are you loved up these days as well?' asked Ethan.

Nico was taking a sip of his beer and almost choked.

'Right,' announced Ryan. 'Let's get dealing.'

Joe broke out the deck of cards and began to deal.

'Just so you know, Ethan is excellent at bluffing,' said Ryan to Nico.

Ethan laughed. 'I just like to keep my cards close to my chest. Literally,' he said, clutching his hand up against his T-shirt.

'Hit me,' said Ryan, taking another card from Joe.

'So, Harriet was telling me that Flora's gone out on a date tonight,' said Joe, looking at Nico.

He nodded, feeling a dull pain in his chest. 'A local farmer. Tyler something.'

'The cattle farmer?' said Joe, in a thoughtful tone. 'Nice guy.'

Ethan rolled his eyes. 'If you like talking to a brick wall. The guy is yawnsville. Have you ever tried to have a conversation with him? Hit me.'

Another card went across the table and Nico felt slightly better. If Flora's date was that dull, then surely the relationship wasn't going anywhere.

'Hey, are you folding?' asked Ryan.

Nico blinked back to life and saw everyone looking at him. 'Nope. I'm in.'

'Of course, Tyler's a very nice guy and I've never seen muscles like his,' carried on Joe. 'The man is the size of a barn.'

'Well, if Flora is only interested in him for his physique, then maybe she's onto a winner,' said Ethan. 'I see you and raise you a whole pound.'

'Check.'

The game carried on, but Nico wasn't following it at all. Was that true? Was the guy Flora was seeing some kind of macho guy? And a farmer too? It was like night and day, the difference between them, he thought.

Why should it matter? He reminded himself.

The trouble was, the sick feeling in his stomach reminded him that it really did matter. A lot.

'Dealer takes two cards.'

Nico was still stewing over his inner thoughts when he realised it had gone quiet. He looked around the table.

'What's it going to be?' asked Ethan.

'Sorry, I lost what's going on,' said Nico.

Ethan smiled. 'The other two have bowed out, so it's just you and me, pal.'

Nico nodded and glanced at his cards once more. He felt riled up. A need to feel the release. 'So if it's just you and me left, do we still have to play for only a pound?'

Ethan's smile widened. 'Bring it on,' he said.

'Fine,' said Nico. 'I see your twenty and raise you fifty pounds.'

'What's going on?' asked Joe, looking at Nico with raised eyebrows.

'Well,' said Ethan. 'I see your fifty and raise you one hundred.'

The surprised looks went table, raised eyebrows, but, to their credit, the other men didn't tease him.

'Okay,' said Nico. 'I call it.'

Ethan spread his cards out on the table. 'Royal flush. Read it and weep.'

Nico glanced down at his hand before throwing his cards onto the table. He was beaten fair and square. 'Well played,' he said, trying to put a brave face on the loss.

'Not really,' said Ethan. 'It was like taking candy from a frustrated, jealous man.'

'I'm not that,' spluttered Nico.

'Yeah you are,' said Ethan, tapping him on the shoulder with a pity smile. 'And I don't blame you. Flora's lovely. Not like that, of course. She's like our little sister.'

'So break her heart and we'll throw you off the side of the hill,' added Ryan.

'I'm not going to break any part of her,' Nico told them. 'She's out on a date with someone else,' he reminded them.

'Yeah. Too bad. Well, there's always Libby,' said Ryan, throwing a glance at his younger brother.

Ethan scowled. 'I wouldn't go near Libby,' he muttered. 'She'll eat you alive. The woman's meaner than my big brother and that's saying something.'

Nico had already picked up on some kind of underlying tension between Ethan and Libby and wondered what had happened there. Besides, as gorgeous as Libby was, it was Flora whom he couldn't stop thinking about.

As he paid his dues to Ethan over the loss of the poker game, Nico realised that he had enjoyed his evening. It was nice having men of his own age to chat and banter with. He had missed that. He had missed having a family, friends, that comfort of knowing that people were looking out for you. And he was beginning to think he'd found it in Cranfield.

He was gradually beginning to hope that not everyone

thought of him as Paolo Rossi's son. In fact, when he thought about it, nobody had even mentioned his famous dad for weeks. Nico could feel himself relaxing and beginning to trust. For the first time in a very long time, he was beginning to make friends.

And that particular thought made him smile all the way back to Strawberry Hill Farm, right up until the moment when he remembered that Flora was on a date and the dull ache returned.

48

As Flora walked into Cranbridge, she felt cross with herself. She was an idiot. In her embarrassment after dancing with Nico, she had made an impetuous date with Tyler. Thus making a difficult situation even worse.

She wasn't even sure she wanted to see Tyler again. At least, not on a date. But if Nico wasn't interested in her romantically, wasn't it best that she try and move forward with her life?

She groaned and picked up her speed, ensuring that she was actually early and waiting for Tyler at the bar when he arrived.

She saw a few women look over appreciatively as he crossed the floor towards her and was reminded that Tyler was an attractive man. Anyone else would be glad to be on a date with him.

But her pulse remained resolutely steady as she smiled up at him.

'Sorry I'm a bit late,' he said. 'I was waiting for the vet.'

'Everything okay?' she asked.

'One of the calves,' he told her. 'So, what would you like to drink?'

Flora ordered a gin and tonic, Tyler bought himself a beer and they went to find a table outside.

It was another beautiful midsummer's evening and Flora found herself thinking back to the picnic she had shared with Nico under a very similar clear darkening sky.

There had been no awkward small talk with Nico. No need to get to know each other. After spending so much time together, they both knew each other's strengths and weaknesses almost as well as their own.

She tried to concentrate her mind back on her date and began to chat about the campsite.

'I think you're very brave,' said Tyler, nodding thoughtfully. 'Not sure I'd take our farm down that route.'

'Why not?' she asked.

He was silent for a while before answering. 'I guess I only know about cattle,' he eventually said.

He was quiet and considered, she thought. Steady. No surprises. What you got with Tyler was exactly as you saw him.

For a moment, she tried to imagine him behind the wheel of a red Ferrari, but she couldn't see it. It wasn't in his DNA. Behind a tractor, yes. A fast car? Absolutely not.

'Well, for us it was a matter of survival,' she told him.

'Of course,' he replied. 'The farm is all that matters.'

Flora gave a start. It was true to a point, she thought. The farm, her home, was terribly important. And yet she had begun to realise that there were other things to bring a richness to life. She smiled to herself as she remembered Grams all dressed up in her finest ballroom dancing outfit, so far removed from the farming overalls she had worn for many years. Sometimes, a change really was as good as a rest.

After ordering their food, they chatted, but it was mainly about farming. Flora tried to bring him out of himself to talk about hobbies or interests. But Tyler was comfortable and happy just being a farmer. And there was nothing wrong with that, she reminded herself.

After finishing their meal, she went for broke. 'So what about future dreams?' she asked. 'A bigger farm? Or somewhere completely different?'

'Oh no,' said Tyler, shaking his head. 'I'm not so good with change. I like it here.' He looked at her with questioning eyes. 'Don't you?'

'Yes, of course,' she said.

'Must be hard, though, things changing so fast for you and Grams,' he said. 'Not sure how I'd cope.'

'I'm not really sure that I am coping,' she admitted. 'I've spent so long trying to save the farm that now that everything's changed, I'm all aflutter. I mean, it's exciting. The thought that Strawberry Hill Farm could have a different future. It's been so hard all these years. I feel like it's a new opportunity.'

Tyler frowned. 'Really?' he said. 'I'd be in a bit of a mess, to be honest.'

Flora laughed. 'Well, I'm not saying I haven't let off steam and gone a bit crazy a couple of times,' she told him. And propositioned Nico, she added silently.

'We've all done that,' he replied, looking at her with softening eyes.

He was a decent man, she thought as she walked home. He had offered to drop her home, but Flora had told him that it would only take ten minutes on foot.

Truth be known, she was avoiding the difficult end-of-a-date scenario. What if he tried to kiss her? What would she have done? Backed away or accepted it?

She groaned as she walked down the track towards Cranfield. There was absolutely nothing wrong with Tyler, she reminded herself. He was a kind and lovely man. A few months ago, she had considered him a good prospect, someone to even think about having a relationship with.

But that was before she had met Nico.

Nico had changed everything. He had changed the farm. And changed her, she admitted. She liked slightly more reckless Flora.

And she liked Nico too. In fact, she was pretty certain that she liked him an awful lot more than she had let on to anyone, even herself.

49

Despite another gloriously warm and sunny start to the day, Nico was still feeling grumpy when he woke up the following morning.

He had deliberately gone to bed earlier than normal, reluctant to hear how much Flora enjoyed her date. In fact, he was really hoping that it had been a disaster and that she wouldn't meet Tyler again.

Deep inside, he knew he was being unfair. He was only there for the summer. They had a tentative friendship, and from all that he had discovered about the sacrifices she had made so far in life, she deserved every chance of happiness.

And yet, the thought of Flora being in anyone else's arms apart from his filled him with despair. They hadn't even kissed. Perhaps they weren't even compatible. But as time went on, he found himself wanting to get to know her even more. And thinking that perhaps he should be the one kissing her.

Downstairs at breakfast, he looked up and automatically smiled when Flora came into the room. 'Good morning,' he said.

'Good morning,' said Grams. 'Did you have a nice time last night?'

Flora nodded. 'Morning,' she said, heading across to pour herself a coffee. 'I did, thanks. Really great.'

Nico looked down at his plate of pancakes and lost his appetite.

'Right,' he said, suddenly standing up. 'I'm just going to have a walk around and check on things in the campsite.'

Flora looked a little surprised but didn't say anything.

He stepped outside of the cool farmhouse and straight into the warmth of the July heatwave. The long-range weather forecast was for the sunshine and heat to continue, perfect weather for camping.

As he crossed the courtyard, he came across Tyson tinkering with the motorbike.

'Hey,' he said. 'You're up early this morning.'

Tyson looked up and nodded at him. He was dressed in his school uniform and had obviously cycled over before classes. 'Was thinking about the gearbox and needed to check something out,' he replied, looking back at the bike.

'What about school?'

Tyson checked his phone. 'I've got five more minutes.'

Nico leant up against the wall and watched as the teenager began to reconnect the gearbox. 'So do you enjoy school?' he asked.

Tyson shrugged his shoulders. 'Not really,' he muttered.

Nico nodded. 'I found it pretty boring myself,' he replied.

Tyson looked up at him surprised. 'For real?' he asked.

'I was never one for writing everything down,' Nico told him. 'Carpentry, on the other hand. That I loved. Anything where I could make something with my hands, get them dirty.'

Tyson nodded. 'Yeah. Same.'

'Are you starting your GCSE courses in the autumn?'

Tyson made a face. 'Teacher keeps nagging me to choose

them, but I haven't had time to look. Kevin's back in hospital and I don't want to bother Mum.'

'I'm sorry to hear that. I hope he's okay. Well, if you want to run the courses past someone, I've always got time for you,' said Nico.

Tyson looked pleased as he stood up. 'Cheers,' he replied, grabbing his bicycle.

'Any time,' Nico told him.

As the teenager cycled up the lane and away from him, Nico nodded thoughtfully to himself. It was nice to give something back, he thought. He was pleased to be able to support Tyson wherever he could. He didn't appear to have many male adults in his life to guide him. Nico was thankful once more for the lifelong support he had received from Lorenzo. Heaven knows he never got any support from his own father.

The voicemails and missed calls had finally slowed down and Nico didn't know whether that was a good or bad thing. Perhaps Paolo had given up on his beloved supercar. Truth be known, Nico didn't want it. Other things were much more important to him now. Even more so than revenge on his father. Unfortunately the one thing he really wanted though, which was Flora, he couldn't have.

He took in a breath of the fresh country air as he walked past the barn and waved at a few of the campers beginning to step out of their tents and into the fresh air. Nico stopped at the top of the hill and looked out across the hill to where he could see Harriet and Joe setting up the stall in the lavender field for hopefully another busy day.

He hadn't bargained on making friends when he had first made the long journey to Cranfield. He hadn't thought about staying on and enjoying himself that summer. He had been so low, so grief-stricken, and slowly Cranfield had brought him back to life. And perhaps, given him a new life as well. He yearned to stay on, to see and enjoy the changes of the seasons and perhaps make his next home there.

He suddenly saw Flora come out of the farmhouse and turned around to head further into the camping field. For once, he didn't want to talk to her that morning.

Of all the things he hadn't bargained on when arriving in Cranfield, beginning to fall in love was one of them.

50

Flora found that July was rushing past and suddenly, the following week, all the state schools would be breaking up for the holidays and the campsite would be completely full.

She decided to take advantage of the last couple of days of having a tiny bit of free time and went to grab a takeout coffee from Platform 1 to enjoy whilst she painted a new canvas.

Inside the coffee shop, she found Libby dressed in her flight attendant's uniform with her mind also on a strong coffee.

'Mmm, that's better,' said Libby, after taking a sip. 'Have you got five minutes spare? My taxi isn't due until quarter past.'

'Sure. Where are you off to this time?' asked Flora.

'Jamaica,' replied Libby as they headed out onto the station platform. 'This week has been exhausting. I signed up for extra time because, you know, the money, but ugh, the hours have been relentless.'

They sat down on one of the benches on the platform and looked across at the view. The lavender fields were a blur of purple now and lit up the landscape with their incredible colours.

'So,' said Libby, after another sip of coffee. 'I've been so busy, we haven't had time to catch up. How was your date?'

'It was fine,' replied Flora quickly.

There was a short silence.

'Just fine?' prompted Libby.

'I know,' said Flora with a huff. 'I expect all your dates are expensive dinners by candlelight, but I'm not that kind of girl. You know that.'

'I know that any date I describe as "fine" isn't worth a second date,' Libby told her in a pointed tone.

Flora didn't reply and sipped her coffee instead, looking out across the lavender fields once more.

'Is this to do with Tyler or the handsome Italian?' she heard Libby say.

Flora kept her eyes on the landscape. 'I don't think Nico thinks about me that way,' she replied.

'I've seen the way he looks at you,' Libby replied. 'There's something there. You know there is. What's the problem?'

Flora looked beyond the lavender fields to the grass and trees beyond. The brighter emeralds of early summer had now faded to a softer green, and even a pale yellow here and there. The year was rolling on under the heat of summer. And soon Nico would leave. The dull ache in her heart reminded her how much pain that would cause her.

'He's leaving at the end of the summer when the campsite closes,' she finally replied. 'It was only ever about the investment.' She turned to look at Libby. 'He lives in another country.'

Libby's blue eyes blazed at her. 'So ask him to stay,' she said.

Flora sighed. She hadn't seen Tyler since their date. She knew that he wasn't the right person for her and didn't want to lead him on any more. It wasn't fair. But there was a distance now between her and Nico. She wasn't sure what had happened, but he had suddenly backed off. Their cosy chats and the easy relaxed atmosphere had changed in the past few days. Perhaps he wanted to leave anyway.

A car horn at the front of the building broke into her thoughts.

Libby quickly stood up. 'That's my ride,' she said.

Flora stood up to give her a hug. 'Have a safe journey. We'll see you when we get back. Although I'm not sure when that'll be. We're full from this weekend, so it's likely to be crazy busy.'

'More reason than ever to try out those strawberry margaritas.' Libby searched her friend's face. 'Take a chance,' she said, before giving her Flora another bear hug. 'What have you got to lose?'

Only my heart, thought Flora.

As Libby walked away through the station and got into her taxi, Katy came outside.

'Phew, it's mad today. You okay?' she asked, looking at Flora with a frown. 'You look all serious.'

Flora considered Libby's advice. The month of August was likely to rush past as quickly as July. Then September would arrive, the campsite would close and Nico would leave forever. She needed to say thank you whilst there was time. To thank him for all that he had done for her and Grams. In encouraging her to paint. In bringing her back to life. And she knew just what would make him happiest.

Flora looked at Katy. 'Are you fully booked for tonight?' she asked.

It was one of Ryan's Italian cooking nights.

Katy shook her head. 'Actually, we've just had a late cancellation. I have a waiting list, but you're welcome to jump right in if you don't tell anyone.'

'Table for three, please,' said Flora.

Katy looked delighted. 'Of course,' she said. 'This is great. You've never been in before, have you?'

'Never had the time,' said Flora.

But it was more than that. Of course, money had been tight too, but it was that she hadn't thought to have a nice night out. But thanks to Nico, she was feeling a little more free to make impetuous decisions, something that she had never done before.

* * *

'We're going out to dinner tonight,' Flora announced with a flourish when she found Grams and Nico back at the farmhouse.

Grams looked at her in astonishment. 'Since when?' she asked.

'Since I decided about half an hour ago,' replied Flora. 'All three of us deserve a break from time to time, don't we?'

Nico looked delighted. 'Well, that sounds great,' he said.

But Grams was shaking her head. 'Wish you'd told me sooner. I've made other plans.'

'With who?'

'Bob, Maggie, Eddie and I are off to a special dance class tonight,' said Grams, looking excited. 'We're going to learn the American smooth!'

'Oh. I wish I'd known,' said Flora.

'Anyway, you youngsters go and enjoy yourselves,' said Grams.

Flora looked at Nico and felt a little embarrassed. So much for being impetuous, she thought. Now it appeared that she'd planned a sort of date in an Italian restaurant.

51

Nico looked around, somewhat amazed by the difference in the way Platform 1 looked that evening.

Having only ever seen it as a coffee shop by day, and the pizza counter open at the weekend, he hadn't imagined it would look so soft in there by night.

Although the sun was sinking down slowly outside, there were fairy lights across the ceiling and tea lights on every table, giving the whole place a romantic atmosphere.

'I had no idea it would be like this,' he said, pleased.

He looked across the table at Flora who smiled. 'I'm glad you like some of my interior design ideas,' she told him.

'You helped decorate in here?' he asked, not surprised. 'You did a great job.'

'Thanks.'

She shuffled awkwardly in her chair opposite him. They were surrounded by couples and the occasional table for four, but the atmosphere was cosy and warm.

'You look very pretty tonight,' he found himself saying. It was true. In the soft light, with her hair down, she looked very attractive. She had caught some sun and her skin had begun to take on a glow.

She blushed. 'I'm wearing an old top and skirt. I had no time to get ready properly as it suddenly got busy this afternoon. I look a bit of a mess.'

'Not to me.'

She studied him with humour in her green eyes. 'Is this your seduction technique?' she asked, with a smile.

He shook his head. 'If I were wanting to seduce you, believe me, you'd know about it.'

She looked away and reached out for her wine glass.

He reached out and held her hand over the cold glass. 'Why can't you just accept the compliment for once? You look lovely. There, I said it. What's the matter?'

'I don't know.'

He let go of her hand and watched as she took a large sip of wine.

'Maybe it's been so long since I received a compliment, that I don't know how to accept one when it comes along,' she finally said.

He frowned. 'You've clearly been dating the wrong men.'

'I haven't been dating any men. Well, except Tyler, of course,' she added.

Nico suddenly felt his humour drop away. 'Yes, let's not forget Tyler.'

'What about you?' she asked. 'When was the last time you dated anyone?'

He hesitated. 'Five years ago,' he told her.

'Wow, that doesn't sound like a very positive hit rate,' she said, laughing.

'Well, that one stung a bit,' he said. 'I found her in bed with my father.'

Flora's face turned to shock. 'No!' she spluttered.

Nico shrugged his shoulders. 'I know. Tell me that it serves me right. That I'm just like my father and deserve it.'

But Flora shook her head. 'I don't think you're like your father at all. Look at what you've done for Grams. For my home. You're not the selfish man you think you are. You're not your father.'

Nico took a deep breath. Was she right? He wasn't sure.

He glanced at her face and found that the minutes ticked by as he stared into her eyes, unable to look away.

Finally, she was the first one to blink. 'For the record, Grams agrees with me and so do quite a few other people here in Cranfield. You've made good friends.'

He nodded, noticing how she had moved the conversation on.

He was almost pleased when Katy delivered their main courses to the table. Flora had chosen an asparagus risotto. Whereas Nico had been amazed to find lamb tagliata on the menu. It had been a favourite dish of his grandfather's over the years, with his grandmother making it with watercress and tomatoes.

Nico stared down at the plate for a moment, inhaling the sweet scent of rosemary and garlic. But he hadn't been prepared for the first mouthful. It tasted of warm summer evenings, of smoky air, of grapes being harvested and of his grandmother's delicate perfume. It tasted of Tuscany. And of a home that he would never see again.

The food grew thick in his throat, despite the delicious taste. He almost felt overwhelmed by it.

'Are you okay?'

He looked up to find Flora watching him with a worried expression.

'I'm fine,' he told her, picking up his glass of red wine but almost spilling it down himself. He sighed and leaned back in his chair. 'Or not, I guess.'

She took his hand across the table. 'What is it? What's wrong?'

He took a deep breath. 'The food,' he said, his voice full of emotion. 'Food was always a huge thing at home. Like your grand-mother's cooking. It just reminds me, that's all.'

She gave his hand a squeeze. 'Tell me,' she said.

And so, whilst they carried on eating, he found himself talking of the rolling hills of Tuscany. Of his grandfather's serious nature but gentle eyes, of his grandmother's huge bear hugs. Of the way the grapes tasted when they were warmed in the sun. Of the first taste of the wine vintage each year.

The meal rushed by in a blur, with maritozzo con la panna for dessert. Even that was a revelation, the classic Italian dessert filled with cream and the traditional honey. Nico was almost dumb-struck for a second time.

But still, he found himself opening up to Flora, talking of times gone by, happy times, mostly when his father wasn't around.

By the end of the evening, he felt even closer to her. As if had bared his soul, which he normally didn't do. And he knew that he had fallen a little bit more in love with her.

52

Flora had never known a meal out quite like the one that she had just enjoyed.

The food, of course, was superb. She had known that Ryan was a great chef and that evening in Platform 1 had proved the rumours true. She didn't know that much about traditional Italian cooking but judging by Nico's reaction, it was certainly spot on.

Most of all, she was feeling stunned by what he had shared with her. Stories of his family, of the past, of the home that he had lost. She finally understood that the playful exterior belied a sensitive, somewhat bruised soul underneath and she longed to take his pain away. So she let him talk and talk over dinner, sharing everything with her.

When they got up to leave, the last ones still at their table, Ryan came up to them.

'So? How was it?' asked Ryan, looking a little nervous.

Nico took a deep breath. 'Superb,' he told him. 'It tasted...' He hesitated before carrying on. 'It tasted like home.'

His voice broke on the last word and a brief silence ensued as Flora looked from Nico to Ryan. In the end, Ryan stepped forward and gave Nico a hug. He then slapped him on the shoulder. 'That is the best compliment I could ever receive, mate,' he said.

Nico nodded, seemingly unable to speak for the emotion.

Ryan stepped back and gave Flora a nod of his head. So Flora took Nico's hand and led him through the waiting room and out onto the platform. They walked back hand in hand, under the darkening sky, Nico seemingly still in a daze.

'Are you okay?' she asked softly, turning in the darkness to face him when they reached the back door of the farmhouse.

He nodded. 'I think so,' he said, with a small smile. 'Thank you for listening tonight. I'm sorry if I bent your ear off with all things Italian.'

'I loved hearing your stories,' she told him truthfully. 'It made me feel closer to you. To understand you better.'

He took a step forward. 'And now that you know me, what do you think?'

'I think that I'm very glad you came here to the farm, for both of our sakes,' she said softly.

He looked surprised but pleased. 'I'm glad you said that,' he replied, stepping towards her. 'Because there's something I've wanted to do all evening and I shall regret it for the rest of my life if I don't act upon my impulse.'

Somehow, she knew what he was going to do. She didn't turn away. She could barely breathe. Anything to let him do what she had been dreaming about for so long.

He took a step forward, taking her chin in his fingers. He searched her eyes, as if waiting for a refusal. When he received none, he leaned down and their lips met.

At first, it was soft, almost gentle. But pretty soon the chemistry between them fizzled until his arms wrapped around her and her hands crept up behind his head to pull him even closer to her.

Eventually, after she had lost all sense of time, he leaned back a little to stare at her with eyes that were almost black in the darkness.

'You told me a while ago that I needed to be honest with myself,' he said, his voice low and rough. 'Well, this is what I wanted and I figured you did too. Was I right?'

Her breath was still coming in shallow gasps at the magnitude of their shared passion.

But her hesitation gave him the wrong impression.

'Then I apologise,' he told her, breaking the eye contact and moving to step away.

Suddenly, she couldn't bear him leaving and found she couldn't stop herself from grabbing hold of his shirt and dragging him back up against her.

He stared into her eyes and drew a sharp breath at the intensity which was mirrored in his own.

'We'd better make sure,' she told him, reaching out to draw his head down towards hers.

His eyes softened as he leant forward to kiss her again.

This time, she lost all sense of time and reality. This time, he didn't hold back and neither did she.

Minutes, possibly hours passed until finally they drew apart, both breathlessly staring at each other. He studied her, his eyes unfathomable in the darkness now sweeping over the landscape around them. Then, with a soft smile, he took her by the hand and led her through the kitchen and upstairs, their journey punctuated by many stops and short, sweet kisses, often accompanied by murmured Italian words whispered in her ear.

It was only once they were in the darkness of the upstairs hallway, that the kisses once more deepened back into pure passion.

But the sound of Flora's phone ringing brought her back to earth with a bump.

'Don't answer it,' urged Nico, as he dropped a line of kisses all the way down her neck.

'I must,' said Flora, despite every fibre of her being just wanting to stay in the moment with Nico. 'It might be Grams. She's still out.'

Nico swore in Italian before straightening up. 'You're right,' he said. 'Answer it.'

She brought out the mobile and in the darkness the name Tyler lit up on the screen. Flora glanced over and saw that Nico was looking at the mobile as well.

She quickly pressed the button for the call to go to voicemail, but the moment had been broken.

'*Scusi*,' he said, dragging a hand through his hair. 'It's been an emotional evening and I got carried away. I apologise. It won't happen again.' He turned and went into his bedroom, closing the door behind him.

'Nico,' called out Flora, but there was no reply.

In a daze, she turned around and went into her own bedroom, sagging against the doorframe after closing the door. She didn't think she could even take a step at that moment, such was the power of his kiss. The chemistry between them both excited and terrified her. What if she had ruined everything by not pushing him away? What if she never stopped wanting him and gave into her true feelings for once?

She shook her head. He was right, of course. It had been an evening where he had been terribly homesick. They had both got carried away, that was all.

But, right at that moment, all she wanted to do was to drag him back into her arms and kiss him once more.

53

Flora came from the camping field one afternoon to find Nico and Tyson standing next to the old motorbike. The Ducati had received a major overhaul since being dragged out of the old stables. Now it was polished and, she realised as Nico turned the key in the ignition, working as well.

He looked delighted. 'This is great,' he shouted above the noise.

Tyson merely nodded and smiled.

It was wonderful how much the teenager had come out of his shell since the beginning of the summer when he had first begun to visit the farm, she thought. Nowadays, he was always popping in, eager to help wherever he could. She and Nico had even discussed giving him a Saturday job, such was the amount of work and help he had been around the place. Nico had told her that it would give him security and routine which he seemed to be badly craving in his life.

Nico turned off the engine once more and looked over to see Flora. He smiled at her, but it didn't reach his eyes, she noticed and immediately looked away.

Neither of them had discussed the kiss after their meal out a couple of days ago. But she had done nothing but think and dream about it every hour since then. It had affected her so deeply, changed her, it almost felt. It had made her feel things, a passion, that she had no idea she had even had.

Despite the awkwardness she still felt, she wandered over to join them, as if pulled towards Nico by an invisible thread.

'I can't believe that old thing is finally working,' she said, smiling. 'Well done, Tyson. You've worked a miracle.'

'*Old thing!*' Nico pretended to look offended. 'I'll have you know that bike is a classic.'

'Too right,' added Tyson.

'And, as such, a classic bike like this deserves a good run-out,' said Nico.

He walked away towards the Ferrari to open up the car door. Then he pulled out a large box and carried it towards them.

'I got these last week,' he said, pulling out two crash helmets. 'Just in case.'

Tyson's eyes grew wide. 'You're going to actually ride it? You trust me?'

'Of course I trust you,' Nico told him. 'It's not licensed to be on the main roads yet, but I think we can give its maiden voyage this century around the farm, don't you?'

Tyson's face lit up and he nodded eagerly. 'Yeah. I do.'

'Right then,' said Nico, climbing onto the bike to study the dials and switches. 'You grab your helmet and get behind me.'

After a short while as he got used to the feel of the bike, Nico started up the engine. He gave Flora a wink and, with Tyson holding on to the bike behind him, they set off.

Flora watched them head off around the corner and slowly ride down the hill out of sight. She stood for a moment, thinking back to Nico's kisses. She had thought of nothing else since. Then she sat down on the bench in the sunshine, something she had rarely done in the past summers, just to watch the fluffy white clouds drift by across the blue sky high above. But her mind still drifted back to Nico.

She didn't know how long she sat there, but soon she heard the motorbike engine begin to grow louder once more and stood up, eager to see how they had got on.

Nico brought the motorbike to a halt in the courtyard and turned off the engine.

'How was it?' she asked, heading over to see them both.

'Epic,' replied Tyson, climbing off and staring at the bike in wonder. 'Even better than I thought it was gonna be.'

'That's great,' Flora told him. 'I still can't believe it's working. When Grams gets back from her shopping trip, she's going to be amazed.'

'Well, if you want proof, hop on board,' said Nico, with a grin.

Her automatic response was to shake her head and say that she didn't have time, to deprive herself as she had always done. But instead of saying no, she found herself nodding and saying, 'All right then.'

Nico looked delighted and so did Tyson as he handed over the helmet for her to slip on.

She swung her leg over the back of the bike and tried to place her hands where Tyson's had been, on the back of the bike. But she quickly discovered she felt too precarious like that and moved her arms to close them around Nico's waist and hung on to him for dear life.

They went a different way than he had taken Tyson, heading up the hill this time. Flora grinned to herself inside the helmet, loving the feel of the fresh air and the sense of freedom as they went.

All too soon, they turned around and headed back to the courtyard.

'This was amazing,' she said, just as soon as Nico had switched off the engine and she could hear herself speak once more.

'I'm glad you liked it,' he said, taking off his helmet.

She let go of his waist to dismount before taking off her own helmet.

'Told you so!' said Tyson, with a grin.

'It needs a bit of tweaking, but I reckon it'll be roadworthy before too long,' Nico told him.

Tyson nodded. 'Me too,' he said, before his face creased into a frown. 'Oh, hey. I forgot. A taxi came whilst you were gone. There's a guy asking for you.'

Flora followed her gaze to where Tyson was pointing and saw a strange man by the back door watching them. 'Who's that?' she wondered out loud, running through her mental list and thinking that perhaps she had missed an appointment.

But the instant Nico spun around next to her to see who it was, she felt his whole body grow rigid with tension.

'It's my father,' he replied, walking away from them and towards the infamous Paolo Rossi.

54

Nico couldn't quite believe his eyes as he walked towards his father. What was Paolo doing in Cranfield? And how had he found him after all this time?

'*Ciao*, Nico,' said Paolo, giving his son his brightest smile. 'Good to see you, son.'

Nico desperately wanted to believe that was true, but history reminded him otherwise.

Paolo stepped forward to give his son a warm hug, but all the time Nico was aware that his father was looking over his shoulder.

As he stepped back, Paolo asked, 'So aren't you going to introduce me?' he asked.

Nico turned around slowly and locked eyes with Flora. Of course his father was going to run true to form and focus on the beautiful woman rather than on his son whom he hadn't seen all summer.

'This is Flora Barton,' he said in a dull tone. 'She owns the farm. And this is my friend Tyson.'

Paolo gave the teenager a curt nod, but Flora had the full

works, from the wide winning smile to taking her hand and brushing his lips across her skin.

Nico was ready to explode. However, he kept his temper in check, because Flora was there. And Tyson too.

'Nice to meet you,' she murmured.

She flicked a concerned glance at Nico, but he kept his face as a mask of neutrality. The last woman who had stolen his heart had ended up in his father's bed. He knew that would never happen with Flora. He trusted her, body and soul. It was his own father that he didn't trust.

'Can I offer you a drink?' she asked.

Paolo was about to rave about how generous she was and of course he wanted a drink, but Nico cut him off.

'Perhaps after we've caught up,' he said, taking his father's arm and beginning to lead him away. 'It's been so long, Papa. Excuse us. We'll see you in a while.'

Paolo must have been trying to get on his better side because there were no protestations about being led away from the beautiful woman. Instead, he walked alongside Nico as they went across the courtyard and up towards the gate into the strawberry field.

'It's quite an operation they've got going on here,' said Paolo, reverting back to Italian. He looked at the camping field beyond, as well as the number of people picking strawberries in the field in front of them.

Nico leant against the gate and kept quiet. He thought he knew why his father was there, but the child deep inside of him was still hoping that he might just want to catch up with his only son.

'And this is where you've been all this time? Since you left?' asked Paolo, with raised eyebrows.

Nico turned to look at him. 'Yes. Why would that surprise you?

I grew up on a vineyard. A farm isn't that much of a difference.' He hesitated before asking, 'How did you find me?'

Paolo gave a grunt of ill humour. 'It took some time,' he said, his eyes growing narrow. 'You should have left me a note.'

Nico gave a shrug of his shoulders. 'Why? You didn't give me any warning when you sold the vineyard out from under my feet.'

'I told you why I needed to do that,' snapped Paolo.

'Yes, I remember,' drawled Nico. 'It was to invest in the next big thing.'

Paolo nodded. 'Yes, it was.'

Nico sighed heavily. 'So what was it this time? A woman? A rare antique?'

His father hesitated. 'Listen, son, life is complicated. Can't you trust me to do the right thing with the money from the vineyard?'

Nico turned away to gaze out over the field instead. Trust had been broken a long time ago.

'You know that I would've been there when you were growing up if my career hadn't had to come first,' he heard Paolo say.

'Rubbish.' Nico spun to look at his father. 'It's always about you.'

Paolo sighed. 'I can't change the past. But let me make it up to you.'

Nico shook his head. 'I don't need anything from you. Not any more. You lost that chance a long time ago.'

'We're the same, you and I,' Paolo told him.

'We share a surname,' said Nico. 'We're vastly different in every other aspect. In how we treat people.'

'You're not so well behaved yourself,' said Paolo, with a scowl. 'I remember all those girlfriends you had.'

'That was years ago, Dad,' Nico reminded him. 'A lifetime ago. These days, I treat people better.'

He was surprised to see Paolo laugh. 'No, you don't,' he said. 'You don't treat me any better.'

'You don't deserve anything from me,' said Nico, feeling irritated now. 'What is it that you want? What are you really doing here?'

But as his father hesitated to speak, Nico felt the truth hit him squarely in the stomach.

'It's the car, isn't it?' he said, in a dull tone. 'That's the only reason that you're here now.'

'You stole my Ferrari!' said Paolo, his good looks lost in a fit of temper. 'That was my car. You had no right.'

'I had every right,' snapped Nico. 'You took everything else from me.'

'Didn't I make sure that you were brought up right?'

Nico almost laughed. 'That was nothing to do with you and everything to do with Nonno and Nonna. They brought me up. They fed and clothed me. They made sure that I knew right from wrong. They made sure that I care about the right things in life, not money and fast cars. But about people.'

Paolo shrugged his shoulders, confirming what Nico already knew. That his father didn't care about anyone but himself.

Nico felt around in his shorts pocket and brought out the car keys. 'Take the damn car,' he said, shoving the keys into his father's hand. 'I don't care. It means more to you than I ever will.'

And then he walked away, the tears pricking at his eyes as he did so.

55

Flora hadn't meant to overhear Nico's conversation with his father. But after Tyson had left, she had gone to water the pots at the side of the house and had suddenly been aware that she could hear what they were saying to each other.

She sank down onto the bench, not wanting to invade Nico's privacy but desperate to make sure that he wasn't being hurt any more than he already had been in his early years.

The conversation was conducted entirely in Italian, but the harsh tone of their voices confirmed her fear that the hurt was very much real.

Nico suddenly appeared around the corner and Flora gave a start, not realising that the discussion between father and son would end so abruptly.

He stopped when he saw her before giving her a small sigh and sinking down onto the bench next to her.

She could feel the tension in his body, as if he were trying to keep his emotions in check after such an upsetting conversation.

Unable to stop herself, she reached out and took his hand in hers. She held it, willing his hand and body to relax, but he was obviously still upset.

A sudden roar of an engine confirmed that Paolo had started the Ferrari. A moment later, the car began to move away and they both listened until there was no sound in the air but the farm and the countryside around them.

Flora glanced at Nico and saw that he was looking down at their entwined hands.

'Did you hear everything?' he asked. It wasn't an accusation. Rather, she felt, he couldn't bear to repeat it over again.

'It was in Italian, but I think I got the gist of it,' she told him. 'I'm sorry.'

'It's only a car,' he replied in a dull tone.

'I didn't mean about the car,' she said softly.

He finally looked up at her and she could see the pain in his dark eyes.

He gave a shaky sigh. 'For a moment I thought that he was here to see me. That he had been worried about me for once in his selfish life. But no. It was just about the car.'

She stroked his hand with her thumb, wishing she could take his pain away. 'It seems that both of our fathers are selfish creatures.'

He nodded. 'Yes, but at least you've got Grams. With both my Nonni gone, it's just me now. I'm alone.'

'You're not alone.' She squeezed his hand. 'Not any more.'

His eyes blazed as they looked at her. She couldn't bear to see the pain in them and leaned forward to kiss him. To kiss away the hurt and betrayal from his heart. To comfort and heal him.

Their lips met and immediately she heard him groan and felt him pull her closer. They wrapped their arms around each other and kissed until she didn't know where her body stopped and his started. They kissed each other until nothing mattered but the two of them.

Finally, after many minutes, they drew apart. He looked down at her with soft eyes, reaching out to stroke a stray lock of hair that had caught on her forehead.

'*Grazie*,' he murmured. 'But we shouldn't have done that.'

She was surprised and a little upset when he sat back, letting go of her. Suddenly she felt colder, despite the warmth of the afternoon sun.

'I think that's why I feel so at home here,' he said, looking across the countryside. 'It reminds me of Tuscany with the rolling hills and greenery everywhere.'

'Are you homesick?' she asked, suddenly feeling a dread in the pit of her stomach.

'A little,' he replied eventually. 'But I guess there's nothing left for me there now.'

'So stay after the summer finishes,' she told him.

Stay forever, she thought.

He was quiet whilst she held her breath, desperate for him to take her back in his arms and tell her that he never wanted to leave. That he wanted to stay. With her.

'Thank you for the offer,' he said, after a short pause. 'Of course, I'll stay until the end of the busy season to help out. Then I guess I have to work out where my future lies and leave you and Grams in peace.'

He stood up suddenly.

'Well, I'd better check on the campsite,' he said.

'Right. I'll go and see how Grams is getting on with the jam making class,' said Flora, her bright tone belying the piercing heartache inside.

But Nico was already halfway around the corner and had disappeared before she had even finished the sentence.

Flora sank back down on the bench, unable to find the strength in that moment to act normally. They had kissed, truly kissed as if there was nothing else in the world but the two of them. And yet he was leaving anyway. He didn't feel the same way, he didn't feel as strongly about her as she felt about him.

It was the sensible thing for him to do, of course. Totally the right thing to do. There was nothing for him here come the autumn.

So why did her heart feel so awful? Why did she feel like the whole world had just fallen apart?

56

August went on with Flora feeling as if she were in a daze. From feeling everything all at once, she now felt nothing.

Nico was fine with her but there was no more flirting. No kissing. No heat. Just a dull nothing. And she missed him terribly.

She had tried to reconcile herself to the fact that this was the right decision. That their delicious kisses, although they left her wanting more, weren't the right way forward for her.

So she had ignored the ache deep inside of her and gone out for a couple more dates with Tyler. They had been pleasant evenings, but she knew that he wasn't right for her and that she had to end it, for his sake. She didn't feel anything for him. Wasn't sure she would ever feel again once Nico left the farm forever.

At least the campsite had been fully booked throughout the summer. And now they appeared to have gone full circle as Tyson's family had returned for the end of summer break. Nico's idea had been welcomed by all the needy families in the community who couldn't afford to go away on holiday. It had been a good idea to give back to the community that had supported the farm for so many years.

Much like the wildflower meadows which were now giving much-needed nutrients and pollen to the insects and pollinators whom the heavy farming might have scared away. They were back in abundance now, even though the meadows would probably be more full of flowers the following summer, after their late sowing in the spring. But Flora had been overjoyed with the way that the soil had responded and come back to life. The meadows were a sea of tall green grasses dotted with brightly coloured wildflowers, from which the air was alive with the buzz and flutter of the bees and butterflies who had wandered over from the lavender fields to take on yet more nectar.

Everyone had been amazed at the transformation.

'I can't believe the difference from our soggy holiday in May,' said Tyson's mother, staring in wonder at the colourful fields in front of them.

'It's great, isn't it?' said Flora automatically.

But her eyes couldn't help but stray to look at Nico as he bent over the motorcycle, tinkering with the engine with Tyson.

'I wanted to say thank you,' carried on Tyson's mother. 'Tyson's like a different boy these days. He's happier now and that means the world to me.'

'You're welcome,' said Flora. 'But we're so grateful for his help around here. He's a genius with any kind of engine. Only last week he fixed a fault on the tractor for me.'

Tyson's mother smiled at her. 'He's always been the same, mad about anything with moving parts. I guess people don't really change, do they?'

She walked away, leaving Flora mulling over her words. Deep inside, however, Flora knew that she was wrong. Because Flora had changed. She had learnt to go with the flow, roll with the changes and embrace them. And because of that, she was happier in herself.

Except she wasn't. Because she wasn't sure what she was these days, except miserable. Luckily, she was hopeful that she was hiding it pretty well.

'Hi,' said Harriet, suddenly appearing from nearby.

'Hey,' said Flora, giving her a hug. 'I didn't expect to see you here today.'

Harriet gave a happy sigh. 'It's starting to wind down on the lavender fields now that summer's nearly ending. And thank goodness, we're absolutely shattered!'

Summer was nearly over. Flora gave an involuntary gulp at the thought which made Harriet frown.

'Are you okay?' she gasped, studying her friend's face.

'I'm fine,' said Flora quickly. 'So the visitor numbers over there have calmed down?'

'At last,' said Harriet. 'It's been great, but truth be known, I'll be grateful for a few days off! You must be the same.'

Flora nodded. 'I guess so.' Although in truth, it had been good to be so busy on the campsite. She looked at Harriet. 'I was thinking I might even book myself into the spa as a treat.'

'Wow! I mean, of course!' said Harriet. 'But you can always have a massage on the house.'

'Absolutely not,' said Flora. 'We've made a small profit this summer and I promised I would treat my myself at the end of it.'

'Okay. Well, I'd love to see you over there,' Harriet told her. 'Is there anything in particular that you'd like? Or needs attention?'

Only my heart, thought Flora, but she shook her head.

'How about I treat you to a manicure before Saturday's end of summer party?' said Harriet with a smile.

'I think they're beyond repair at this point,' said Flora, glancing at her torn and ragged nails.

'Nonsense,' Harriet told her. 'Besides, everyone deserves a treat.'

Flora hugged her friend, thankful for her support. She was going to need it even more so over the autumn. The farm was safe, it had a secure future now with the campsite. It was just her that needed saving now and she wasn't sure anything or anyone was going to be able to do that for her. Except Nico.

He had done so much for her that she wanted to thank him in some way before he left. She had an idea as to what kind of goodbye present she could give to him. She owed him so much, for teaching her so many things. And she knew just what would please him the most.

The trouble was that the only thing she really wanted to give him was her heart, forever.

57

It was a great party, thought Nico. So why did he feel so utterly miserable?

The party was a celebration that it was the end of the summer season. The lavender fields were now closed to the public and would be harvested for their flowers within a couple of days before the weather turned as September arrived. That would herald the closing of the campsite as well.

His time in Cranfield was coming to an end.

But at least the campsite had been successful, he thought. And he was glad because it meant that Flora and Grams could stay at Strawberry Hill Farm.

He gulped. Without him, of course. Life would carry on. Perhaps Flora would get married and have a family. Grams bouncing the baby on her knee. For a second, he could hardly breathe. Everything he had, everything he wanted, was right here in Cranfield.

But Flora wasn't his. He watched her now chatting with Tyler, smiling and looking happy. But he could feel his whole body growing rigid.

He missed her. He missed kissing her. He wanted her like he'd never wanted anyone or anything before. It was love, that much he knew.

But she was seeing someone else, had had a couple more dates with Tyler.

'You know, we could always push him into the lake if you like.'

Nico spun around to find Ethan next to him. He hadn't even heard him arrive.

'I mean, the guy is built like a barn, but between us we could probably find a way,' carried on Ethan. 'Maybe we could use the tractor.'

Nico sighed and shook his head. 'She's happy.'

'With that guy?' Ethan made a face. 'I don't think so. And there was me thinking that you knew women.'

'I'm not sure I know anything any more,' said Nico.

'So stay on for the autumn and learn something,' Ethan told him softly.

Nico shook his head. 'I've outstayed my welcome as it is.'

'I think all that sun has gone to your head,' said Ethan, rolling his eyes.

But Nico knew that it wasn't the sun, nor the glorious countryside, or even the sweet smell of lavender still wafting over from the nearby field. It was Flora.

But at least he had got one thing right, he thought, watching Tyson kick a football around with Ryan and Joe. The teenager had flourished. Nico found himself wishing that he could take Ethan up on his offer and stay on. He'd like to see Tyson progress and perhaps help some other troubled young teenagers by showing them life on the farm. Maybe even starting some kind of machine workshop.

But he had to leave. The campsite would close at the end of the season and then what would he do?

'There's our gorgeous girl,' said Ethan, smiling at someone behind Nico's shoulder.

He spun around with hope in his heart, but it was Grams not Flora.

She reached up to pat Ethan on the cheek. 'Dear boy,' she said, with a wink. 'This purple dress does suit me, doesn't it? Now, be a dear heart and find me a drink, would you? I need a quiet chat with our Nico.'

Ethan nodded and walked away, leaving Nico warmed by her turn of phrase. 'Our Nico.' He belonged somewhere again. He was part of a family, of a community, and it had healed him. He could trust again, trust other men like Ethan, Ryan and Joe with his thoughts and feelings, hopes and dreams. He could trust strangers because not everyone was like his father, he had discovered. He could even trust women – and one in particular.

'It's a great party,' said Nico.

Grams nodded. 'It always is when friends and family get together.' She turned to look at him. 'But you know that already.'

'Of course,' said Nico. 'It's been one of the best summers of my life.'

It was true, he realised. He had relaxed, worked hard and discovered things about himself that he had never known or wanted to admit.

'You've done wonders,' said Grams. 'We'd never have survived without your investment. Hopefully, we'll make a profit too each year going forward. Strawberry Hill Farm is safe at last.'

'I hope so,' he told her. 'But, for the record, it was never about the money.'

'So why did you invest in us?' Her eyes twinkled as if she already knew the answer.

'A mixture of reasons,' he replied. 'Most of them about you and Flora.'

She smiled and reached out to squeeze his hand with hers. 'I'm sorry that we can't persuade you to stay with us.'

'I guess I need to stand on my own two feet at last,' he told her.

'You can do that here, can't you? You have done so far anyway.'

'I know,' he replied. 'It's complicated.'

'If it's true love, then it shouldn't be,' she told him.

He gave a start, but she merely gave him a sad smile and walked away.

It was true, of course. It was love.

And, he had to admit, he was in love with Cranfield too. It had become like a second home to him. Everything had been so uncertain and now it was stable. The farm had healed him.

There was just one part missing. He had backed off for Flora's sake at the cost of his own heart. And it ached to hold her just one more time.

But he couldn't be like his father and steal another man's girl-friend. It wasn't his style and he certainly wasn't his father. But the pain he felt was worse than anything Nico had ever known.

58

Everyone was merry and having a good time, thought Flora with a smile. Extremely merry in Libby's case. She was laughing and dancing in the middle of the lavender field, her laughter drifting across to where Flora was standing.

She watched as Libby danced with Harriet, then Joe and finally Nico.

Flora shivered suddenly, despite the warmth of the night. Libby flirted with everyone, of course. It didn't matter. And why should it? She had professed long and hard that Nico absolutely wasn't her type. That he was only a good friend and business partner. That was all.

Why would she mind if he and Libby got together? And in that moment, she knew. She knew she minded more than anything.

But he wasn't flirting with her any more. And she missed it. The banter. The back and forth. She wanted Nico to flirt with her again, to make her feel wanted and special. To look at her with those dark eyes with something akin to desire.

She was still watching them when Grams wandered over to her.

'Well, that's summer done and dusted,' she said.

Flora smiled at her. 'We've had worse,' she replied.

'We certainly have.' Grams sank down on her chair and Flora sat down next to her. 'Far worse. Especially the last few years. They were the hardest.'

Flora nodded. 'But it feels like there's a future for the farm now,' she said. 'If we can have another successful summer next year with the campsite, then we'll have enough for a steady income.'

Grams turned to look at her granddaughter. 'I wasn't talking about the farm,' she said, with a sad smile. 'I was talking about your grandad.'

Flora blinked. 'Of course. I miss him too. Although not as much as you do, I'm sure.'

'He'd have liked the changes we've made these past few months,' said Grams.

Flora was surprised. 'Really? I thought he loved the steady rhythm of the seasons and the same crops each year.'

'Oh no,' said Grams, shaking her head. 'He only did that to keep our heads above water so we could keep the farm. Before that, he was ever so impetuous.'

'Grandad?' Flora blinked rapidly. 'Are we talking about the same man?'

Grams laughed. 'You know, we were all young once. I bumped into him one day in Aldwych. Literally, as it happens. I was rushing out of a shop on my lunch hour and he was heading in. He stepped on my foot and apologised. Then I found myself looking up into the bluest eyes I'd ever seen.'

Flora smiled to herself, remembering those same eyes twinkling down at her from an early age.

'He asked me to lunch!' Grams laughed once more. 'I'd seen him at school, of course, but we were so young then. Now we were in our late teens, but within five minutes I was sitting down opposite him in the café on the corner and he had persuaded me to have a large slice of cake, even though I was supposed to be watching my figure.'

'Maybe he thought your figure was just right,' said Flora, nudging her grandmother with her shoulder.

Grams smiled. 'He always liked my curves, that's for sure. Anyway, we talked and talked and I was late back to work. Do you know, I had a date that night? A young man in the solicitors where I worked. Nice lad but ever so dull. I ended up pretending to be sick and went out with your grandad instead! My mother was scandalised, but I didn't care. He had something, a special air about him. I couldn't keep away. Next thing I knew, I was jacking in my job at the solicitors and joining him on the farm to help with the strawberry picking that summer.' She turned to look at Flora. 'And I never left.'

Flora was amazed. 'I never knew that,' she said.

Grams nodded. 'The young man I'd been stepping out with was a kind soul and he would have given me a steady, secure life. It was certainly the sensible option to choose. And yet, your grandad made me laugh. Made me feel alive. I loved him so very dearly. I could have chosen another path, but I wanted – no, I *needed* your grandfather. He was my soulmate.' She gave a little shrug of her shoulders. 'When you know, you know.'

Flora was stunned, trying to take in what her grandmother was telling her.

'At one time, Lorenzo and I hoped you and Nico might end up together,' carried on Grams. 'Why do you think I invited him to stay? I hoped, we all did, that the two of you might...' Her voice trailed off.

Flora suddenly remembered something. 'The letter Lorenzo sent you with the shawl?' she asked.

Grams nodded. 'He asked me to keep an eye out for Nico. Said that his father was hopeless and if we could give Nico a home, then he would sleep at peace.'

'But we did all that and he's leaving anyway,' said Flora, a pain piercing her heart.

'Not if you ask him to stay.'

Flora looked at her grandmother, the tears pricking her eyes.

'Together you can get through everything that life throws at you. Much like those two, I reckon,' said Grams, gesturing at Harriet and Joe, who were standing nearby on their own. 'They're two parts of the same heart.'

Flora followed her gaze but didn't really register what was happening, such was her mind churning over what she had been told. So it wasn't until Joe suddenly bent down on one knee that she, and everyone else, realised what was happening and gave a little gasp.

'Harriet, will you marry me?' asked Joe, his voice a little wobbly as the nerves obviously kicked in.

But he needn't have worried. 'Yes! A thousand times yes! Of course I will!' squealed Harriet, dragging him up off his knees to fling her arms around him.

Everyone rushed over to congratulate the happy couple. Flora didn't think she'd ever seen Harriet look happier, wear such a wide smile. She was pleased for her friend. She had found the other half of her coin, just like Grams had said.

She spotted Nico in the crowd and they looked at each other, the hubbub around them carrying on despite the unsaid words they exchanged with their eyes.

She reminded herself that he was leaving and broke the eye

contact, beginning to move away. But a hand caught hers and she turned back to find Grams studying her.

'My dear girl, a sensible life is all very well, but it's not a full one,' she said softly. 'Go, live your dreams. Wherever they lead you.'

Then as the congratulations grew louder, Flora suddenly found that she couldn't bear it. That she wanted so much to have what Harriet had been blessed with.

So she turned away from everyone to speak to Nico but found her path blocked.

She stared at Tyler aghast. He was on one knee, kneeling down in front of her.

'Flora Barton, will you marry me?' he asked.

59

Flora was completely stunned as she stared down at Tyler, who was still kneeling in front of her.

She glanced around and, yes, everyone was staring at them. Her eyes caught Nico's for a moment before he turned away. Then she looked back down at Tyler.

'Get up,' she said softly.

Tyler looked confused. 'Really?'

'Yes,' she told him, taking a deep breath.

He stood up and looked at her. 'Flora Barton, would you...?'

'Stop!' she said, holding up her hand to interrupt him before taking his hand and leading him away from everyone. Once they were apart from the main group, Flora shook her head at him. 'You don't want to do this,' she said softly. 'Firstly, you're stealing their thunder.' She glanced over at Harriet and Joe, who were still hand in hand watching them. 'This is their time.'

Tyler looked downcast.

'Second, you're not proposing to me because you love me,' she carried on. 'You just think we could be a great team on the farm. And I love having you as a friend. But nothing more. I'm sorry if I muddled things for you and the last thing I wanted to do was hurt you.'

Tyler nodded slowly.

'You're kind and steady and a good man,' she told him, taking his hands in hers. 'We'd make a good partnership and that would be the sensible choice.' She gulped. 'But that's not what I want. I want enduring, passionate, silly, impetuous, can't live without him love.'

She caught a look from Grams and turned back to Tyler.

'You don't deserve a lifetime of being married to someone who wishes...' Flora's voice trailed away as she looked around once more. But she could no longer see the man she was thinking of. She focused back on Tyler. 'Who wishes she were with someone else. You're too good for me. You'll find someone who loves you wholeheartedly because that's what you deserve.'

She was grateful to see Tyler nod slowly. 'But what about you?' he asked.

She shrugged her shoulders and took a deep breath. 'I guess I'll just have to do something spontaneous for once.' She kissed him on the cheek before walking away.

Flora looked around the crowd for Nico's face, but he was gone.

Grams tilted her head in the direction of the farmhouse and Flora rushed away across the field lit by the setting sun to find him.

* * *

Nico felt ill as he stood outside the farmhouse.

He had seen Tyler propose and had walked away before the double engagement celebrations could commence. He'd left it too late. He'd backed off so far that Flora had moved on. And his heart ached for her.

Nico stared down at the motorbike, the keys in his hand. It was time to leave. Flora had her happy ending. Heaven knows she deserved it, but he would be lost without her.

He certainly couldn't bear to stay in Cranfield with her and Tyler so happily engaged. His heart had just shattered into a million pieces and he needed to get out of there fast. He knew it was running away, but what else could he do?

'Hey.'

He looked up suddenly to see Flora standing hesitantly nearby in the courtyard. She was obviously worried that he disapproved about the engagement. Well, he did, but not in the way that she imagined. He looked back down at the bike, unable to make eye contact without her seeing the truth in his eyes.

'Congratulations.' He was so desperately miserable that he couldn't even instil any fake happiness in his tone of voice.

He heard her take a sharp intake of breath but still didn't look at her. He couldn't bear to see the happiness in her eyes at marrying someone else.

'On what?' he heard her ask.

Confused, he finally looked up at her. 'On your engagement. What else?' he said, forcing a smile on his face. 'I hope you'll both be very happy.'

She stared at him with wide eyes. 'Do you?' she asked.

The question drifted in the air between them and he looked at her with a frown. 'I don't understand.'

'Do you wish us well and to have a happy life together?'

The silence stretched out as he struggled to find the lie with which to reply.

'Because I'm not going to marry him,' she blurted out. 'I don't love him.'

'Thank God,' he said. His words came out choked as his throat was thick with emotion as he sagged against the motorbike with relief.

Flora began to walk towards him. 'It's you,' she said, beginning to cry. 'I love you.'

'*Dolcezza*,' he said, rushing over to draw her into his arms. '*Ti amo*. I love you too. Don't cry. It's always been you ever since I saw you in that pond. And it always will be.'

Their lips automatically found each other and the kiss was the sweetest one he'd ever known. He realised this was it. This was where he belonged. Forever.

When he finally let her go, she smiled despite her tears. 'Look, I don't want romance from you. I don't want any of that. I just want you.'

'Well, that's tough,' he told her, wiping the tears from her cheeks with his thumbs. 'I'm giving you romance whether you like it or not.'

She laughed and leaned forward to kiss him again.

'I'm going to give you a thoroughly insensible life, Flora Barton,' he said, in between kisses. 'We're going to be silly and laugh and enjoy life. That's my vow to you.'

'I adore you,' she told him, looking up at him with stars in her eyes.

'Are you sure it wasn't just the sexy motorbike?' he asked.

She laughed. 'Oh, I'm sure it's partly down to the bike.' She grinned. 'Do I get equal driving duties?'

'You get everything,' he told her, holding her close. 'Including my heart.'

'I'm glad to hear it,' she said. 'Now kiss me again.'

As she drew his head towards her, he replied, 'Yes, boss.'

* * *

When they drew apart, Flora knew that they were together forever and her heart was full to bursting with happiness. She completely adored him.

'You know, I did have a leaving present for you,' she told him, stroking his cheek. 'But I want to give it to you.'

'Do I still have to leave to receive it?' he asked, with a smile.

She shook her head and leaned up to kiss him on the lips. 'No. But I want you to have it anyway.'

She headed inside the farmhouse to where she had hidden the double package under the stairs. Nico looked bemused as she handed it over to him when she came back outside.

But as he unwrapped the brown paper, his expression went from intrigued to amazed. He brought out the painting, which was of Strawberry Hill Farm. Flora had made sure that she had included the little campsite in the background, as well as the strawberry field.

'Thank you,' he told her. 'It's wonderful.'

'I wanted you to take the farm with you, to remind you of us all,' she told him.

'I'd have never forgotten you,' he replied, drawing her close and kissing her with such passion as to leave her breathless.

When they finally drew apart, Flora was almost too dazed to hand over the other package, such was her love for him. But she managed to place the second wrapped paper into his hands.

'I hope it's a self-portrait of your beautiful face,' he told her, unwrapping the paper. 'Although I'm happier looking at the real thing every day.' He gave her a soft smile, but as he looked down at the second painting, his face fell.

'I hope I got the details right,' she said quickly. 'I wanted to do the vineyard justice, so I got an old photo from Grams. It wasn't in colour though.'

She watched Nico take a deep breath as he stared at the

painting for a long time in silence. When he looked back at her, there were tears in his eyes. 'The light. The way the sun peeks through the tall trees. It's just like being there,' he told her. '*Grazie.* I was worried that I would start to forget it. You've given me back my home. My other home, I mean.'

'You're sure it's okay?' she asked.

'It's perfect,' he told her, placing it down carefully to draw her into his arms. 'Just like you.'

'I love you so much,' she told him, reaching up to pull his mouth down to hers.

And then she lost herself in his sweet kisses, knowing that she would stay as happy as she was at that moment forever.

60

Nico took a step backwards and stared at the old barn.

'It's looking more secure, don't you think?' he said.

Joe nodded. 'I reckon it should withstand any winter storms, if we get any,' he replied.

Nico was pleased that his friend agreed. The barn had played an important part during the summer for the campsite, as a place to gather and meet people. The cooking area had proved popular for those who didn't want to head out for something to eat and so he had plans to install a more permanent outdoor kitchen over the winter.

The games area had also helped, especially when the weather had turned at the beginning of the summer, so that too would be shored up in preparation for the following season.

'How's the planning application going?' asked Joe.

Nico nodded. 'The shower and toilet block look like they're going to get the seal of approval over the next week, so I can make headway with the foundations.'

They glanced over to where there was now a gap where Dodgy Del had removed his flamboyant cabin which had gone back to wherever it had come from. Nico was grateful for the loan though, whatever its dubious connection.

He and Flora had decided to apply for a permanent campsite licence which was being processed. It would ensure that the business would continue to thrive and breathe life back into the farm and Cranfield.

It looked like it was going to be a busy winter of renovations, but with bookings already coming in for the following summer, it seemed the next season for the campsite was going to be even more successful.

'What about the additional plans?' asked Joe, as they walked across the field.

Nico looked across. 'If I've got my figures right, then I think we might just be able to afford a couple of shepherd huts to place over on this near side,' he said. 'If the wood-burning stoves don't cost too much.'

It was another plan to extend the season, as well as helping with some all-year-round income. If the tents remained warm at night, then they could prolong the camping season, starting at Easter all the way through to the end of October, they hoped.

'I've got the figures on my phone somewhere,' said Joe.

'That's great,' said Nico, glancing at his watch. 'I can't look at them now, but how about I buy you a pint tomorrow at the Black Swan and we can chat then.'

Joe nodded. 'We can meet a little earlier before others get there,' he said, before laughing. 'And before the match starts!'

'Excellent,' said Nico. 'We can talk wedding plans as well.'

Joe laughed once more. 'I was hoping the big football match would be a wedding-free zone,' he said. 'Just for a little while in any case.'

'Then we'll make sure it most definitely is,' said Nico.

But he knew that Joe was looking forward to the big day later that year because he had talked to Nico about it. They were friends, as were Ryan and Ethan. He had real friends now, friends he could trust and who didn't care about his background. He wasn't Nico Rossi, son of Paolo Rossi to them. He was Nico, campsite owner, carpenter, handyman and sometime poker game winner. He could finally relax and be himself because they liked Nico for who he was and that meant more to him than a thousand flash Ferraris ever would.

He hadn't heard from his father since he had driven off into the sunset with the Ferrari. But Nico had learnt to forgive him on some level and move on. And he had begun to forgive himself for the loss of the vineyard. He had proved to himself that he wasn't his father's son and that his own destiny was whatever path he chose, including the way in which he conducted his life.

Nico was grateful that he had Grams as his surrogate family, although Bob and Eddie were also filling that gap as well as they became closer.

He waved to them both now as they headed into the railway workshop. He was hoping to find out later how close they were to getting the old steam train going as Ryan had told him the previous day that it might even be seen out on the railway tracks very soon.

Nico was looking forward to it. In fact, he looked forward to every day in Cranfield now, especially when each one started with a kiss from Flora.

She had made him a part of her home, assured him that it was his home too. He loved her so much and made sure he told her at every opportunity.

He still couldn't believe that he had found the love of his life in such a tiny village in the middle of nowhere but he was so grateful that he had. He was home now and had no intentions of ever leaving.

The sun broke through the trees and warmed up the cool late September air. Nico glanced at his watch once more and began to walk down the hill.

He didn't want to be late. After all, he had a date with the woman he loved.

* * *

'I think lilac as our wedding theme, don't you?' said Harriet, looking at her friends.

'Don't you mean lavender?' asked Flora, laughing.

'That was the point!' replied Harriet with a wide smile.

Flora had never seen her so happy, but the wedding chat was all-encompassing until they all got her to relax.

Thankfully, it had been another bumper harvest year for the lavender so there would be plenty to keep Harriet occupied in the spa. But every coffee session and gin night were all about the wedding. The old Flora would have rolled her eyes like Libby and railed against it all. But she had changed. She relished a little bit of romance in her life now. Nico gave her flowers every week. 'Just because,' he told her, and she began to look forward to receiving them.

He had helped her change in so many ways. The previous evening, he had taken her out on the motorbike to a pub for dinner. No reason, he had told her. Just because.

She was still getting used to life being not quite so structured. Not quite so certain. But she was certain of his feelings for her. And vice versa. He was the love of her life. The one that Grams had taught her to believe in.

She looked up at the clock in the waiting room and stood up. 'I've got to go,' she told them. 'Gin night tomorrow?'

'Of course,' said Libby, with a grin.

'With a little bit of added wedding talk,' said Katy, giving her a wink.

Flora gave them all a kiss and rushed out onto the station platform. She waved at Ryan down at the train workshop but didn't stop.

It was nearly sunset. Her favourite part of the day, along with the sunrise, and she had an urgent appointment to get to.

She headed down the lane and went past the farmhouse. Grams was out in Aldwych, having an evening of bingo. Now that the pressures of farming had dissipated, Grams was enjoying her retirement and had begun to venture out more, for which Flora was glad. She had worked so hard for so many years that she deserved it.

The strawberry field was still producing fruit, although that would stop in the next couple of weeks once the weather turned. But she was grateful that the strawberries would be there next year, just like the farm. It was all safe. She would be forever grateful to Nico for that.

Flora smiled at the view as she headed down the hills. The colours of the trees were turning now and a kaleidoscope of green and yellow had begun to form. Soon, autumn and the cooler days would arrive and life would move inside more and more. But, in the meantime, her fingers itched to paint the scene. That was another thing that Nico had given her: she had found her love of painting once more and often took an hour out of her day to sketch a different scene. She was even going to offer painting classes the following summer at the campsite. It had been a spontaneous thought the previous evening, but she was finding that she was prepared to take a risk now and then. To embrace spontaneity and the thrill of not being quite so certain as to what each day would bring.

She headed through the trees and finally arrived at the

clearing by the pond. Even in late summer, it was still stunning. The sun peeped through the leafy branches of the trees as bird-song filled the air and butterflies fluttered along the banks.

Nico was sitting on the deck at the edge of the water.

'You're late,' he told her, with a smile lighting up his handsome face.

'Sorry,' she said, shrugging off her boots as she joined him on the jetty. 'The girls were chatting and then I just received a late booking for tomorrow night.'

'That's great,' he told her.

The camping business had not only survived the summer but was thriving. Strawberry Hill Farm was safe. Their forever home was secure.

They sat down for a while, their feet dangling in the cool water. Flora leant against Nico and drew his head down for a kiss.

'Mmm,' she murmured against his lips. She didn't think she'd ever be able to stop kissing him, such was the love and desire she felt for him.

'Let's stay here for the evening,' he whispered, dropping light kisses all the way down her neck.

'What about clearing out the barn?' she asked, only half-heartedly.

'It can wait,' he said. 'I've got more important things to do.'

She looked at him and saw a familiar gleam in his eyes.

'I'm a playboy, remember?' he said, with a grin. 'Bad to the bone.'

'Thank goodness,' she said, leaning forward to kiss him once more.

For a while, there was only him and his sweet embrace before Flora leant back to look at him.

'I have an even better idea,' she said, his eyes sparkling as she began to undo the buttons on his shirt.

'What if someone's nearby?' he asked, despite slipping the shirt from her shoulders.

She glanced around, but it was just them in the sunny clearing. She shivered, not because it was cold but from the feeling of his hands on her skin. She knew he would always make her feel that way.

'I don't care,' she told him, with a shrug. 'Do you?'

Nico laughed. 'No,' he said, shaking his head as he stood up. 'Not in the slightest.'

He then held his hands out to pull her up next to him.

He was impetuous, exciting and she loved him for encouraging her to be the same. He supported her every step of the way and she felt as if her life were fuller and far better now than ever before. It was to be an exciting life together and she was ready for it with Nico by her side.

So she took him by the hand before they both turned and jumped into the lake.

ACKNOWLEDGEMENTS

A huge thank you to my lovely editor Caroline Ridding for the continued support and encouragement!

Thank you to everyone at Boldwood Books for all their hard work on my books, especially the fabulous marketing team and Jade Craddock for her wonderful copy edits. Thank you also to all my lovely fellow Team Boldwood authors for their support and cheer.

Thank you to all the readers and bloggers for their enthusiasm and reviews for each new book, which is so important to so many authors, myself included.

Thank you to all my lovely author friends who understand the madness that lies within, especially members of the RNA, DWLC and the Surrey Buddies.

Thank you to all my friends, especially Jo Botelle whose encouragement remains as steadfast on this fourteenth book as it did for the very first one! I owe you a large piece of cake with our next cuppa!

Thank you to my wonderful family for all their continued support, especially Gill, Simon, Louise, Ross, Lee, Cara and Sian.

Special thanks once more to my fantastic husband Dave, who persuaded me to go camping for the first time all those years ago, leading to many happy family holidays since then. As always, this book could have never been written without your love and support and cups of tea.

ABOUT THE AUTHOR

Alison Sherlock is the author of the bestselling *Willow Tree Hall* books. Alison enjoyed reading and writing stories from an early age and gave up office life to follow her dream. Her series for Boldwood is set in a fictional Cotswold village.

Sign up to Alison Sherlock's mailing list for news, competitions and updates on future books.

Follow Alison on social media:

facebook.com/alison.sherlock.73

x.com/AlisonSherlock

ALSO BY ALISON SHERLOCK

WHERE ALL YOUR ROMANCE
DREAMS COME TRUE!

THE HOME OF BESTSELLING
ROMANCE AND WOMEN'S
FICTION

 WARNING:
MAY CONTAIN SPICE

SIGN UP TO OUR
NEWSLETTER

https://bit.ly/Lovenotesnews

Boldwod

Boldwood Books is an award-winning fiction publishing company seeking out the best stories from around the world.

Find out more at www.boldwoodbooks.com

Join our reader community for brilliant books, competitions and offers!

Follow us
@BoldwoodBooks
@TheBoldBookClub

Sign up to our weekly deals newsletter

https://bit.ly/BoldwoodBNewsletter

Printed in Great Britain
by Amazon